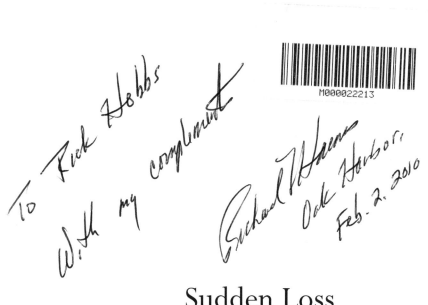

M000022213

Sudden Loss

Earthquake Realities

Richard F. Haines

Copyright © 2009 Richard F. Haines
All rights reserved.

ISBN: 1-4392-5279-3
ISBN-13: 9781439252796
Library of Congress Control Number: 2009907914

To order additional copies, please contact us.
BookSurge
www.booksurge.com
1-866-308-6235
orders@booksurge.com

Contents

Acknowledgements

Neither a bridge nor a story about one is constructed by a single person. I am indebted to many people who have contributed their suggestions on how to make this a better story. Each contributed something that was unique and important and I want to acknowledge them. First, to Dave Crawford, who shares my passion about the need for a new bridge to Whidbey Island goes my sincere thanks and mutual support. I also want to thank Marvin Koorn, North Whidbey Fire and Rescue Fire Chief, Deception Pass Park Manager Jack Hartt and Law Enforcement Park Ranger Jason Stapert for supplying useful background information. James Tartas challenged me to rewrite, rewrite, and then rewrite again to add more human interest and for that I am most grateful. I hope that the bridge itself might have taken on a bit of its own personality as well because of his advice. Other valuable technical assistance was given by former Island County Commissioner Bill Byrd, Todd Carlson of the Washington State Department of Transportation, Marilyn Dobbins, Mike Frost, Peter Hunt, Tom Johnson, Theodore Newstad, Mary Rose of the American Red Cross, Clark Schroeder, Tim Verschuyl, and my Creative Writing group. To Reverdy Allender go my grateful thanks for the exceptional cover photo and to Daniel Sirak of Jolt Studios for producing the excellent cover. Finally, to my wife Carol go my deepest thanks for her encouragement and insightful editorial advice over several years.

Foreword

It's just human nature to put off until tomorrow what we should do to-day, to overlook the obvious and see the minor details, to rationalize about why we don't need to do things rather than why we do, and to think that a gigantic earthquake will not happen where I happen to live, at least in my lifetime. Yet, our procrastination and rationalizations can also end up killing us as they have done in so many instances of natural disasters around the world. We can live in our own world of fantasy and denial if we want to and take our chances or we can be proactive and get as prepared as we can, given our individual circum-stances. We still have that choice. But immediately after the "big one" hits it will be too late. Our choice is gone, nulled out, voided. What remains is only a reverberating series of silent haunting taunts…"if only I had…".

All events and people portrayed in this book are purely fictional. Any similarities between them and real individuals are purely coincidental. Of course, I must also acknowledge that any and all errors of omission or commis-sion are mine alone.

Richard F. Haines
Oak Harbor, Washington
September, 2009

Chapter 1
Day 1 Tuesday Morning

As this day in mid-March dawned the sun was supposed to have risen at 6:24 am but a cold blustery gray overcast kept it invisible anywhere on Whidbey Island, a long, thin, snaking island some sixty miles north of Seattle, an island that sits resolutely in the cold lead-colored waters of Puget Sound. The sun hidden by thick dark clouds, turned day into a prolonged faint twilight at best, a twilight that was familiar to everyone who had lived there for more than a few months. House and streetlights were still on everywhere.

Yet island residents who were familiar with the air of Puget Sound might have noticed that something was different this morning; its speed and direction, its humidity, its sounds, even its smell. The air was troubled by something and this trouble was transmitted to the surface of the water; strange concentric wavelets radiated outward from many thousands of different points each several hundred yards apart; they were something like those produced by a handful of small pebbles tossed into a pond. They came and went at random locations that covered many square miles of water and they continued over the course of an hour before finally dying away, but because of the hour and the darkness no one noticed them.

Every weather system has no beginning and no end; every system changes constantly, yet every system is also fundamentally the same as weather experts like to point out. Nevertheless, the weather that was now engulfing Whidbey Island and most of the upper Puget Sound region was different. It was the result of one of the strangest the Pacific Northwest had ever experienced. As with most previous weather systems this one developed far to the northwest and that from yet another even farther west over northern Siberia. This one took on its particularly ominous features a week before as the gigantic storm descended slowly to the south and east. All of the weather experts thought that eventually it would collide with the Northwest Coast of Vancouver Island and move directly inland, yet they were to be proven wrong.

The closer that this weather pattern got to the mainland the more moisture and energy it picked up which is normal; yet it was marked by two things in particular that were not normal: the first was an alarmingly high-pressure leading-edge followed almost immediately by an area of very low pressure. The gradient between them was steeper than had ever been recorded before. The air pressure behind the front was so low it pegged all standard barometers. Their thin black needles were forced hard against tiny brass stops inside their cases. Only scientific instruments having extreme range capability could accurately register the extent of the low pressure.

Its second unusual feature was its massive size; it would require an area of almost ten thousand square miles to reasonably enclose it. These two particular features were captivating meteorologists in many different locations. Naval Air Station Whidbey Island's Station Weather and Emergency Advisory website was preparing to issue a special alert as was the Federal Emergency Management Agency on their site. In addition, the National Weather Service in Seattle as well as researchers at Boulder were watching the progress of this alarming phenomenon but feeling powerless to really do anything about it.

The room had no windows; it didn't need any. It was a room buried deep within the very center of a massive three story concrete and steel building set into the eastern base of the Rocky Mountains. There were more than three dozen multicolored computer-graphic screens positioned around the room that displayed the whole world's weather. They were its windows and they lit up much of the room with bright colors that flickered and flashed from time to time. Thirty feet of wide screens like those at mission control at Houston filled one entire wall. Their images changed much more slowly. One of the sixteen staff personnel on duty this morning was hunched over a particular barograph display. Except for taking some notes, he'd been sitting there motionless for almost an hour, fascinated by what he was seeing.

"Hey Tom, come take a look at this."

Tom was the watch supervisor on duty at NOAA's Earth System Research Laboratory at Boulder. As Tom approached the console where the younger meteorologist was sitting he heard him whistle; a long, low sound, the kind that was meant only for ones self, the kind of whistle one makes when totally absorbed.

"Yeah, what's up, Rich?" he said.

"Take a look at the northern Puget Sound frontal profile here. I've been watching it since I came in this morning and it's something else. I've never seen anything like it in my eleven years," he exclaimed. "Look along here, he said," pointing to a thick brown dashed line with the letters TROF hovering nearby. "This trough of low pressure is over three hundred miles long. Man, what a gradient! Look how thin it is right here, only about five to fifteen five miles wide!"

Two more staff members who were sitting nearby got up and walked over to look at the colored coded display as he said this. They also studied the symbols carefully, silently. Each was evaluating the thick brown dashed line with small red triangles spaced along its length. It was progressing across the screen downward and to the right. Both of the newcomers also whistled under their breath. One of them was an extremely thin young man with a freckled face and bright red hair who looked like he was fifteen or sixteen at the most. He was an intern working on a two-year post-doctoral fellowship he had received from the National Research Council on the topic of ultra low frequency behavior of substrata. The other was an attractive young woman in her early thirties; she had brunette hair (short-cropped) with a little curl, a good figure, and was neatly dressed. She was a final year graduate student at Boulder working on her dissertation.

Tom had not only been Rich's supervisor for several years, but he had considered him to be a younger version of himself, a guy to watch as he climbed his way up the organizational chain slowly but quite surely. More importantly he was his friend. Tom studied the display for a long time without saying a word, and then finally he spoke.

"We're going to have to put out a special alert and we also need to contact Seattle center and Silver Springs right away. They'll probably have been watching this as well, but it never hurts to back 'em up." His voice was tinged with alarm as he turned to face the younger man at the console. "Do it right away! And have them…"

He was interrupted by the red head who said, "Chief, I've been watching the same region. Our geophones are quiet so far, however there's been a slowly increasing ULF activity in the 0.01 to 12 hertz bands." He paused but didn't notice any particular response from the group so he went on. "And one more thing, our QF stations are continuing to detect an increasing number of short duration pulsations, anywhere from one to thirty seconds long."

Tom didn't say anything. He only smiled briefly at the young man as if to say, "so what?"

Red head looked at Tom, paused as he took a long deep breath and answered, "Well Chief, I have a hunch that it could be leading up to an earthquake. A group in California has recently reported the same kind of profile on their QuakeFinder sensor network. You probably read their article. Theirs peaked only days before they had a 5.4 near San Jose. I don't remember how many days."

Everyone in the group went silent and looked at one another not quite sure of what to say. At length, the young woman jumped into the discussion with all the self-confidence that the uninitiated often displays.

"Ah, I've been watching this area on our air conductivity monitors, those two over there," she said pointing off across the room. She didn't notice the barely concealed smiles on the faces of the experienced staff members who knew the location of every monitor on the whole second floor much less those here in the "command room," as everyone called it. She was referring to measurements that were being made periodically by three special sensors, sensors that recorded relative concentrations of airborne ions. Unfortunately or perhaps fortunately, the three sensors were spread very far apart, one at the north slope of the Olympic Peninsula, a second one hundred miles to the east in the Skagit Valley basin near the town of Mt. Vernon on the mainland, and the third placed between Seattle and Tacoma, again, another 90 miles farther south of it. NOAA had simply run out of money before it could install any more; everyone who really understood geophysics (an extremely small handful of people it seemed) knew that three sensors weren't enough to really do much good but it was a start.

She bubbled on. "Well, there's something strange going on. I've checked these three stations every day since I got here and there's never been any significant shifts in their output...until now!"

Tom studied her face intently, waiting for the answer that everyone else was also waiting for. He studied it not only expecting to hear her explanation of what she thought might be happening but because she was just a pleasure to look at.

She ignored his typical silent male response and went on, "Yes, ionic concentrations have been fluctuating within their normal ranges, an almost classic gaussian distribution, at each of these three stations for weeks now...only yesterday I began noticing that one of the stations had suddenly pegged for several hours. The others hadn't changed their pattern at all. I'd bet a lot of money that there's been significant radon emissions there."

"Where?" asked everyone almost in unison, a little frustration hidden in several voices.

"Oh, didn't I say? It was the sensor on the Olympic Peninsula," she answered.

Seattle issued a special alert on the National Weather Service's website as well as over the National Oceanic and Atmospheric Administration's Weather Radio, WWG-24 Puget Sound; but relatively few people heard the warnings. For one thing the news networks picked it up slowly because of other competing stories: flood watches, high winds, power outages and hazardous driving conditions; but for another NOAA's Weather Radio is broadcast over VHF frequencies that standard radios cannot even receive. Few people owned the special weather-tuned radios that were needed. The result was that almost no one was as prepared as they could have been. It was the proverbial calm before the storm, so to speak. To most people this one seemed just like any other major weather system coming in off the ocean; however the professionals knew that this particular system was virtually unique. It hadn't been propelled by a high altitude jet stream like previous storms had; rather, along its edges it had moved in small epicycles at an oblique angle to the jet stream as its core moved forward. It seemed to be guided by invisible rails at ground level or below. It was almost as if the system was slowly being dragged forward toward the northwest corner of Washington by some other mechanism, a mechanism that the professionals were still trying to figure out.

The system had moved forward steadily at between forty and sixty miles per hour over the past week and had finally passed the southern tip of Vancouver Island when, for some unknown reason, perhaps a backing pressure or other force caused the mass to veer suddenly to the east. The center of its energy cell was aimed half way between Bellingham and Seattle, an area bordered by Puget Sound and populated by well over two million people. The experts knew that this was going to upset most if not all of the weather records. They also knew that they were powerless to do anything about this system other than try to give people as much warning as possible. After that it was up to the resourcefulness of the citizens.

The front of the storm was now so broad that its northern flank passed through southern British Columbia while its southern edge passed through northern Oregon as far as the Columbia River over three hundred miles away. The system was moving inland toward the Cascade Mountains and centered just north of Mt. Rainier where the flooding was rapid and extensive in all the major river basins.

The winds that finally came through the region were not as strong as predicted but they were more variable. Gusts of over one hundred twenty miles per hour were recorded at Naval Air Station Whidbey Island at one point yet they had quickly fallen again to only small craft advisory levels, about 30 mph. Interestingly, the winds caused only isolated power outages, mostly due to trees falling on power lines; the main highways in the Pacific Northwest were opened by the time of the morning commute but even then motorists had to meander slowly around trees and litter. Most of the secondary roads were closed by tree falls and downed power lines. Fortunately most of the small boats moored in the numerous marinas that dotted the San Juans were protected from the winds and high surf while many others riding at anchor farther out were beached.

Nevertheless, the two things that triggered the devastating chain of events that followed wasn't the wind at all, but the huge area of ultra-low air pressure that accompanied this storm coupled with a series of three unusually low tides around Whidbey Island where this story largely takes place.

Tuesday 7:35 am

One Mile South of the Deception Pass Bridge
on the Main Highway on and off Whidbey Island

It had rained most of the night and the ground was covered by puddles and small tree branches. The roadways were slick yet not that treacherous for the hundreds of local commuters on the highway, commuters who were already familiar with their local climate and driving conditions. They knew how to drive in western Washington's winter weather. The highway department had only begun to clean up the trees and larger debris that littered the roadway from high winds of the night before. Yes this day had started out like most others in the late winter; but it was to become the worst day in anyone's memory, indeed in the recorded history of the whole region.

A solid stream of cars and trucks was headed north out of Oak Harbor along State Route 20 toward the well known, even beloved by some, Deception

Pass Bridge and beyond. The steel cantilever truss bridge drew more sightseers during the year than any other place in Washington State. Indeed there seemed to be pedestrians standing somewhere along its 976 foot long main span or its 511 foot long second span over Canoe Pass to the north at any hour of the day and sometimes even after dark, in good weather at least; and this single, steel-linked artery carried well over fourteen thousand vehicles every day! The traffic this morning was no different; moving steadily but not evenly spaced.

Someone looking down on this stretch of highway at night would have seen an undulating string of luminous headlight "pearls" punctuated by periodic dark stretches caused by the few stoplights along the route north of the city of Oak Harbor. These traffic lights caused the pearls to bunch up and then expand again until the next light was reached; they were like pearls strung on an elastic cord.

Only nine miles north of town Kate Anders, a cute twenty-six year old blue-eyed blond wearing a smart, trim outfit, was in her virtually brand new silver SUV, her pride and joy. It had only three hundred and eighty five miles on it and she was determined to keep it in perfect condition for as long as possible. She loved the smell of its new leather and had settled herself into its soft yet firm contour seat for her daily commute to work. The rain and mud splashed up by passing cars annoyed her but there was nothing she could do about that; she was going to her job in Mt. Vernon over on the mainland. She was a legal secretary in a small practice there; perhaps, she hoped it might be a stepping stone to a bigger firm someday. Kate felt more secure in knowing that the SUV's heavier weight would make her commute safer if she ever did have a collision. She also liked sitting higher above the roadway than in her old car. It made her feel taller and safer. She felt good this morning in spite of the heavy traffic. Kate had driven this same route for over two years now and was familiar with its many turns and dips, its left-turn lanes, and newly installed center turn lanes. State Route 20 was the only route off the island to the north. It was a really beautiful drive but it was still too dark a morning to see very much of it.

She lived by herself in Oak Harbor having moved to Washington from Boise, Idaho to take this job several years before. It was only coincidental that she came from Dutch stock. Soon after arriving in Oak Harbor she learned that she wasn't particularly unique. Dutch names seemed to blanket the countryside. Women of Dutch extraction were usually fair skinned, usually blond, and ruggedly healthy. She was no different.

Kate took pride in staying fit, eating right, exercising, drinking only in moderation and definitely not smoking. "I hate the smell of tobacco," she would tell her small group of friends. Some of them pretended to make an allowance for her personal view by backing a few feet away while they continued to smoke their cigarettes. Then she'd usually smile at them weakly and wonder to herself why she hung around with them at all. Their stale tobacco odors grated on her sensibilities.

She and her family were very close. She still looked forward to their weekly telephone marathons when she would bring her Dad and Mum, as she called her, up to date on the latest events in her life. Inevitably, she would hear her Mum ask, "Katy, have you met an eligible man yet?" She found it humorous how direct her Mum was with her over the phone but never face to face. Kate hadn't found any guy who really appealed to her so far. In fact she didn't date much at all despite her beauty and poise and the normal urges that accompanied her biology. She was maturer for her age than most and was still content to be single, finally out on her own.

By 7:35 she had just passed the entrance to the Deception Pass State Park a mile south of the bridge and began to climb a slight grade. Her windshield wipers just kept time with the music on her CD. She was in a continuous line of traffic, all-moving about 35 miles per hour. Suddenly she thought a tire had blown out. Her vehicle seemed to swerve sideways to the right for a second and then back to the left but she hadn't moved the steering wheel! It really seemed strange, something she had never experienced before. As she instinctively slowed down she noticed brake lights coming on ahead of her. Rather quickly she slowed down to twenty miles an hour not knowing what was happening. That was when she was hit by another kind of motion that felt like all four tires were being lifted up off the surface of the road at the same time, like being levitated. It seemed like she was on a giant roller coaster. In the roadway ahead of her she could see the blacktop surface begin to ripple like wavelets, wide chunks of roadway surface were thrust up like blackened whitecaps on the waters of Puget Sound around the island. She was confused and just jammed on her brakes. She came to a stop so fast that the pickup truck behind her, driving too fast and too close, ran into her bumper with a painfully sharp thud. She sat still for a moment before the reality of what was happening hit her. She didn't hurt anywhere although her upper body and head had been thrown forward almost to the steering wheel. Dazed, she felt the tremors lift her SUV several more times even higher than before. All she could do was cling to the steering wheel and hold on.

She saw that most of the cars ahead of her also had come to a complete stop. Their taillights were rising and falling as if they were riding on top of a very long carpet that was suddenly yanked up and down at one end. Kate didn't know what to do. She just sat and prayed that whatever was happening would stop. She had to get to work and now she had a rear-ender to deal with. "Could things get any worse?" she wondered.

Just over a half-mile ahead of Kate in the same undulating line of northbound traffic Bill Arnold was nearing the southern end of the Deception Pass Bridge just before the first tremor hit. He was travelling about thirty miles an hour and it was 7:37 by the dashboard clock of his late model, extended cab pickup truck; his clock was several minutes fast. He had driven this route so often that he knew that at this speed he would just make the 8:00 o'clock check-in time. Even if he was late he and his boss were on good terms.

Bill was enroute to Anacortes where he worked full time as a powerboat mechanic in a large leasing firm there. He was looking for a better paying job, one in his chosen field of engineering, not one that sent him home at night with thin lines of black grease under every fingernail, but hadn't been able to find anything yet. He loved this drive for it gave him time to be alone and think; he usually drove with his radio and CD player off.

His friends and coworkers liked him; he was glad that he could make friends so easily. He'd learned years before while serving as a Navy Chief onboard a large supply ship that a calm, unruffled front could stave off a lot of potential problems. He was a tall, thin, quiet man with black hair and bushy eyebrows that set off his striking hazel-brown eyes. He thought things out before speaking. It was yet another trait that had saved him from trouble in the past. It was surprising that Bill had never come to see himself as being gifted both with common sense and a sharp intellect but his friends and coworkers had. They had many reasons to like him.

Bill's father was of Portuguese extraction (several generations earlier). His mother came from poor Irish stock (also many generations before). Their genetic contributions had survived in Bill in whom was found a healthy mix of stubbornness, a sense of humor, and an easy-going friendliness.

For some reason he couldn't explain the bridge just up ahead of him always reminded him of a mature woman. He loved her smooth curves and inner strength and he appreciated her complex "underpinnings." He laughed to himself as he considered his choice of this word. Perhaps she was worn, but cosmetically she was still very beautiful…as long as one didn't look too closely. While her lines, her beams, were clearly visible, few people seemed to notice them. They were probably more captivated by the fantastically beautiful surrounding environment in which she was nestled. Physically speaking she wasn't visibly weak. "Nevertheless, she had to be life-worn and tired deep down in those invisible places," Bill had reasoned. "Her frame may still look sound but inside her assembled parts must be slowly, surely disconnecting, rusting, fracturing microscopically. She certainly carries more than her fair share of the load," he thought. Yet the Deception Pass Bridge also had another dimension that he thought about from time to time.

"The bridge somehow seems to me to possess a deep and wonderful spirit of quiet strength. Sure she has her hidden weaknesses but doesn't everything built by man? Nothing lasts forever." He pondered.

The bridge was a prime example of structural steel engineering typical of the 1930s. Each time he drove across its two spans he tried to visualize its design, but he was usually distracted by something. Most often he was distracted by the nearness of the oncoming vehicles. The lanes were very narrow with no room for a center barrier to keep traffic apart.

Bill had received his degree in civil engineering five years before with special emphasis on bridge design. Bridges had always fascinated him. He wondered just how strong this seventy-plus year-old bridge really was; he asked himself this same question almost every time he drove across it. It was funny that he never worried much about the second, shorter span that linked Pass Island with the rocky ledge of solid ground just to the north. "Shorter is always better when it comes to bridges," he had reasoned.

During their first several years of living on Whidbey he took his wife Nan and little Patricia (still in a backpack baby carrier) on a walking tour all the way across the bridge and back. Timothy hadn't been born yet. To Bill at least it had become an annual event; a family photo session always took place at mid-span.

Each succeeding photo showed a typical American family a little older and a little more timeworn but the bridge never seemed to change.

After five years Nan finally mustered the courage to tell Bill that she really didn't enjoy these annual bridge walks that *he* considered to be a family tradition. He'd shown genuine surprise when she told him this. She'd never been so—to the point—with him before. Then she finally explained, "I don't know why but I'm terribly afraid of heights. I always have been...I don't want to go out on the bridge anymore. It makes me feel sick and dizzy to look down."

Bill tried hard to understand her fear that seemed a little irrational to him. He found himself shaking his head, at least inside (out of her sight) and making a curt, disparaging remark (out loud) that only drove her farther into a politely expressed but sullen silence. They finally stopped taking these family trips altogether.

So, when the weather permitted, Bill began to hike by himself along the many park trails that bordered both bridges. On several of these walks that passed directly under the low, green beams of the bridge he used the blade of his jackknife to probe beneath the many thick layers of paint, paint that was supposed to protect them. He was just curious. He'd read that the bridge was last painted back in 1998; for the nearby beams that he could see clearly the paint was thin and bleached and salt corrosion was clearly obvious in some spots. Yet he knew that water could find its way into places man never thought of; few metals tolerated water well. What he found worried him. In several different places he dug out thick brittle layers of flaky orange scale, oxidized iron—pack rust—but he couldn't tell how deep the rust went. It brought to mind the slow, invisible build-up of plaque in human arteries that, if not dealt with, can lead to death. He wondered how extensive was this corrosive, weakening plaque? It was an important question, but because there were usually other people around he didn't want to be noticed inspecting the structure too closely. Concerns about terrorism were still running high after the 9-11 disaster. Each time he drove over the spans, he flashed back to those vivid mental images of painted-over orange rust that he had discovered. Many other thoughts cascaded into his mind as well.

During his college studies he had learned a lot about rivets and bolts that were used to connect all of these beams. One seemingly inconsequential fact he had read suddenly popped into his mind without warning, "Riveted structures may be insufficient to resist seismic loading from earthquakes if the structure

wasn't engineered for such forces. It's a common problem of older steel bridges."
At first he couldn't remember why this was true; but finally he remembered. It
was because a hot rivet cannot be properly heat-treated to give it sufficient hardness and strength. As Bill looked around he noticed that almost every beam of
this bridge was connected with multiple rivets, their factory heads bulging from
one side in precise, equally spaced geometric patterns. He knew that if one rivet
broke before the load on it could be redistributed to adjacent rivets at that joint
a catastrophic failure could occur. He'd remembered this particular fact because a question about it had been asked on a mid-term exam during one of his
engineering courses. When he had jotted in the margin that "All joint fasteners
should reach capacity simultaneously," his professor had written A+ beside it.

Bill had also read somewhere that the two spans had been completed by
a bridge construction firm in Seattle back in the mid 1930s, but how well it
was designed and how structurally sound its construction was originally didn't
matter as much to him now as how it had weathered the corrosive, saltwater-
contaminated air and rain over the years and whether its hundreds of joints
had remained sound from the almost constant vibrations from the continuous
stream of traffic it had to carry.

"The fact that there are more than two hundred other bridges in Washington older than the Deception Pass Bridge doesn't make me feel any safer
either," he thought. "The island's population has continued to skyrocket in the
past ten years." These and other thoughts only contributed to his misgivings
related to the increasing vehicle loads that crossed its concrete decking. He had
read that almost 350 large semi-trucks and another 1,285 busses, campers, and
smaller trucks crossed the bridge every single day!

Each time he drove across its main span Bill felt several sharp bumps
(about four seconds apart) caused by his tires and, he reasoned, "...the tires of
every other car and truck as well. These vibrations couldn't be doing the bridge
any good." Once in a while he tried to calculate the total number of axles that
passed over the bridge in a day because, logically, each one would trigger its
own set of small tremors. He was an analytical kind of person who enjoyed
reasoning things out systematically and carefully. He started with the fourteen
thousand five hundred vehicles a day that went across the bridge. This multiplied out to 5.3 million cars and trucks every year! At this point he gave up on
his mental multiplication, feeling a little frustrated. Almost without realizing it
Bill counted each of the bridge surface jolts that his own truck produced every

time he crossed the span; it was just a part of his compulsive nature. It was as if he was adding them all up somewhere deep within his subconscious to see what his own contribution was to the total.

The periodic bumps that he felt reminded him of a special computer analysis program he'd used in his college studies. It had been developed by NASA many years before. Designed to analyze every member of a steel building or bridge, the NASTRAN program, as it was called, could pinpoint structurally weak members by using precisely known vibrations introduced artificially at certain key locations on a bridge or a building. He hoped that someone had used that program here.

He'd also read somewhere that Washington State's Department of Transportation was responsible for inspecting and maintaining almost three thousand five hundred bridges and structures on state highways. "That sounds like an awfully big number to me for even a large crew to be able to inspect," he thought. The article said that all of them were inspected and maintained; this called for another mental calculation. "Let's see, assuming that every bridge is inspected every other year, that's three thousand five hundred divided by seven hundred thirty days…which equals…about four and a half bridges and structures inspected every day!" He felt a little better until he worked out the rest of the calculation. If there were eight-member teams for each inspection, travel time was added, no one took any vacations or weekends off, and the number of useful daylight hours was subtracted, the resulting number of possible inspections was much less encouraging. He hadn't even included the equipment set-up and takedown time required at each location, assuming there was any. Bill had gone through this calculation before and usually gave up because of distractions. This morning was no different.

Bill also knew that truck traffic over the bridge had been climbing about two or three percent each year for a long time. "The total weight of all these trucks must be enormous," he thought. He hoped that the bridge would never be crossed at the same time only by trucks. Still, he knew that trucks and cars could also get onto the island by taking one of two ferryboats, one located near the southern end and the other about halfway up its fifty-mile length. These thoughts passed through his mind incredibly fast, one after the other, like the traffic that crossed the bridge. Suddenly his mind-wanderings were over. Now he had to concentrate on his driving; he was nearing the bridge and the traffic ahead of him had slowed down considerably.

For some reason that only God knew, there was a tall, apparently young man standing on the right side of the road several hundred feet ahead of Bill's truck. He had barely been able to make him out through his smeared windshield. It was obvious that the guy was waiting for a break in the traffic so that he could run across the highway to the parking lot on other side. Bill couldn't see his face because he was turned away and wore a thick, dark colored coat with a parka pulled up over his head.

"Why would anyone be at the bridge at this hour of the day…almost before the sun was up…and in such cold, wet weather?" he asked himself. He hadn't seen anybody else here at this early hour for months and this guy just didn't fit. The fact that the young man was standing at the top of the stairs that went down under the bridge never even registered in Bill's mind.

As the cars ahead of Bill began to slow down it was clear that none of them was going to stop for the pedestrian, so Bill decided to do so. It was his turn to be mister nice guy; so Bill braked and the cars behind him slowed and then came to a complete stop as well. The guy looked over at Bill, gave a grateful wave, paused, and then walked briskly across the highway, dodging the oncoming traffic. No more than eight to ten seconds later the northbound lane began to move forward again.

He could see the red taillights of the string of cars that were just ahead of him now already several hundred feet out onto the bridge. There were also many oncoming headlights, probably commuters who worked somewhere on Whidbey. "Why doesn't everybody put their headlights on low beam?" he muttered to himself. Then, without any kind of warning, all of the vehicles out on the bridge began to slide sideways several feet, first to the right and then left. A small car that was coming toward him slid so far to its left that it collided with a northbound car near mid-span; both sliced diagonally up and through the steel-cabled railing. They came to rest part way on top of the raised pedestrian sidewalk. It was lucky that no one was walking out on the bridge yet.

"Both cars must have been travelling at least thirty to thirty-five miles an hour," he reasoned. Within several more seconds all the other cars travelling in both directions came to a screeching stop on the wet pavement, several colliding with others in front of them. Bill jammed on his own brakes with his front tires only yards back from the bridge deck. He was the last vehicle still on solid ground. He had the front row seat for what happened next, a scene that would haunt him forever.

Bill sat watching in fascinated awe and increasing fear, as the pavement on the surface of the bridge ahead of him now seemed to rise and fall in long undulating roller coaster waves. What he had learned in his bridge design courses suddenly came back to him; he held his breath without realizing it. "It just shouldn't be doing this; the Narrows Bridge was much longer and designed to be flexible, this one was designed to be rigid; where is the sheet motion they told us about?" Just for a moment he thought he could make out some horizontal swaying but it was hard to tell. The roofs and in some cases even the headlights and taillights of cars and trucks out on the span rose up into view and then disappeared again behind nearer cars until the undulating wave finally reached him. He knew that they must be rising and falling at least five or six feet to be visible above the roofs of the nearer cars! Then it was his turn and he felt his pickup truck quickly lift and fall within a second, a second that seemed like an eternity. Huge similar motions were repeated several more times. Then, abruptly, he came back into a present in which ordinary time flowed steadily again.

He noticed a muffled thunderous sound like a chorus of deep kettledrums coming from somewhere nearby. In his rear-view mirror he saw the solid rock hillside on his right side begin to collapse over the tops of several cars and a large delivery truck. Within seconds only its crushed white top was visible anymore, covered by the rain-softened earth and jagged granite boulders. Several other cars were no longer visible at all! Several small granite boulders crashed against the right rear of his truck jarring him to the left.

When Bill looked forward again he was shocked to see the long string of taillights begin to disappear! Starting in mid-span they just dropped out of sight, seeming to drag those cars ahead and behind them into the dark depths of Deception Pass 180 feet below. It was as if each vehicle was fastened to the next with an unbreakable chain, each being dragged forward against its will and then dropped! He cried out in raw fear as he grabbed the door handle to get out. He might somehow be pulled over the edge, too, along with the other cars, he thought. His rational thought was evaporating.

It was over in less than fifteen seconds. A large section at the center of the main span of the Deception Pass Bridge had just broken apart and fallen into the swirling black waters below taking many cars and several large trucks with it. Most of the lucky drivers in line behind Bill were in shock, others were crying uncontrollably or swearing or praying, overcome with horror. Many of them were asking why they were even ten or twenty seconds late and had been spared such an awful death. Bill asked himself the same thing and why a lone pedestrian had wanted to run across the highway just then, just when *he* was about to cross the bridge. He looked to his left around the parking lot briefly but couldn't locate the man.

7:35 am

Naval Air Station Whidbey Island—Runway 07

When the first quake struck Whidbey Island several seconds after 7:35 a U. S. Navy EA-6B Prowler jet with its four-man crew had just begun its takeoff roll down runway seven more than a mile and a half in length. The airplane was enroute to an aircraft carrier cruising off the southern Oregon coast. A light rain was falling and visibility was about three miles. The experienced pilot had reached a speed of 95 knots when, like Kate in her SUV, he felt a slight, unusual, sideways jolt as if a tire had blown out, but since he felt no roll or any other sign of a blowout he continued to accelerate. Seconds later he passed his max abort speed, the speed at which he was committed to take off. Reaching 145 knots (just beyond the three-quarter mark of the runway) he saw its surface begin to rise up at the far end and come rolling toward him in several continuous sine-wave-like crests several feet high! His first rational thought was that it was some kind of trick of optical refraction in his forward canopy. Maybe a maintenance person hadn't wiped the glass completely clean and had left horizontal streaks; but then within several more seconds, just as he pulled back on the stick to lift the nose of his aircraft, he reached the nearest of these rigid incompressible travelling waves. The crew heard and felt a loud explosive crash as both of its main gear were instantly driven upward and back blowing out both tires by the tremendous force with a shattering jolt. What the crew couldn't see was that one wheel strut was severely bent, the rubber tire on the opposite side was flailing backward in the wind-stream, and that both of the wing tanks had been punctured and were leaking fuel! He quickly and instinctively added more power and regained pitch control but couldn't get his main gear to retract. Several red panel indicators flashed at him along with the red and white barber pole indicator that he had learned about several years before but, thankfully, had never seen come on in flight…until now. He also heard the incessant, repeating, grating sounds of several of the aircraft's auditory alerts. A quick systems check told him that the electrical, fuel, and hydraulic systems all seemed to be functional, as was his attitude control system. He began to relax a little. He was airborne, accelerating, had a positive rate of climb, and was already three hundred feet above the ground. He and his three crewmen were heading east, just approaching State Route 20.

He relaxed a little more as he watched his airspeed continue to climb over 180 knots, yet hovering just below his immediate awareness was his concern over what had happened. He was able to take a quick glance below him through the side of his rain-streaked canopy at the heavy traffic heading north and south. It seemed somehow different from what he had seen during any of his previous flights. Some of the cars had stopped while others were moving very slowly. Still others had swerved sideways onto both shoulders, one was completely off the embankment, nose down in a cow pasture. The young ace didn't have time to see more than this. He instructed his electronic countermeasures officer number one, ECMO-1 for short, who was sitting to his right to radio the tower. Moments later only static was heard in response. The pilot decided against continuing his climb straight out over Dugualla Bay as he might have done had the aircraft's damage symptoms been worse than they seemed to be. This would have been SOP. So far at least, his airplane seemed to be OK; so he banked left following the Navy's standard landing pattern. He intended to fly closer to the tower for a visual inspection of his airplane. He changed his down-wind heading a little farther left than usual. Then he had his navigation officer broadcast in the blind on their assigned com frequency. Maybe that would get through and the tower guys could signal him with a colored light gun or a flare or something. He knew that he had to land somehow, someplace but he didn't know when or where.

The thin rain and haze of the overcast blocked him from seeing very far horizontally in any direction. Anyway he had to concentrate on keeping his airplane under control. He glanced ahead and to his left as he passed just north of the Naval Air Station's control tower at five hundred feet above the ground. The tower looked OK as did all the other hangers and support buildings below him; but there was still no response at all from the tower. "That's strange," he said out loud, "the runway lights are out and none of the building floodlights are on either." Now he knew that something was really wrong. In a louder voice he said, "Well guys. We're going to go around again. Maybe we can find out what's happening down there." He glanced down at his fuel capacity indicator and was relieved to find that he had 15,100 pounds of fuel.

7:38 am

South of the Bridge

Kate felt angry and frustrated as she got out of her car to inspect the damage to her rear bumper and to size up the guy who had just rammed her. She walked to the rear of her car as he climbed out and walked toward her. She glanced at the front end of his truck but couldn't see any damage at all. "Isn't that always the way?" she mumbled. She saw wide, deep creases in her own brand new bumper with another vertical crease running half-way up the rear door. Even without any knowledge of what the repair costs were these days she knew that it would cost somebody many thousands of dollars.

She turned toward the young man, obviously in his early twenties. He wore faded jeans and a red checkered wool shirt. Even some distance away from him she could see that he hadn't shaved for some time. She was getting more and more upset, almost on the edge of tears. She got hold of herself but all she could say was, "Look what you've done to my brand new car." She was feeling angry now and began to cry; the young man didn't know what to say or do with an older woman who was crying because of him.

Within herself Kate knew that her words alone couldn't fix the problem, her Dad had taught her that long ago, but she was still angry with this nerd. "Why do young guys always drive so fast and so close?" she said quietly with clenched teeth.

They were just starting to take each other's license numbers and insurance information when the second quake struck. It was far more violent than the first. It happened unexpectedly a little over three minutes after the first one had ended, as people were still wondering what had happened. The earth shook once again only this time the movement was far more furious than before with a stronger horizontal movement in the east—west direction. It began with a strange, faintly audible rumble coming from deep down in the earth, a sound vaguely like a huge nearby diesel locomotive at low power idle. Within seconds everyone on Whidbey Island and all of the surrounding islands in northern Puget Sound heard this totally foreign sound. It rose and fell in intensity as if the locomotive engineer was playing with his throttle. Some said that they even heard this sound on the mainland as far as fifty to one hundred miles to the south and east. Yet even if these outlying areas didn't hear the sound they all felt the tremendous jolts that lasted for thirty-two seconds.

Without any warning at all both Kate and the young man found themselves flat on the ground. Neither of them had noticed that most of the other drivers nearby had also gotten out of their vehicles, as if it was somehow safer there; many of them had also toppled over. Kate was scared and cried out; the young guy lying several feet away from her only whimpered, a tight grimace plastered on his pink young face.

All of the vehicles in Kate's direction began to slide part way across the pavement trapping several people underneath them. A fully loaded cement truck several cars behind Kate's SUV was jostled sideways (its brakes were still fully set). With each new powerful sway of the ground it worked its way backward, down the slight grade striking a small foreign car and crushing its front end... its driver trapped inside. The lateral swaying went on and on as time seemed to stand still. The amplitude of each lateral wave must have been fairly constant as the rows of cars in both the north and southbound lanes all slid back and forth in unison pretty much by the same distance; first west, then east, then west again by a yard or more each time. One might have been watching a chorus line that was out of practice. Little by little each vehicle changed its direction on the pavement until it wasn't possible to tell what direction they had been travelling in the first place. They were all headed in every which way and spread across the two-lane road.

Soon after the earthquake began Kate became aware of the strange noise whose volume seemed to ride the waves that continued to sweep over the earth. She was afraid because she'd never heard such an ominous sound before. She looked all around her but couldn't see anything that would cause such a deep throbbing; the sound also seemed to her to produce a sensation inside her body, something like deep heat. Apparently the other drivers nearby also heard it because they were also looking around to find its source.

After what seemed like an eternity the ground suddenly stopped moving and the noise stopped almost at the same moment. Finally, Kate and the young man were able to stand up, both thankful to be alive. She held on to her roof rack for support. She had no idea how much time had gone by and, since there had been two separate earthquakes already, she was sure there would be more.

She was afraid and when she looked down, she saw blood. Her left thigh was bleeding badly and her pants were beginning to seep blackish red, warm and thick. Yet she didn't feel any particular pain there only a tingling sensation in her left wrist. She was unaware of why but thought she must have tried to break her fall with her arms and hands. Her skin abrasions would be the least of her concerns.

Farther up ahead in the same line of traffic Bill had gotten out of his truck to run across the now empty southbound traffic lane to the parking lot area, to be farther away from the granite hillside that was close beside his truck. He didn't want to be buried if that part of the hill decided to come down like it already had on those poor people behind him. Bill knew that the hillside across from the public parking area at the south end of the bridge was almost solid granite. "How could it crumble like that?" he asked himself. For decades second growth evergreen trees had discovered ways to cling to the solid, fractured faces of the granite, but now several of them lay part way across the highway, their roots exposed like bleached bony fingers. Bill's rational mind tried to convince him that solid rock can't split apart and fall down but he'd just seen it happen. He ran across the roadway to the parking area as several people ran towards him off the bridge.

Even though it was still quite dark and misty out Bill could see all the way across the main channel of Deception Pass and down to the water's swirling surface beneath the bridge. The temblor had conspired with gravity and the very deep channel to swallow up over a hundred foot-long center section of the span. The bridge's roadway in front of Bill's truck still hung out over open space for a hundred yards or so; many cars and trucks were stranded and unmoving on it. Beyond them there was nothing at all. For some reason the grayish concrete vertical support column at the north end of the main bridge span hadn't fractured and still supported another section of roadway facing out in his direction. Bill couldn't see the bridge's foundation on his side but it must still be there too, he reasoned. He could see people running off of both spans toward firm ground.

Across the mist-filled pass he could just make out the twisted, gaping end of a huge water pipe that was hanging down at a steep angle from the end of the bridge that was still standing. Water poured out of it into the salt water below. Its fresh water would no longer reach Oak Harbor or the Naval Air Station.

He was relieved that the first tremor had stopped, that the earth was firm and fixed again, and that noise had also stopped. It seemed to him like it had lasted less than a minute but he couldn't be sure. A few of the people behind him were beginning to gather in the parking lot near the highway; all of them stood in a strangely muted silence. There was nothing to say. No one panicked. The only sound that he heard was some soft muffled moaning and cries coming from an older car that had been behind him and that now was almost totally buried beneath huge granite boulders. He could see that there was nothing he could do to help them.

Bill walked carefully toward the brink of the hillside that dropped steeply down to sea level. He wanted to get a better look at the tragedy he had just witnessed. That was when the second tremor hit with a violence that was truly unbelievable and far more terrifying than the first. The dark evergreen trees around the parking area started to sway under the influence of some invisible force that wasn't the wind. In fact, there was almost no wind at all, and that awful noise came back!

Bill had never been in an earthquake before. He didn't realize how they can quickly undermine one's confidence in reality and shake one's fundamental belief in the permanency and stability of the earth. His first experience with a constantly moving deck had been onboard a Naval supply ship in the South Pacific at the far edge of a typhoon. It was only when Bill had been a landlubber crewman on board a friend's small cabin cruiser in heavy seas that he had really begun to understand how hard it is to stand up and walk on an irregularly moving surface. Now he had to face this new reality on land, a reality where the tops of trees swayed back and forth twenty feet or more while the ground beneath them moved in the opposite direction. Somehow he managed to stagger over to the trunk of a young fir tree at the very brink of the cliff and wrap his arms around its rough bark, feeling its various twisting vibrations against his chest. It made him feel a little more secure than standing out in the open for some reason. Small branches started falling on him from above, bruising his head and shoulders, but he decided that they were probably better than what might happen to him over there, out in the open, near that hillside. He didn't see what the other people were doing behind him but only heard their cries of fear and panic along with that terrible, oscillating roar from deep underground.

The noises of this second earthquake were truly awesome and continuous. To him they began a second or two before the temblor was felt and stopped abruptly just as it ended. It was as if the earth was crying out in anguish at the pain it felt deep deep underground, the pangs of change and new birth. These sounds were terrifying not only because they were so unnatural but also because of their incessant, very low frequencies that seemed to vibrate and warm his viscera. The earth wasn't supposed to have a voice but it did; but what happened next literally froze him in disbelief.

As he clung to the base of the tree he could see everything. The two ends of the main span that were still in place began to whip back and forth, literally tossing all of the cars and trucks off into the water below. As the mechanical forces became too great for them sections of concrete pavement began falling between the parallel steel beams beneath them; more cars followed them down. Finally, both ends snapped off and followed all of the vehicles in a vertical dive that seemed to take place in ultra slow motion. Within ten or twenty seconds time, he couldn't tell for sure, there was nothing at all left of the main span except twenty feet of naked twisted steel sticking out at odd angles from the formerly solid concrete foundations near him!

Bill wrapped his arms around the trunk even more tightly and looked out across the opening to the solid jagged dome of rock called Pass Island that was over 190 feet high. It anchored the northern end of the main bridge span and the southern end of the shorter 511 foot-long span over Canoe Pass farther to the north. As far as he could tell the shorter bridge span was still in place, thank God, with a solid line of unmoving automobile headlights facing in different directions on its pavement, pavement that was lashing back and fourth savagely. He could just make out a streaming mass of people trying to run back across its span onto solid ground as the second jolt continued to pummel the earth with gigantic, sideways blows.

"They probably didn't know what had happened to the cars ahead of them," Bill reasoned, "now all gone." As more and more people reached solid ground at the far north end of the bridge the force of the quaking grew to such an extreme magnitude that the fifty foot high cliff of gray-brown solid granite beside the road began to fracture diagonally, vertically, and in other directions just as it had done near him. He watched the huge jagged boulders fall onto the cars and many scores of people, burying them quickly and completely without any hope at all. He couldn't see many details but he could imagine the terrible toll over there. Bill's emotions had not yet caught up with the first deaths he had seen on his side of the bridge. These new deaths only added to his feeling of numbness and denial. He wondered if the earth would ever stop its rocking.

Then, staring in utter disbelief, Bill watched in horror as the shorter span of the bridge over Canoe Pass twisted and buckled and very slowly came apart; like a young boy might twist paper straws just for the fun of it into forms that are no longer recognizable. He knew that it was the horizontal whipsaw motion of the ground that forced it apart. It didn't take an engineer to understand that it just wasn't designed to withstand this kind of extreme lateral displacement.

For a second time within minutes existence seemed to slow as if to make this visual nightmare even more permanent, more indelible; he watched help-lessly as car after car dropped vertically out of sight behind the rocky island that separated him from them. Then the screaming of the crowd in the parking area behind him penetrated his consciousness; they were screams of helplessness, utter terror, and realizations of what might lie ahead for each of them. He knew that even though he couldn't hear them the screams of the others out there across the pass were just as loud and soul wrenching.

So many were gone so quickly. Men, women, and even some children had gone to meet their maker in the freezing waters beneath the bridge without any hope at all of surviving the vertical plunge or the crushing deceleration at impact or the suffocation of drowning that took place within a minute or two under water even if they had somehow survived the fall...and Bill realized that he could do nothing to help! He began to feel an awful burning in the pit of his stomach. It would stay with him for a long time.

After what seemed like an eternity in slow motion the temblor finally ground to a stop. That awful noise stopped with it. Time started up again. He didn't dare let go of the only firm thing he had found. "It could happen again," he reasoned. After five more terrifying, now deathly silent, minutes he loos-ened his bear hug around the tree trunk and stepped back onto the parking lot surface several yards and took a deep breath. Then he got an idea.

Bill pulled out his cell phone and quickly punched in a single, auto-dial number. "Yeah, Denny, this is Bill...it's happened!"

The voice on the other end of the line asked rapidly, "Is this Bill?...What do you mean? You mean the earthquake...are you OK?"

"Yeah, but I'm shaking pretty badly...there are a lot of others here much worse off than me...sorry, I've got to go. I'll call you later."

The other voice cried, "No, wait! Where are you?"

Bill sobbed, "I'm at the south end of the bridge! It's totally gone. I, I almost went with it!"

He barely heard Denny's voice. It was as if his words were drifting through a very thick fog. Bill heard him say, "Call your wife man. Get home right away. It's already terrible here in town. Fires seem to be starting up everywhere."

Bill's heart skipped a beat. Then he said, "I'll try to call you later Denny," and hung up abruptly.

While Bill and several others nearby had done what they could to rescue people trapped under huge boulders they had absolutely no success at all. They didn't have any way of lifting tons of rocks off the cars and trucks all by themselves. The victims who were still alive had to be left. This only contributed to Bill's growing feelings of guilt.

Meanwhile, the EA-6B crew was busily checking all of its complex, aircraft subsystems. Had the loss of the main gear caused a slow leak in the hydraulic lines? Had a power control cable been severed or bent into uselessness? Why didn't their radios work? The ECMO1 switched frequencies again and everyone was relieved to find that their radio actually did work. He was able to reach an air traffic controller for the northwest sector of Seattle's TRACON. He informed the Navy jet that there had been an earthquake but didn't know anything more than that. He suggested that Navy jet "Five-One-Eight" continue to try to reach its own base's controller and to let him know if there was anything he could do to help. Even during his second circuit of the landing pattern the pilot had failed to look at the fuel indicator.

Now that the pilot thought the rest of his airplane was reasonably sound he could concentrate on isolating the problem and also take a look outside the cockpit. When he did he saw that the jet was surrounded only by gray clouds and mist that became lighter and lighter as they rose in altitude. He couldn't see anything else outside.

Checking his compass he was now heading west-northwest out over Puget Sound eight miles from the shoreline and climbing through an altitude of 4,500 feet. He had reduced his airspeed back down to 185 knots due to a strange vibration that began whenever he increased it more than that. Although he was pretty sure he was the only Navy jet in the air at that time he decided to extend his downwind leg farther than normal as they continued to try to contact the tower. There was no way he could know that although still standing upright the

Air Station's control tower was no longer functional. When the bridge collapsed the main electrical power lines strung high over the water at the pass nearby also snapped; the base's emergency power generators hadn't yet switched on.

There was also no way that the pilot could know that he was literally on his own if he decided to return and land at Whidbey. He still hadn't noticed that he was leaking fuel at a pretty high rate and could never reach the carrier at sea; he did know that his first alternate runway was Paine Field south of Everett, yet they didn't have any arresting gear stretched across the runway to stop his aircraft. He would have to fly to his second alternate, McCord Air Force Base south of Tacoma where they had a trap. The difficulty there was that it took twenty minutes to get it set up and he might or might not have that much time left.

Back on the island Kate sat in her car. She had finally swapped all of the required accident information with the young man who had hit her. She was shaking and feeling weak more from the collision than her roller coaster ride during the quake. She spread out her plastic raincoat beneath her to keep the blood from reaching the new tan leather. To be sure that it didn't she also put a plastic bag under that. Her wrist throbbed and she rubbed it with her other hand. The minutes clicked by slowly and she wondered what she should do now. Kate finally noticed that the traffic had stopped coming down the grade from the direction of the bridge for some reason. That was strange. Something was probably blocking traffic, probably another accident like hers. She wondered if she should wait for the traffic to begin to move north again? "It shouldn't be too long," she reasoned. "I still have to get to work."

Most of the other drivers had also gotten back into their cars to keep warm, all of them wondering what had caused the traffic tie up.

After several more impatient minutes Kate finally saw the headlights of a single vehicle coming from the direction of the bridge. It was the first one since the second temblor and it had its emergency flashers on. It didn't look to her like a park ranger or a highway department truck. Kate was a take charge kind of woman and she had to find out what had happened, so she opened her door, got out, and limped out into the oncoming lane to flag down the approaching pickup truck as it wove its way slowly between the other cars that were still spread across the pavement. The pain in her thigh was beginning to come on stronger now.

Bill saw her and came to a stop. He was shaking so much that he had trouble rolling down his window. His face was ashen white and his voice trembled; all kinds of thoughts crowded into his head and there were tears in his eyes. Before Kate could say anything he looked at her and just said, "It's gone down." His voice cracked unnaturally. It was all he could manage to say.

Kate looked at him intently. She could see that something was terribly wrong. She noticed him shaking his head back and forth slightly, almost out of control. "What? What's gone down?" She asked, looking into his eyes for some kind of nonverbal explanation.

He couldn't speak for a long time. He could only swallow as he bent his head down, his eyes shut. Finally he lifted his head and looked at her and stammered with a voice that showed that he was suddenly awfully tired and afraid. "The whole...the whole bridge!

Kate felt her knees go weak and she cried, "Oh my God, no...When?"

Then Bill realized not only what he had said but also how he had said it. He shouldn't have been so blunt; yet he had to...facts are facts. There was no other way but to tell her the truth straight out. His voice softened a little as he choked, "I was there. I saw it all...just now." He couldn't hide the terrible burning anguish he felt inside. Finally he was able to focus on Kate's face through his blurred vision; his hands trembled although he was still clutching his steering wheel. He was so caught up in his own images that he hadn't thought about what might have happened to her.

Kate just stood there beside his truck shaking and crying for a long time. Finally she managed to say, "My sister...and her son...they were just a little ways ahead of me." She sobbed again. She couldn't say anything more.

Then, without any forethought Bill reached out of his window and took her hand in both of his huge hands like a loving older brother might have done. She continued to sob uncontrollably. He didn't know what else to say or do so he just held her hand, feeling her warmth and softness. Bill didn't know why but her touch helped him push those images away for a few brief moments.

Finally a few more cars began to approach them from the direction of the bridge.

Bill let go of her hand gently, slowly, as if to try to give her some kind of reassurance even though there was no way that he really could. As he began to process what she had just said to him he realized that she was starting to grapple with death and grieve the possible loss of her sister and nephew. She was at the early stages of processing the harsh reality of death, death that he had just witnessed himself. He had been the one to force that awful possibility upon her.

The news of what had happened to the bridge spread quickly to the other drivers still waiting in line. A few of those returning from the bridge stopped along the way to tell them. Most had been so far back around the curve, however, that they hadn't seen it happen themselves but had only learned the basic facts from a few others who had. They'd felt the ground shake and heard or even seen the rock cliff fall, but everyone had heard that awful noise coming from underground. Other than that they only repeated what they had heard from a few others.

The two major tremors had been followed by dozens of smaller aftershocks that continued for several more hours. Nevertheless, it was becoming apparent to everyone (except perhaps the experts far away) that the worst was finally over.

Soon after the two major temblors had stopped vehicle traffic began to surge back south away from the terrible gap where the Deception Pass Bridge had stood less than an hour before. Most of the drivers were orderly but some drove as if their lives depended on getting away from the ruins of the bridge. There were over a dozen accidents within a ten mile long stretch of two lane black top. While most of the drivers obeyed the law and exchanged the required accident information many others didn't and merely drove away quickly as hit and runs. It was clear that emotions were running high; and the main source of these emotions was raw fear, a fear that lay barely hidden below the surface of most of them. Other drivers were still headed north toward the bridge because they didn't yet know that it had collapsed. They only contributed to the growing traffic problems.

Still, news of the disaster spread like the high winds of the night before.

Now, like everyone else, Kate was determined to get back home at all costs too. She was a strong and self-reliant woman but now she needed the quiet protection of her own home. More importantly she knew that she had to find out if her sister and nephew were OK, she would phone them. Finally, with huge tears streaming down her cheeks, Kate thanked Bill and turned slowly away. Returning to her car she noticed that her thigh was beginning to throb in time with her heart beat.

Like many others who were driving south Kate's thinking was confused and slow. She wondered about what the earthquake and the loss of the bridge might mean, but foremost in her mind were her sister and young Jim. Where had they been when the earthquake struck? Did they make it across? If they were alive where were they? Sometimes the unknown carries with it much greater anguish than the known. Imagination carries with it its own peculiar penalties. She noticed several emergency vehicles speeding past her in the direction of the bridge, units from the North Whidbey Fire and Rescue station, their sirens blaring and lights flashing, but they were strangely muted; she was in a state of shock that dulled the rest of her trip home.

7:38 am

Strait of Juan de Fuca near Port Angeles

Normally it was the tremendous weight of seawater in the Strait of Juan de Fuca pressing down on the firm bedrock below that helped keep the subterranean plates locked together. This vast downward pressure, spread out over so many square miles of sea, was transmitted to the plate-rock almost sixty miles farther down. There happened to be unusually low tides for several days before this earthquake. When both the atmospheric pressure and the volume of seawater decreased by so great an amount, their combined downward pressure also decreased greatly. This reduced pressure was transmitted to a particular region where the two massive plates met. Experts called it a reverse fault. The upper plate had interlocked with the lower plate aeons before in a kind of stair-step shaped grip. Ancient mariners would have called it a ratchet and pawl. The experts had long surmised that potential energy had been building up slowly but steadily within these plates but couldn't be released because of the extreme rigidity of both masses. Rather than fracture into many smaller volumes within the two plates both had remained integral until now.

The energy that was released by the sudden snap slippage was so great in magnitude that a gigantic shock wave was sent upward at the speed of sound finally arriving at the surface of the earth, in this case the Strait of Juan de Fuca. The fluid sea had to give way!

A tremendous bulge rose from below the surface of the strait centered seventeen miles west of Whidbey Island, the earthquake's epicenter. The surface of the water became as smooth as plastic wrap stretched over a rapidly inflating balloon. Within a minute this mound of seawater rose upward over seventy feet before falling into its own perfectly round, smooth, deep crater again of almost equal depth. The result was a tidal wave that moved concentrically outward in all directions, a towering wave that moved at over forty miles per hour. The first wave would reach the nearest points of land (the southern coastlines of San Juan and Lopez Islands) in a matter of minutes. The easterly portion of the first surge was approaching the northwest coast of Whidbey Island where the Naval Air Station was located. Much of the air base stood only 50 feet above mean sea level. What was even more crucial was the fact that when the waves reached land there had been almost no energy loss within them because the distance it had to travel was so small.

No tsunami alert was issued on the island! There wasn't time and, even if there had been, there was no electricity to operate its sirens. Both sets of high-tension power lines that came across at the northern end of the island just east of the bridge had snapped off in the earthquake. Their tall steel towers had simply collapsed. The northern ends of the many cables sizzled for some time deep under water.

The tidal waves reached around into the snug, hook shaped harbor of Victoria, British Columbia only minutes before it also crashed over the lowest sections of Port Angeles, Washington on the south side of the strait. Residents of every low-lying, coast-side town on southern Vancouver Island and the north-facing shores of the Olympic Peninsula experienced significant destruction from the gigantic surges. Some of the residents in Port Angeles (the city that directly faced the approaching waves) saw it coming but couldn't rationalize what they were seeing at first, losing precious minutes of escape time in the process. Everyone had felt the two strong earthquakes and wondered whether something like this might happen; nevertheless, most of the people were just trying to dig out from the earthquake's destruction. Some just went on about their usual business of living while others tuned their radios to try to get more news. Unfortunately, only a few made their way to higher ground. When the tide, already unusually low, drew out even farther they saw all the litter that lay on the sandy bottom of the bay; litter than never should have been dumped there in the first place. By the time they watched the water ebb far out into the harbor and then begin its inward race (the tall gray wall of water finally becoming visible) it was too late to escape. The slope of the beach there caused a run-up factor of two or three which multiplied the height of each of the three waves even more.

7:48 am

Naval Air Station Whidbey Island

Fortunately the base's Commanding Officer was on site when the two powerful earthquakes hit even though it seemed like he spent most of his time in Washington, D.C. The Captain, his adjutant, and entire office staff managed to get out of the headquarters building a minute before the second quake occurred. At first glance, the initial tremor seemed to have caused more noise and confusion than anything else on the airbase. The Captain was relieved to see more and more people pouring out of the buildings near by. When the second shock struck, however, everybody knew immediately that it was far worse than the first, but everyone rode it out sitting on the ground or hanging onto nearby tree trunks.

Most of the larger and newer concrete buildings appeared to have survived; if the many wide stress cracks didn't count, if tilted concrete-block end walls on many buildings didn't count, and if geysers shooting columns of water into the air from broken water mains didn't count. The control tower was still standing, a clear tribute to the structural design engineers and talented men and women who had built it; but the group of uniformed men and women could only look around them in awe as the power beneath the earth's surface had its way with man's puny, constructed things. They knew that there was absolutely nothing they could do right now, only wait it out and hope that the earth under their feet didn't open up and swallow them.

Everyone knows that the U. S. military is well prepared to cope with all kinds of emergencies, not least of which is loss of electrical power. It was just over four minutes after the main temblor had stopped that the sounds of diesel fueled generators could be heard starting up from different locations around the base.

One of the flight operations officers standing beside the C.O. had watched the sole EA-6B take off minutes earlier. "Man is he lucky to be up there right now," he reflected. He wouldn't know for several more hours that that very airplane was doomed.

The Commanding Officer, recently appointed to Naval Air Station Whidbey Island said, "We have to contact Washington immediately...and I need a preliminary assessment of the injuries and damage as soon as possible. Be sure to contact flight operations and ground all aircraft too." As soon as he had uttered these words several officers and enlisted men ran off in different directions (with an almost simultaneous ripple of Aye Aye, sirs and smart salutes).

Over the next fifteen minutes he discovered that eighty percent of their power had come back on, injuries had been relatively light considering the huge magnitude of the quake (the death toll had not yet come in), and the base had gone into a one-hundred percent lock-down at his command. No one would come aboard or leave the base until further orders.

Just as he was about to issue more orders he was abruptly cut short by the stifled cry from a Chief Petty Officer standing nearby who happened to be facing the coastline. He was the first person to see the tall, steep wall of sky-gray water approaching them from the west. Its upper edge was smooth and almost merged imperceptibly with the lead sky; it looked like it was moving in very slow motion and there was no line of white water frothing along its upper edge as is usually seen. Unexpectedly there was a new edge to the world. As everyone turned to see what he was looking at it became clear that the wave was so high that it would breach the level land and come far inland.

"Oh my God," was all the chief could say, his emotions taking complete control of his speech. The others around him could only stare in disbelief at the fluid mountain that was rolling directly toward them.

In less than three more minutes the first gigantic wave reached the shoreline and smashed down silently (sound travelling so much slower than sight). Finally the group heard its muffled roar. Up until now the tsunami had seemed like some kind of bad dream but its sound had finally confirmed its reality. It's so easy to deny something that had never happened before.

Finally the men and women started running for higher ground toward the south but they realized it would be a touch and go thing because of the long gradual slope ahead of them. The wave was still over fifty feet high and came crashing inland over the low beach area at high speed. The huge, low building nearest the coast took the brunt of the wave almost immediately. It housed the ultra secure Naval Ocean Processing Facility where acoustic information arrived from a vast array of sensors designed to provide continuous maritime surveillance against attack.

None of their own sea sensors had given any warning of the waves that had originated less than eighteen miles away. It was as if no one had considered this possibility; it was too close a threat to be concerned about! Without warning it was impossible for the building's evacuation plan to be followed by the almost four hundred souls who worked inside. Even if they had had several minutes advanced warning they couldn't have outrun the first gigantic surge because the land was so gently sloped upward. A hundred feet of running would only gain them three, four, or five feet of elevation at the most.

The crushing weight of the seawater collapsed over half of the roof area of the NOPF building within seconds, flooding most of the interior compartments and drowning more than forty-five personnel. It was fortunate that the primary electrical power had already gone out all over the base and that only those emergency generators designed to come on immediately (to keep the computers running) had functioned. Otherwise many people would have been electrocuted. It was also fortunate that the bad weather had affected the arrival of some of the men and women who commuted from off island. At least seven U.S. officers, eight Canadians, and twelve civilians had not yet shown up for work!

The force of the gray water-wall was tremendous, reaching the broad, flat ends of the western most hangers and other buildings first. It slammed against the heavy sheet metal skin of the buildings like the fist of a giant prizefighter sending airplanes and people tearing away to the east, a flood of living flailing flesh and silver mangled metal.

The C.O. and others outside of the administration building had been able to run only a hundred yards to slightly higher ground before the first wave finally reached them. Its height had diminished but was still several stories high; its force literally swept them along, many underwater, over a quarter mile before depositing them like driftwood on the earth. As the first of the three gigantic waves retreated slowly back in the opposite direction several people found themselves deposited almost where they had started! They were the lucky ones, alive and freezing cold. Others had drowned. The survivors didn't know what would happen next but they tried their best to reach higher ground. Only a few of them noticed the terrible devastation the first wave had produced. Only the buildings and equipment located at higher elevations had survived.

Located a little farther inland from the beach was the square concrete base of the control tower. It withstood the water's impact but there was a long white wake that streamed around both sides of it toward the east. Looking down from the top of the tower (and now surrounded completely by water) several air traffic controllers felt as if they were looking down from the bow of a large ship steaming at high speed. Both small and large airplanes parked neatly in their assigned spots were forcibly spun around or pushed up against others nearby. When the water had finally subsided several of the airplanes were lying upside down a quarter-mile from where they had been parked.

It had taken almost four minutes for each of the three primary waves to come ashore and then go back out again. The slowly receding water of the first surge had lured some personnel to go back inside their offices. Most of them had been drowned without any warning whatsoever by the second wave that returned. All three waves inevitably took more lives and destroyed more valuable hardware all over the base until they, too, subsided as the sea finally came to rest again.

7:49 a.m.

West Beach

The last several miles of Whidbey Island's northwestern coastline is generally low, lying not more than twenty feet above sea level. A low, flat valley about three and a half miles long and almost a mile wide runs east and west across the entire island (four miles south of Deception Pass). This valley was selected to be the site of Naval Air Station Whidbey Island at the outbreak of WW II because of its good weather and many other important factors.

The West side of the island, immediately south of the air base, rises up steeply from the beach to form a bluff more than two hundred feet high in some places. It is composed mostly of pure sand and faces the Strait of Juan de Fuca squarely. An official tsunami evacuation sign is posted prominently on West Beach Road that runs along the top of the bluff where many old and new homes have been built treacherously near its edge. When the first gigantic wave approached this shoreline the beach run-up caused the water to slow down while its height was multiplied by seven or eight times. The result was a tremendous compression that forced the wave up and over the top of the bluff in many areas! Its impact caused scores of houses along the top of the bluff to come off their foundations or simply collapse altogether. Numerous others slid down the almost vertical bank as the sand fell away beneath them. Some of the aftershocks of the earthquake broke more of the sand loose, which slid down to bury several of these houses. Houses that were set farther back from the cliff's edge survived with less damage.

What the earthquake didn't demolish near sea level the tsunami did. When they finally reached Whidbey Island's northwestern coast the three towering waves produced massive damage to property and terrible loss of human and animal life. Their force carried sea water completely across the low section of the island where the Naval Air Station was located with a wave that was still over fifteen feet high by the time it finally emptied into Dugualla Bay to the east.

The most awesome destruction, however, occurred to the homes sitting just above sea level along West Beach Road. Most were completely demolished as they were first swept inland a quarter of a mile and then sucked back out to sea by the initial wave. Tragically, some of their occupants were still trapped inside them when the wall of water struck. Where there had been a continuous row of homes now there was only lumber and furniture, books and clothing, junk from garages and every other sort of object imaginable. Their colorful remains floated in hundreds of thousands of odd shaped pieces. The area was marked by occasional brick chimneys, still standing like silent sentinels on guard of the now vacant land. Huge driftwood logs were deposited far inland. Even the paved roadway was no longer visible. Such was the force of the initial wave.

Yet two more tidal waves, also of extraordinary height and power, were to arrive before the sea finally settled back to its own level. What had not been demolished near sea level by the first wave was utterly destroyed by the next two.

The beautiful and historic portion of Whidbey's western coastline south of the sandy bluffs that were so devastated, known as Ebeys Prairie, were not damaged significantly except for flooding in the low-lying areas. This was because the waves struck only an angled, glancing blow along the more east trending coastline there; the long majestic rollers lost most of their energy as they produced the surf. It was only by chance that the ferryboat that ran between Whidbey Island and Port Townsend was not in either dock when the waves arrived. Its captain just had time to turn the boat into the oncoming waves and ride them out. He was to receive a medal for taking such "immediate and effective action with foresight and bravery."

Because much of the West side of Whidbey Island was hit by the wave head on, so to speak, short wave radio and other calls for assistance arrived at the Island Communications 911 office over a relatively short period of time. The last was separated from the first by about twenty-five minutes; yet the earliest calls went unanswered. The on-duty staff didn't have time to get their emergency power generators working. The already minimally staffed island emergency services office was simply unable to cope with the magnitude of the disaster.

Meanwhile, the Navy jet's flight crew continued to try to isolate the cause of the caution alert indicators that wouldn't go out. It was 8:20. Fortunately, the pilot had had several thousand hours of pilot-in-command time in this model airplane and knew it very well. The four crewmen worked efficiently as a team going systematically through each subsystem using only their NATOPS pocket checklists and knowledge of the airplane that they had gained through the years, but as the minutes passed they began to realize that something was fundamentally wrong. The plane's power and attitude control systems worked normally, as did the electrical and hydraulic systems. It was when they were still in the clouds that the pilot had finally looked carefully at his fuel indicator display, three numbers displayed in small windows near his center panel. What he saw sent a brief wave of panic through him. He said, "Guys! We've got another problem." He paused briefly and then said, "Main Bag, four point eight thousand pounds and zero left in our wing tanks! We've picked up a pretty strong headwind and I've left the flaps down." ECMO-1 turned and said, "Our BINGO for McCord is about five thousand pounds."

The pilot glanced over at him with pursed lips and responded, "Then I'm afraid we can't make it to McCord...our fuel's dropping very fast." They would either have to attempt a crash landing someplace or eject.

When the jet reached twenty two thousand feet altitude it suddenly broke out into clear air. The crystal blue sky around them appeared unexpectedly; instantaneously visibility went from zero to over sixty miles with the snow tipped Olympic Mountains on their right side poking through the sea of ultra-pure white cotton. The scene gave each of them a much needed, if short lived, boost in morale.

Their remaining fuel would give them only about ten more minutes of flight, twelve at the most. Now headed almost due south and well out of commercial flight paths east of the Olympic Peninsula crest, Navy Jet "Five-One-

Eight" seemed under control, for the time being. The pilot said to the navigator, "Call McCord with a dirty BINGO." Then to himself, "We just crossed over from a land as soon as practical to as soon as possible...only I don't think we're going to land."

The airplane's crew didn't know that the air station had gone into a complete lock down, as if war had suddenly broken out. In fact it was very much like a war minus the bullets.

Chapter 2

Forced Changes in the City of Oak Harbor

Oak Harbor began as a typical Northwest pioneer village in the mid 1800s. Many people had hoped that its incorporation in 1915 would bring in more but it wasn't to be. It took the completion of the Deception Pass Bridge on July 31, 1935 and World War II to bring about this result. Although the Navy built a seaplane base near town and a larger land-plane base several miles north seven years later in 1942 it was really the opening of the bridge that permitted all of them to function well. The population and prominence of the village (and its land values) rose quickly thereafter. Yet, as the decades slowly passed relatively little changed in Oak Harbor. More and more of its roads were paved and electricity (and all that it makes possible) finally arrived along with a citywide water and sewer system. Of course, cosmetic changes came to building facades, yet pretty much everything else stayed the same. Deep down in its heart Oak Harbor remained a pioneer town; it was as if its citizens somehow needed to cling to its now accepted virtues; virtues of slow change, quiet streets, friendly neighbors, and oak tree-lined streets that look out over the sheltered, crescent shaped bay to the south. Yes, Oak Harbor embraced its small town flavor throughout the years.

The Irish came in the 1850s to farm and fish, but the most lasting impact upon its culture was made by the Dutch who arrived forty years later, mostly from Minnesota, Michigan, and other northern Midwest states. They found the farming conditions far more supportive here than there. The founding families of Oak Harbor brought with them solid traditions of hard work, high quality, and social cohesiveness. They also tended toward pride in their own European heritage, a pride that largely excluded other nationalities.

Yet to really understand Oak Harbor on the day of the great earthquake one would have had to have lived there and experienced its quiet charm and seen how it clung stubbornly to the past more than aggressively seeking its future.

Oak Harbor's destiny as the largest municipality on Whidbey Island was suddenly about to change.

With a land area of just over nine square miles, Oak Harbor's population density was only about 2,200 people per square mile, however this fact doesn't adequately describe the concentrations of newer neighborhoods that are packed much more closely together. Several large, new housing developments were built, occupied mostly by naval families stationed at the air base and retirees who came to Whidbey, just because they loved it.

Although State Route 20 runs generally north to south through much of Oak Harbor's length, Pioneer Way is a two-lane road that runs east and west through the oldest business district. It parallels the shoreline of the harbor. In earlier days Pioneer Way boasted rough sawn, false-front buildings like any other American town of the mid and late 1800s, some painted, others left to weather naturally in the rain. Most of its original business buildings were one story with a few of two, packed almost side-by-side, without fire hydrants or water mains. Yes, Oak Harbor held all the promise of growth and prosperity that many other small American towns held back then.

Yet even today Pioneer Way seems to symbolize more of its past that its future. Historic photographs taken early in the twentieth century show the settlers standing proudly outside buildings that were located just above the tide line; later land fill created many more acres of valuable land.

Today Oak Harbor boasts a Wall-Mart, Home Depot, and several other large and modern stores along with the usual assortment of small specialty shops and restaurants, fast food stores and markets, strip-malls, banks and savings and loans, realtors, and scores of others businesses. Oak Harbor has grown into a town of over twenty thousand people, but beginning at 7:35 on this particular morning further progress would come to a violent and sudden halt.

Tuesday 7:35 am

Downtown Oak Harbor

The first earthquake shook down several of the older brick and poorly reinforced concrete block buildings along Pioneer Way as well as some older homes in surrounding neighborhoods. It also started a number of fires.

The first telephone call that was routed to the city's Fire Department communications center pin-pointed one of the earliest fires even though the caller didn't know there was a fire. A natural gas line in the furnace of a small dress shop had ruptured before its pilot light flame went out. It's still a mystery how the call even came through.

For some reason Fran had arrived earlier than usual this morning. She was a friendly, outgoing, and attractive California transplant whose instant smile and relaxed manner had drawn many customers into her shop over the years (along with her selection of trendy fashions). As the building began to shake she was arranging new mannequins in her front window display, a long way from the relative safety of a doorway. She could only crouch down and ride it out hoping that the plate glass windows didn't fracture. Fran knew what was happening right away having lived through many before this. As the tremor grew in force most of her shop's false ceiling and a small section of the roof above it fell. Fran was fortunate to not have been hit by one of the main ceiling joists that came crashing down not twenty feet away from her. She was safe and covered only with plaster dust and debris; she choked on the thick dust-filled air. However, she didn't know about the tiny tongue of orange flame from the furnace's gas line that now licked against dry boards, far out of sight beneath a pile of rubble at the rear of her store.

Fran was able to find her phone under a heap of dust-coated ceiling tiles and somewhat to her surprise, it had a dial tone! She blew the dust off and punched in an auto-dial number that she had installed only months before, the Icom-Police Department's non-emergency number! She thought it was 9-1-1. Without even thinking anything about it, she expected the call to go through. It did! For some unknown reason her telephone was still working. Fran felt some relief when she found herself speaking to an actual person and not to a computerized voice; but she was so intent on giving her information to the anonymous female on the other end of the line she didn't notice how frightened the other woman sounded, a voice that should have remained cool, calm, and under control. Fran didn't think to mention that she had just survived a large earthquake.

"My name is Frances Williams and I own the Woman's Mode Dress Shop on Pioneer," she said, "my roof has just collapsed but I'm OK." Then she abruptly hung up.

Fran had lived through two large earthquakes in the San Francisco Bay area that had left her with surprisingly little fear of them, at least not the same kind of fear that many other natives of Oak Harbor were now experiencing. After she hung up she rather calmly looked around for her purse and plowed her way through piles of merchandise that was scattered everywhere. She moved in the direction of her cash register to remove the day's operating cash that she had just put in its drawer; but there wasn't any electricity! It wouldn't open! This made her more angry than anything else. So, as she heard the faint siren of the first emergency vehicles approaching, she resigned herself to getting out of the building as fast as she could. "There might be more aftershocks," she said to herself. She was right! Fran never did smell the smoke that began to rise from the pile of debris in her back room.

Just as she reached the sidewalk the second awful temblor hit; she knew right away that it was much worse than the first. She ran out to the middle of the street just as the whole front wall of her shop and others beside it collapsed outward into the street. Cement blocks cascaded toward her, coming to a stop only yards away! The noises of collapsing buildings kept her from hearing the beginning of the low pervasive rumble all around her. When Fran finally heard it it frightened her more than anything else. It was totally new to her.

As she turned to look up and down the street she saw that most of the other buildings had twisted and already fallen within ten to twenty seconds. They created a surreal landscape out of a wartime picture book complete with choking, swirling clouds of dust that only contributed to a sense of perpetual motion and impermanence. The fires had not yet begun in earnest to replace the dust with smoke. Her adrenaline was beginning to kick in as she began to shake; a cold wave suddenly flooded through her.

She noticed several people down the street who were lying motionless, partially buried under piles of brick and wooden beams; they hadn't outrun their toppling walls in time. Others were moving only slightly in grotesque, limited ways. The fire engine sirens were getting closer now which gave her a kind of comfort that she was not the only whole human being still alive.

Fran ran over to the nearest victim lying on the ground, a middle-aged man whose legs were pinned under a pile of white painted bricks. She began to lift some of them off as she smiled down at him. Most of the bricks were still cemented together and were just too heavy for her to lift so she concentrated on those that she could move. "It'll be OK," she said, yet she wasn't sure if it really would be. The man groaned and then smiled back weakly without saying anything. About then the first firemen arrived and took over. They had the man freed and in an ambulance within minutes. The dozen or so full-time firefighters and almost forty other paid "on call" volunteers would have their work cut out for them today. Finally Fran headed toward her car that she had parked in the lot several doors down but found it had been buried under tons of cement blocks. She walked home discouraged and afraid.

When the initial tremor hit, James McGrath, Oak Harbor's Fire Chief had been on his way to the main station to start his day. He lived in the southeast part of town while his office was in the center of town. He knew that if he was going to go there he would have to cross a massive amount of tree limbs and other debris, vehicle accidents, and downed power wires first. He quickly decided that the first thing he had to do was determine the extent of damage and he could do that via his radio.

It was his responsibility to determine how best to deploy his personnel and their equipment. He had to figure out where his limited resources were best placed before setting up an incident command station. Yet the damage appeared to be so wide spread that it's location probably wouldn't matter. He was thankful he had a short wave radio that worked.

He was heading south on State Route 20 nearing East Whidbey Avenue when the second temblor struck. His red panel vehicle was thrown back and forth almost across the oncoming lanes. Fortunately all of the other traffic was doing the same thing; some vehicles were tossed up onto the sidewalk or against light poles. Within ten seconds he and all the other vehicles had come to a complete stop. He never thought to turn on his red flashing emergency light or his siren. He was too busy hanging on to his steering wheel!

Even as the violent swaying continued for what seemed a very long time other concerns were not very far back in his mind: water, roads that were passable, available manpower. Water was his primary ammunition for fighting fires. He couldn't use dynamite as they had during the terrible San Francisco earthquake of 1906 with awesome consequences. He didn't have anyone trained to use it anyway. "If it gets that bad we might have to contact the Navy's demolition unit, but that would be absolutely my last resort," he reasoned.

As he looked down the highway McGrath saw that the tall metal street lamp poles on the West Side of the road were all swaying back and forth in a smooth, undulating wave. Like tall silver wheat stalks in the wind, each tilted far out over the roadway and then equally far in the opposite direction with each sideways thrust of the ground. The Chief watched in horror as several of them suddenly fractured at their base and fell over, one onto a passing car only a hundred feet ahead of him. The concrete foundations of several other poles simply could not hold them securely and they pulled themselves up out of the earth. Some fell over the highway, others over the sidewalk and nearby buildings. The poles reached almost all the way across the four lanes. They insured that the cars and trucks in both directions didn't move. He didn't find out until later that much the same thing had happened to the highway lamps at several other places along State Route 20 to the north, causing enormous traffic problems and some injuries.

After making sure that the driver was OK inside the partially crushed car ahead of him (he escaped death by inches) Chief McGrath radioed this emergency into his headquarters knowing that the EMT people would be listening as well. An ambulance was dispatched almost immediately. Then he turned on his lights and siren.

He left the scene making his way to the lowest point on Pioneer Way by driving on the sidewalk in places, through back alleyways, and around the stranded traffic in others. He was glad that he knew the city as well as he did. He passed several houses that were clearly ablaze but there was little he could do about them right now.

He had heard the first alarm of the fires along Pioneer Way over his radio and had authorized two trucks to respond immediately. His men and their red vehicles, engines throbbing and lights flashing, were being strategically placed at two points: the location of the most westerly fire and four blocks farther east on Pioneer ready to create a fire break if necessary. Everyone was waiting for further orders from him. It was then that he heard the excited voice of a ranger at the Deception Pass State Park headquarters on his short wave radio say that the bridge had collapsed. The young trembling voice came through clearly but in short punctuated phrases followed by periods of total silence as he tried to control his emotions; he thought that many people might be dead. The ranger had just spoken with several eyewitnesses at the scene, witnesses who had barely survived and then fled away from the terrifying site. The Chief began to feel a cold chill as he considered what would happen now in his city.

Oak Harbor Fire Department's men and equipment had responded to the largest of the early fires within minutes but the hydrants failed to deliver enough water pressure. This was because of fractures in the mains in many places and more importantly because the main water supply had been cut off at the bridge. Fortunately the harbor (only eight hundred feet to the south of Pioneer Way) provided their much-needed water. It was salt water and would not do their pumping equipment any good, but this wasn't the time to worry about that kind of problem. With great effort the firemen dragged the heavy hoses off their trucks and down to the newly constructed city pier that extended just beyond the low tide line. Others carried two Handy Billys, small portable pumps, out onto the dock as well. The minus tide had pulled the water's edge far away from the shoreline which cost them more precious time and energy by the time they finally dropped the suction ends of their hoses into the harbor. Meanwhile fires were clearly beginning to spread. The Chief thought about contacting the other three fire district commanders on the island but decided not to right now. They were probably busy with their own problems.

From his location Chief McGrath could see the hillsides that surrounded Oak Harbor. What he saw filled him with increasing dread. There were scores of houses on fire, some just in the early stages sending up thin bands of smoke and others pouring out thick black clouds illuminated by bright orange tongues of fire. The fires were scattered almost at random everywhere he looked. He was helpless to do anything about them.

The fires along Pioneer Way spread mostly toward the north by flaming tree branches and glowing embers that were carried high up into the air by the superheated currents and then fell onto composition roofs of houses and other buildings; the situation was quickly turning far more serious. The firemen from two stations worked together systematically down Pioneer Way. They were well trained in the basics of fighting fires, but they knew that unless they could make an effective firebreak the business district conflagration would continue to march east and north. Fortunately the wind was fairly mild for the time being and the humidity was high. If only the thick gray clouds that hung overhead would yield their much-needed rain.

Even though the larger more modern buildings in Oak Harbor all had automatic sprinkler systems there was almost no water pressure! Pressure had dropped significantly within ten to fifteen minutes after the bridge had gone down. Not very many people realized that the main water supply for the entire city came across the bridge from Fidalgo Island to the north. Thankfully none of these newer buildings had caught fire yet. Most of the managers and key personnel in them had already arrived for work when the earthquake hit and had gotten their employees out safely after the initial temblor; some also saw to local fire control. The older wooden structures along Pioneer Way and residences up the hill were a different matter.

After three unsuccessful attempts McGrath finally reached his counterpart in Coupeville nine miles to the south to find out the extent of injuries and damage there and whether he might be able to send any equipment up to Oak Harbor. He was relieved to learn that their early estimates showed that relatively little serious structural damage had been done. Nevertheless, there had been many injuries. The Coupeville Chief said he would dispatch three trucks immediately along with a special Emergency Medical Technician squad. Chief McGrath wasn't able to get through to the Naval Air Station.

At the forefront of the Chief's mind were all the complicated details of evacuating everyone from the affected downtown area and rescuing victims still trapped inside the crumpled buildings. Farther back were concerns about several injuries that his own personnel had suffered and whether the really big tremor was still to come. These thoughts rolled around and over one another like the waves from pebbles tossed in a pond.

He considered it to be a little ironic that the huge gnarled ancient magnificent oak tree on the corner near the Post Office had also fallen over in the darkness well before dawn, probably caused by the high winds. Now it blocked two roads although crews had been busy for hours cutting away its massive trunk and branches. "What more could go wrong?" he thought.

The first earthquake-related phone call to reach the Oak Harbor police department that morning wasn't even necessary. The woman who called was so flustered that she forgot to give her name and then hung up abruptly after announcing that there had just been an earthquake where she lived. Everyone realized that this was going to be a very, very long day.

Oak Harbor's Chief of Police, Rollie Townsend, quickly put out an emergency radio call to all off-duty officers and staff to get back into town as soon as they could, after they had made sure their own homes were OK. He realized that many of them might not be able to show up immediately. The Police Department worked closely with the County's Sheriff Department; their combined total number of officers at full force was about sixty on Whidbey Island.

There were another twenty Sheriff's jailers but most of them weren't available when prisoners were kept on the island. Now there was no way to transport any prisoners off the island! Including Washington State Patrol officers, Coupeville Marshalls, reserve deputies and others the total number of law enforcement officers increased to only about 109 or so. He knew that if things turned bad he would be severely limited. He understood the general chain of command that mandated the Sheriff as the single point of contact in an emergency situation such as this one. Chief Townsend knew he had to talk with his counterpart immediately.

Chief Townsend thought about the need to establish an incident perimeter but soon discarded the idea when he saw that the devastation was everywhere; right now at least there was no meaningful perimeter, a conclusion that the Fire Chief had already reached. His next action was to contact all of his patrol cars to issue emergency orders related to traffic management and spectator control in those parts of the city where fires were being fought. Unfortunately this left many damaged businesses without any protection from a very small but determined group of lawless people who, he thought, were going to take advantage of this slowly disintegrating situation very soon.

Fortunately there was minimal structural damage to the city administrative offices on Barrington that overlooked much of the town, but the smoke and flames were gradually advancing up the hill in their direction.

8:55 am

Parking Lot of Oak Harbor City Hall

Standing huddled together in a rapidly growing circle of people was the Mayor, Chief of Police, and several city councilmen and women who had arrived by following very circuitous routes, through streets filled with people, downed trees and power poles, and all kinds of rubble. Also present were several dozen citizens who lived nearby. Sirens could be heard in the distance to the north and west of them.

Mayor William Tate was a man who possessed obvious power as well as the authority that was conferred upon him. Both were apparent in many ways: his attitude toward others, particularly the other City Counsel members who had voted him as their chief administrative officer; his clearly demonstrated talent for cutting to the core of an issue quickly and fairly; his quick wit and al-most perfect memory for names was almost legendary. He wasn't a tall man, as executives go, but his habitual almost military posture hinted at greater height. His very light blue eyes and thick black eyebrows and hair gave his face a most striking look. He also knew what kind of power clothes to wear, and he wore them! William Tate's credentials were also impeccable for the office.

Bill and his wife had arrived on Whidbey twelve years before from Santa Barbara where he had served on the City Council there. During his two terms in office he had demonstrated his ability to make fair and honest decisions and he also understood the essential importance of a balanced city budget.

Now, firmly planted on Whidbey, the Mayor had recently authorized (and found funding for) a new administrative support position with the impressive, if somewhat ambiguous title of "Incident Coordinator." The incumbent, accord-ing to the job description, was to oversee and direct, from the point of view of the Mayor's Office, all emergency situations and provide a more effective single point of contact and interface with the Mayor. The IC who was selected turned out to be Frank Metcalf, a young man of thirty-one years, who was hired away from Seattle's Office of Emergency Management.

Frank hadn't had any experience with real disasters yet but he was bright and energetic. He had first been noticed when he wrote several sections of Se-attle's Disaster Readiness and Response Plan. Later he'd done a masterful job in coordinating a new plan for storing and transporting emergency supplies for the Emerald City. He also seemed to spread an enthusiastic *can-do* atmosphere wherever he went, however the limits of his responsibility hadn't yet been en-tirely spelled out nor had the Mayor had time to formally introduce him to the rest of the city's upper management. What hadn't been made entirely clear to Frank during his interviews was that Oak Harbor's Fire Chief was officially responsible for heading up the city's Department of Emergency Management. Many people in fact had hoped that Chief McGrath would be appointed to the new position. This blurred boundary of Frank's responsibilities couldn't have happened at a worst time; it contributed to a general sense of reserve on his part, limitations on his actual authority, and even more importantly, a certain hesitancy to cooperate fully with him on the part of Chief McGrath.

Frank was standing beside the Mayor who turned to him and said. "Well Frank, you've really got your work cut out for you here."

Some of the people standing nearby heard the Mayor give a slight emphasis to the word "your" and they glanced at the new man for some kind of response. There wasn't any. "It's just too bad you didn't have more time on the job before this happened, but you have my complete support." Then almost as an afterthought he added, "Only check with me first on all major budget matters won't you?"

"What in the world does he mean by that?" the young man reflected silently. "Practically anything I do will cost money and I can't be checking with him all the time. He never mentioned anything about that during my interview." The young man never thought that he should have asked these kinds of questions before he accepted the position.

Standing rather closer together in the parking lot than they would have otherwise—the cold, gray mist and low clouds lending an additional somber feeling to the group—they quickly reviewed their general situation. Virtually all of the city's electrical power was out. Limited emergency power had just been brought on line in the municipal buildings and the buildings themselves were all structurally intact, thank God. As far as anyone knew, all of the available ambulances were already en-route to the hospital in Coupeville but no one was sure how well either of the two major local hospitals (in Coupeville and Anacortes) had come through. The Chief of Police asked one of the bystanders he recognized to go find out if he could. As a third and then a fourth moderate after shock arrived the community leaders realized that nothing was really stable yet. Was the "big one" still coming? One thing was certain, they had to act on this emergency right away. They had to assess the extent of the damage done to all property and focus on lifesaving.

A woman in the rear of the crowd called out, "What are you going to do about the school children?" Her question wasn't addressed just to the Mayor but he answered anyway.

"Well…that's a good question ma'am. We've got over fifty six hundred students in school right now and five hundred employees as you may know. I imagine that the principals are working hard to get them all home safely, just as soon as possible," He replied.

Once again Mayor Tate turned to Frank and said in a low voice, "You'd better contact the Department of Emergency Services in Coupeville right away and the State Emergency Management people as well. For now just say that we've experienced a major earthquake and tsunami and will need assistance as soon as possible. We'll provide more details a little later. Oh yes, contact all the school principals and find out what you can about damage and injuries…and whether the students are being sent home as soon as possible. Then come and let me know what you find out."

Frank nodded with a slight frown on his face and ran inside the administration building to his office, now in total disarray. When he tried to use his cell phone he only heard a muted busy signal. Much to his surprise his desk phone still worked! He managed to get through to his old boss in Seattle who said he would help by getting these emergency announcements sent out from there.

"Well Frank, I'd say you've been baptized under fire," he said with a laugh.

"You can say that again," Frank replied. "Oak Harbor is literally on fire right now, we're going to need a lot of assistance. Do you know how big the earthquake was?"

His boss replied, "Well we really don't know yet Frank. We'll call you when we learn something more, OK? Does your cell phone work?"

"I don't think so. You'd better use my regular line," he answered.

His boss had turned away from the phone for a moment and Frank heard other voices in the background. Finally he returned and said, " I've got to go now. We've had quite a bit of damage here too."

"I can imagine…and thanks for your help," he said as he hung up.

It took Frank over forty-five frustrating minutes to reach most of the school principals. He learned that there had been significant damage to a number of buildings and a lot of injuries but no deaths. He didn't ask them what they meant by "significant." He also learned that the high school's zero period had started at 6:45 am and first period at 7:45 just ten minutes after the earthquake struck. To Frank this meant that it probably would be harder to locate all of the students if they were still inside the buildings. "I'll try to contact the other principals later," he said to himself.

Island County and Oak Harbor city officials had set up a Department of Emergency Management some years before to deal with situations like this one. When everything was working normally its Director could use the special radio communication system, called ICOM, to talk simultaneously with the Naval Air Station, ferry system officials, Washington State emergency personnel and area first responders; but things weren't working normally now. Nevertheless, during the next twenty minutes Frank was able to reach several people off island but no one else for some unknown reason.

It was just after 9:00 am when Mayor Tate learned that the bridge had totally collapsed. A car had pulled up near the group of Oak Harbor officials standing in the parking lot and a naval enlisted man in uniform had gotten out and ran over to them. The sailor didn't know who all these people were but he did recognize a policeman who was a neighbor of his. The sailor had been near the bridge somewhere behind Bill and had seen what had happened. He was still out of breath and his account was gruesome. It was hard to believe, but the vividness of his details and his obvious emotions convinced them all that he was telling the truth. In the midst of his description several people in the crowd standing near him heard him whisper, "Thank you Lord for sparing me."

The Mayor felt a growing sense of dread as he quickly thought through some of the implications of this disaster for Oak Harbor. Soon there would be no more gasoline or food deliveries for a long time and the water supply from the Skagit valley source far to the east would also stop if it hadn't already! He felt some relief in knowing that the city wells would continue to supply drinking water as long as the pumps could be kept working and also that the fire department had stockpiled enough fuel for about four or five days time. Another thought that entered his mind from out of nowhere was that now there would be fewer visitors but nevertheless, still possibly an increase in crime. He would have to deal with each aspect of this disaster as it arose; there were just too many awful possibilities to try to cope with them all right now.

It was nine fifteen. No one in the group had yet noticed a significant darkening that was spreading across the sky to the north, probably because it was still so very low on the horizon. They would not find out for another hour that both oil refineries at March Point east of Anacortes had caught fire and were sending up enormous clouds of jet black smoke, smoke that was being carried inland toward the southeast.

No one in the group had checked yet to see if water actually came out of any faucet. They had been too busy surviving and helping others who were in need of immediate assistance. Finally someone ran up to the knot of people to announce that, in fact, there was almost no water pressure! This news deeply shocked the city leaders. If there was no drinking water they faced real trouble and very soon!

Within several more minutes the Head of the Public Works Department arrived. He was a short, bald headed man in his mid-fifties; he had hastily thrown on blue coveralls that made him look more like a farmer going out to milk his cows than the city's respected and experienced middle manager that he was. Someone quickly explained the current situation to him. Although he was still out of breath he managed to explain that by using their emergency power generators he thought he could start the primary pumps connected to the above ground water tanks. He told them that these tanks were at a high enough elevation that gravity would provide the needed water pressure. Normally there was about two and a half million gallons of water in the three tanks. Then he added ominously, "But I'm not sure that the tanks have survived...they might have cracked and flooded the land around them." He would try and find out as soon as he could. He asserted that *if* their pumps worked and *if* these tanks were full and *if* the primary water mains had not ruptured then he could guarantee at least seventy-two hours of limited water supply for the city. He stressed the word *if* each time. He wondered to himself whether any of these *ifs* would be true. Even so everyone would have to go on immediate water rationing. After announcing his hope-giving statement he realized how ludicrous it was. If the water mains were broken there would be no water, or at least relatively little available to ration! Their supply would have slowly leaked out at each break. He hoped that the citizens had been storing up a private supply of water on their own. He also wondered why the city had not issued detailed instructions to the general public about water rationing before this. Maybe doing so was supposed to have been his responsibility in which case he hoped no one else would ask that question.

With a population of about twenty two thousand and each person normally using about ninety gallons of water a day in the winter along with various other uses he knew that Oak Harbor required approximately twenty million gallons a day. While the city did have three standby wells they could call on, with a combined capability of providing seven hundred thousand gallons a day, it didn't take any genius using higher math to figure out that there would be a huge shortfall once the above ground tanks were empty.

Mayor Tate ordered Frank, who had just returned, to go and do whatever he had to do to establish contact with the Washington State Police headquarters and the Sheriff and have them contact him as soon as they could. Frank turned around again and jogged back across the street into the Police Department building, a one story white building marked by a complex array of antennas that were held up by guy wires running in many different directions. It was more than remarkable that they all were still standing!

The Mayor and many others present knew that the city would need a lot of aid within days: water, food, first aid, and most of the other basics. Personal medical prescriptions were also high up on the list along with public safety and fuel. He hadn't even thought about the possibility of requesting the Governor to call in the National Guard. Whether or not they could be transported over to Whidbey wasn't his concern. At any rate, that level of decision was out of his hands, first things first.

He also thought about having someone develop an evacuation plan for the city, just in case it might be needed. It was ironic that he had never considered the idea very seriously before this. He dropped the idea when he remembered having read somewhere that evacuation plans have limited effectiveness anyway without the use of force at least as one study had shown. At least fifty percent of all citizens will wait to be evacuated until their concerns for loved ones in the area are also addressed. He reasoned that Chiefs McGrath and Townsend could handle it together if such a plan was needed.

Some months before the disaster Mayor Tate had learned about the formation of a group of radio amateur civil emergency service volunteers known by the acronym RACES. They were supposed to man the emergency operations center but he didn't know much more than that. He turned to Frank again with a questioning look and asked him to check it out as soon as possible. His look was answered with Frank's equally questioning look and a shrug of the shoulders as if to say, "I don't know anything about them." He hadn't been on the island long enough. So the Mayor asked if someone in the crowd knew any amateur radio operators living nearby. Five people did and were immediately sent off to locate and bring them back as soon as they could. Mayor Tate didn't discover until days later that a score of amateur radio operators had already gone into action to contact their counterparts outside of the disaster area. They had quickly learned that the earthquake had affected a much larger area than just Whidbey and that emergency officials on the mainland were beginning to swing into action.

His Honor also had heard about the "Voice of the National Weather Service" as it was called, the All Hazards Weather Radio operated by the National Oceanographic and Atmospheric Administration. It was used in circumstances such as this one to broadcast emergency messages in addition to extreme weather conditions. "We've never needed to use it in the past and it would take precious time to find the telephone contact number for the service and then dictate a text to be broadcast...Frank would have their number which's right up his alley...How many residents would be listening anyway with all the electricity out?" His Honor thought to himself before deciding not to issue any emergency radio information at this time.

One of the next persons to show up was the editor of the local newspaper who had never been afraid to voice his opinions on anything. He had a personality that didn't particularly endear him to everyone. He had another even more prominent reputation, namely that he was the man of the moment, Johnny on the Spot. What people meant by this was that he always seemed be right where the important action was, often while it was happening! Nobody could figure out how he did it. Some thought that it was probably a kind of learned skill that was left over from his days as an investigative reporter for a Portland newspaper long before he "retired" to Whidbey. In his distinctively booming voice he said to no one in particular and therefore to everyone, "I just heard that the bridge went down. Is it true?"

Mayor Tate looked at him without any clear emotion and nodded a couple of times. The editor went right on without a pause, "Well, we've really got a tiger by the tail then don't we...I mean with the bridge gone! As you probably know there have been a lot of concerned citizens speaking out in our paper lately about the need for a new bridge of some kind and I, for one, agree with them."

The acrid smell of smoke drifted through the gathering. It reminded everyone that the disaster was for real as if anyone had dared to think otherwise. As sirens were heard coming from several different directions the group felt the first drops of a light rain. Soon people were holding their palms up and looking around at one another smiling just a little. They knew that rain was just what they needed.

Realizing that the editor might be trying to provoke him into a useable quote Mayor Tate smiled toward the crowd and said, "Well, folks, it looks like it's going to rain after all. Let's continue our meeting inside the council chambers. They're pretty beat up but they're better than standing out here." He turned and led everyone back into the flat-roofed building nearby.

Once inside the large room the Mayor motioned for everyone to sit down. It was relatively dark inside and several windows were broken; they let in cold air and the smell of smoke but it was still better than standing outside in the drizzle.

"We should have anticipated this disaster long ago…but," the editor began again, "but right now we've got to get accurate information out to the citizens, immediately! They're either going to be a part of the problem or a part of the solution. Mr. Mayor, you should have prepared for this long ago." He said again as he stared at Tate with his familiar penetrating look for several long moments. Then he looked around at the various civic leaders and others who were present. Most of them avoided his look. He continued on in a quieter voice.

"People need to know what to expect from their leaders and how to help themselves and their neighbors and that law and order *is* going to be maintained. The people should have been told long before now that they aren't supposed to enforce the law!" (He and everyone else in the room knew that many homeowners owned guns, that wasn't news to anyone). Even the Chief of Police nodded in agreement. He continued, "So far at least, I think we've all avoided the question of whether law and order might break down in a situation like this." Actually most of those in the room thought that such an idea was absurd in our day and age; however the editor had pondered it carefully and he wanted them to think about the possibility as well.

Several people were beginning to feel uncomfortable and started to fidget but the editor didn't notice them. He went on, "But it's almost too late now for all these things. I hope we can save our building and get electricity back. We've got enough paper stock and supplies for one or two more issues." Then he paused, cleared his throat as he turned directly toward the Mayor and said in a less strained tone of voice, "Mr. Mayor, I pledge the full support of our paper if you need it…and if we can get a paper out," he added. With that he gave a single sharp nod of acknowledgement to "His Honor" and left the room without waiting for any response.

His Honor turned and watched him leave. He had wanted to thank him for the offer but he had waited too long. The man was out of the door and gone in a matter of seconds. The Mayor felt a little embarrassed but remained mute. It was still the most politically correct thing to do under the circumstances. He could publicly thank him later after things had calmed down.

Meanwhile, as this emergency meeting was going on a rookie Sheriff's deputy in his dark green patrol car was enroute to the scene of a minor collision at the intersection of Ault Road and State Route 20 a mile north of town. When the traffic lights stopped working there two young men hadn't waited for each other and had collided in a minor fender bender. Each had jumped out of his car yelling at each other; this had quickly escalated into a fight. As he approached the officer didn't know what to do first, direct the snarl of traffic or stop their fighting. Compared with what was going on elsewhere on the island it was a fairly minor event but, of course, the deputy didn't know that. The two main quakes had ended less than an hour before yet the rookie hadn't been able to contact the Sheriff's office on his radio so had just continued his regular patrol beat as if nothing had happened. His training hadn't specifically instructed him what to do in an earthquake except for maintaining the peace and enforcing the law.

He separated the two men and ordered them to calm down. He thought that as long as he had gone this far (it was the scene of an accident) he had better go through with all the paperwork in spite of the fact that the traffic jam at the intersection was growing and there no one else there to help him. He did his best to do both, so after another half-hour the traffic began to move again. The presence of his patrol car and flashing lights beside the road encouraged people to obey the rules of the road in spite of the signal being out.

Earlier, just after the first jolt, another deputy was driving south on Taylor Road several miles north of town. Within a minute after the first earthquake had stopped he had tried to radio in for instructions but wasn't able to reach the office, so he turned around and started back south. As he was accelerating the second quake struck causing his patrol car to seem to float up and down on top of a solid wave of undulating blacktop. He quickly lost control, went over the left-hand embankment, broke through a barbed wire cattle fence, and finally came to a stop in a soft muddy field several feet below the roadway level. He was thankful he wasn't seriously injured. He tried a second time to contact his office by radio but again without success. Since both of his doors were now jammed shut he lowered his window and climbed out onto the soft muck and tufts of wet grass. He looked around him for the nearest house that would have a telephone. The officer hadn't noticed that the lights were out in all of the houses and driveways nearby. As the ground continued to rock and lift he just stood beside his cruiser holding on, wondering when it would stop. He couldn't know that only a half-mile behind him to the north the tidal waves would soon sweep over all of the low-lying pastureland and cover the road over which he had just driven.

By 9:00 am the Navy jet was quickly running out of fuel. They had to decide what to do very soon. COMI1 radioed McCord Air Force Base south of Tacoma about their situation and was told that while their main runway was open and available, one of their heavy crash-foam vehicles was temporarily out of commission. They said that they would try to get their trap gear in place as quickly as they could. They also told the crew that the Whidbey Island Naval Air Station tower was out of service as far as they could tell. They wouldn't advise attempting a crash landing at either field, if that were their decision.

The airplane was now at a precise location where (if the plane continued on its present downward glide path) it would impact the ground where very few people lived. The pilot also wanted his crew to come down on land, hopefully soft pastureland and not a forest, and definitely not in the ice cold water of Puget Sound. They radioed their aircraft's location, speed, heading, and altitude; then each man bailed out in sequence several miles southwest of Shelton.

The memory of those few fleeting seconds at 7:35 during takeoff haunted the flight crew for years just as other memories haunted those who were at the bridge, the Naval Air Station, Oak Harbor, and many other places of death and destruction around the Pacific Northwest. It was strange how certain events in life that last only seconds can remain locked forever in one's conscious and unconscious mind and come tumbling out at the oddest moments. The jet's flight crew didn't learn the exact cause of the damage to their landing gear until months later during the extensive accident investigation that was carried out.

When the gigantic tidal waves had finally flooded east over much of the naval base they left a large salty lake covering the low farmland on both sides of State Route 20 which, at this location, was a raised highway on fill dirt. Its pavement stood only ten to twelve feet above the surrounding pastureland. The three waves swept up and over the highway itself, and after finally subsiding for the last time, had left a barely navigable stretch of mud covered blacktop roadway littered with vehicles of all kinds as well as several dead cattle and pieces of dull aluminum colored metal sheeting torn from buildings at the nearby base. Many of the vehicles had been swept off the highway into the now flooded farmland. Several people had been drowned in their cars when they couldn't get out.

Another unexpected event happened hours after the quake had stopped. Asphalt covered Dike Road had been laid along the top of a manmade sea wall about a mile due east of the Naval base. Built originally to reclaim many acres of land that had been under the waters of Puget Sound since the island was formed, the long manmade earthen dam stood fifteen feet above the wetlands and pastures to the west but only several feet above the high tide line of Dugualla Bay to the east. In other words, the wetlands and pastures actually were below sea level. Surely but invisibly, the earthquake had liquefied almost the entire length of this long fill. Already waterlogged, it had been shaken into a soft, muddy ooze in two places in particular so that when the tide finally came in hours later salt water slowly but surely flooded through the breaks toward the west and mixed with the standing water left there from the tidal waves. Many cattle had drowned without warning in the tsunami's earlier flood, their bodies still floating in the icy cold water. Now this second far slower surge of seawater coming from the east forced the rest of them higher and higher up the hillsides until they pressed against sharp barbed wire fences that edged their pastures. Some of them bellowed in pain while the rest continued to graze with apparent unconcern, glancing occasionally at the slowly rising salt water with their huge soulful brown eyes. A few broke through the wire fence for higher ground; others stood in muted silence in the icy cold water waiting to be fed, waiting for help. Yet this was almost a non-event compared with the tremendous devastation that was occurring across much of the Pacific Northwest.

There were only two main power lines supplying electricity down the entire length of the island. For most of the distance they ran side by side, their thick dark wires strung atop heavy wooden power poles planted several hundred feet apart. For some reason known only to the original utility planners both of these power lines ran right along the top of Dike Road (the same road that had liquefied during the earthquake). One set of wires had been strung on each side of the road. Surprisingly, neither set broke when the dike failed. Their poles merely tilted over almost to the ground, leaving the wires suspended just above water level. Yet even if the wires had been submerged they wouldn't have shorted out because there was no current flowing in them. The same power cables crossing over from the mainland at the north end of the island had broken hours before. Many other unexpected things happened this day as well.

For generations, everyone's utter dependency on electricity had lulled them into a complacency that was almost beyond belief. Part of this local complacency was based on the fact that many residents of Whidbey Island had gone without power almost every winter for days at a time and had still survived. Another part was the naïve and unsupportable belief that nothing at all could prevent electricity from arriving on the island sooner or later. Nevertheless, the present loss of electricity, that very likely would last far into the foreseeable future, was totally new to them. Without electricity very little worked in homes and businesses. Because television sets and most radios didn't work this left battery powered radios, short wave radios, and cell phones as the public's sole means of finding out what was going on and for contacting the mainland. It was a godsend that several cell phone towers on the north end of the island were still standing and functioning because they had their own motor generators. However, their fuel wouldn't last for more than a week. After that they, too, would cease working. No one except the Navy had working satellite phones.

The total loss of electricity had other serious consequences. People couldn't cook their meals as they were accustomed to and had to improvise using their fireplaces, gas-fired grills, camping equipment, or campfires in their yards. At night many families used candles or butane camp lights to illuminate their homes until these supplies ran out. They sat in darkness after that, darkness that was accentuated by imagined terrors of the future. A lot of islanders went to bed early each evening. Because most furnaces didn't work without electricity people were cold throughout the day and nighttime. This only contributed to their overall misery. Of course the elderly were affected by these conditions more than almost everyone else was.

Oak Harbor was known for its excellent and professional elder care. These assisted living facilities were an important part of what made retirees want to move to the island and they ranged in size from converted homes with only a few residents to several larger facilities with round-the-clock professional staff and hundreds of residents. Soon after the earthquakes had finally stopped maintenance staff at the larger facilities checked out the safety of their building's wiring and had gotten their emergency electrical generators working. Things inside them returned to a reasonable degree of normalcy. However, when their supply of diesel fuel ran out days later they too lost their electricity which affected everything: meal preparations, leisure time activities, in some cases drug dispensing, and most of all heating and lighting. Winter's cold began to pervade every room and the residents suffered terribly. The low temperature and the stress contributed directly or indirectly to the deaths of some residents.

The small county hospital at Coupeville (a level 3-trauma center with only thirteen dedicated emergency rooms) filled quickly with injured people within an hour of the earthquake. Its 25 in-patient beds were filled almost as fast. First aid and some major triage surgery kept the small medical staff busy around the clock for the next four days. Most of the patients were from the Oak Harbor area. Injuries ranged from minor bruises to major internal injuries, broken bones, and burns; many people were in shock, a few were exhibiting symptoms of heart attack. Fortunately, the hospital itself had suffered only some roof leaks and broken plate glass windows that the staff had cleaned up within the hour. A local lumber store supplied plywood sheets and volunteers from the neighborhood arrived to cover all of the openings before night fell.

It was fortuitous that the earthquake had not done more extensive damage in Coupeville. While a couple of the old homes and a church had literally been shaken apart most of the others in this old and picturesque pioneer town had faired much better than the newer stick-built houses had; perhaps it was a testimony to the boat-building craftsmanship of earlier days.

It was also providential that, like Oak Harbor, the town of Coupeville was located on the opposite side of the island from where the tsunami first struck. When the surge finally reached the east-side towns the tidal waves were only several feet high. The waves had traveled almost a hundred miles around the south end of Whidbey, the second longest island in America.

Kate had gotten back home several hours after the series of earthquakes had finally calmed down to almost nothing. Her return had followed a slow and tortuous route because of so many other drivers doing the same thing and because of all of the debris that covered the roads. One thought kept coming back to her, had her sis and nephew gotten across the bridge in time? That one question kept rising to the surface. It helped her drive more deliberately, more carefully so that she could get home and find out.

As she drove through the outskirts of Oak Harbor she saw groups of people standing by the sides of the road talking and gesturing in the cold drizzle. She thought they must be afraid to go back inside thinking that more earthquakes might still be on the way. She saw several houses on fire and their terrified occupants standing on lawns powerless to do anything; there were no fire engines anywhere in sight! Her heart went out to a middle aged man who was standing with an empty garden hose in his hand looking at his house being slowly destroyed by flames.

As she finally turned up her street on the northeast side of town, off Midway, she was relieved to see that the little bungalow she rented was still standing upright. As far as she could tell it looked pretty much the same as it had when she left. Kate felt even more relief when she saw that none of the other houses on her street had caught fire either.

She pulled into her gravel driveway, got out, and crossed the wet grass to her front door. She expected to find everything inside to be in shambles. The shaking that she experienced at the park was terrible; she could only imagine what it must have been like back here in town. Kate realized that she was still shaking, too, but it wasn't from the cold; perhaps the earth's many after-tremors had been impressed into her as its contribution to her own personal, prolonged after-quakes.

Kate was relieved to find far less damage inside than she thought she would have. Her tall antique bookcase had toppled over and most of her dishes had fallen out of the kitchen cupboard. They covered the floor with thousands of colorful shards. Water covered the bathroom floor as well, having sloshed itself violently out of the toilet's tank. Yet she felt a strange sort of comfort in discovering that her front door still closed completely, its handle and lock appeared to hold firm. She lived by herself and needed the sense of security that they provided. Kate checked each room, stopping and listening carefully and looking around for anything that wasn't as it should be. Other than the myriad of things that were scattered everywhere over the floor and furniture that had rearranged their positions, all in all, the house was OK. When she went to check her refrigerator she was shocked to see it dark inside; she knew that it wouldn't hold the cold forever, but she would deal with that problem later. She didn't think to check to see if she had any water pressure.

Kate hardly noticed her injuries. Her wrist hurt more than her thigh but she didn't want to have it looked at if she didn't need to. She knew that her thigh had been lacerated in several places by the sharp rocks on which she had fallen. Kate slipped her slacks off and pulled down her panties to look at her thigh. The black, caked blood that covered a much larger area than she had imagined shocked her. Both of her garments were soaked through with clotted blood and ripped in several places; it was probably too late now to soak them in cold water, anyway. The realization that she would have to throw her new pants away only added to her vague sense of frustration.

She was getting ready to wash off the blood when she discovered there was almost no water at all from any faucet! She walked through her house to find one that might work; none did except one in the back bathroom. Water dripped out of it in a tiny stream. She grabbed a drinking glass and captured as much as she could. Kate was so focused on getting this clean-up chore done that she didn't think about what having no water would mean to her in the days to come. They would have to be dealt with as best she could one day at a time in spite of the fact that she hadn't stored any water for an emergency.

Using a wash cloth she was able to clean her thigh and leg and put on four small bandages over the area; they were all she had in her little first aid kit. She noticed a few other black and blue marks and broken skin but they looked like they were already beginning to heal a little. No, she didn't need to see a doctor. She suddenly smiled to herself thinking that if any scars did remain they could be her private tattoo, something that she would never have gotten otherwise. Just the thought of having a tattoo, anywhere on her body, made her smile in spite of her shaking. Her Mom would go through the roof if that ever happened!

It was then that her phone suddenly began to ring. It startled her because of the silence that had filled her house 'til now. She finally found it buried under a blanket and newspapers on her couch. "Hello?" She was breathing faster with the hope that it would be her sis saying everything was OK. "Hello?" she said again but there was only silence on the other end like when someone has already hung up, not when they're still on the line listening. After several more seconds she heard the familiar dial tone. Someone had hung up, it was probably Veronica, she reasoned. Just the idea made her feel a little better.

"I'd better call Mom and Dad," she thought, and without thinking anything more about it she speed-dialed their number. After only two short rings she heard her Mom's wonderfully familiar, calming, friendly voice. "It's funny how she must stay glued so near to that phone all day long, it's never had to ring more than twice ever since I moved here." Kate thought. This also made Kate feel better.

"Yes? This is Mary Anders. Who is calling please?" It was her usual greeting that put callers who didn't know her a little on the defensive.

"Mum, this is Katy," she began. "Did you hear the news yet?"

"Katy!" she cried, pure pleasure showing in her voice. "It's funny but I've been thinking about you all morning for some reason. You know the way I am sometimes...just after breakfast...we had a later than usual breakfast...I saw your face so clearly for a few seconds and then you faded out. Are you alright?" she asked.

Kate paused to collect her thoughts. "I should have figured out what I was going to say to them before I dialed." Finally she answered, "Sure Mum, why shouldn't I be alright? I'm fine." She thought she had covered up the fear in her voice pretty well.

Her Mom went on. "Your Dad isn't here right now, Sweetheart. I know he'd want to talk with you. Do you think you'd better call back when he gets home, about two hours from now?" She didn't want to make either of her two daughters spend any more money than was absolutely necessary. That was the way she was. Kate knew it was a byproduct of her having lived through the tail end of the Great Depression.

"No Mum. I need to talk to you. Now!" Kate's voice trembled and her Mom recognized it.

"Katy. There is something wrong isn't there?"

"Uh...yes, I'm afraid there is. I just don't want to alarm you. It's just that...there's been a terrible earthquake here this morning." Her voice cracked again and she began to sob quietly.

Her mother was always the strong one in her family; she said in her most calm and controlled voice, "Yes, Sweetheart. Tell me all about it. You're safe right now aren't you?"

"Yes Mum. I'm home now."

"All right Katy. Just tell me what happened.

They spoke for twenty minutes during which time they were disconnected twice. Kate redialed her Mom each time, her heart trembling that she wouldn't get through, but she did...it was some kind of a miracle. Kate finally found the courage to explain about Veronica and little Jimmy, that they hadn't gotten in touch with her since the quake. That was as far as Kate could go with her Mom. She couldn't tell her that they had been ahead of her in the stream of cars crossing the bridge. It was the truth yet it avoided the awful possibility that she was trying hard to deny.

"Oh my Katy Katy," her Mom began. Gently repeating her name like that was her own special term of endearment with her younger daughter. "Your sister will probably call you just as soon as we hang up. It'll be OK. You'll see."

"I hope to God you're right Mum. I've told you all the bad stuff so I guess we'd better hang up so she can get through, but please give Dad a hug from me won't you? Don't upset him. He doesn't need any more grief from me than I've already given him." Kate said, trying to make a joke.

"Yes, Sweetheart. I'll tell him."

They hung up.

After changing into clean clothes and finding a warm coat in her now dark closet Kate decided to check on Anna and Clarence, her neighbors. She wanted to stay home by the phone when Veronica called but she thought she should go next door for a minute or two. This kind of neighborly concern came naturally to her; it was how she was brought up.

At her knock they both came to their front door smiling. Both had lived through earthquakes before. They were clearly shaken but, thankfully, unhurt as far as she could tell.

Kate had barely said a word when Clarence, a pensioner for over fifteen years exclaimed, "We both ran outside at the first temblor. We held onto each other for support. We were still outside on the lawn when the second one hit." It was obvious to Kate that he was enjoying himself, retelling their thrilling experiences as if he were young again. "Then we both toppled over onto the grass; we were still holding hands," he said with a sly smile on his long wrinkled face. "We knew enough to just wait it out, sitting on the wet grass out there."

"What an amazing couple," Kate thought to herself. "Here they are older than my folks and they seem like they actually enjoyed the whole thing."

"We were outside as I said. I thought it would be safer for us out there." His wife looked at him and beamed. She had always been able to rely on him for protection. He went on, "I'll never forget it as long as I live. The lawn rolled and bucked up and down for a terribly long time. And we both noticed that the roadway out there was bucking up and down too, like big waves on the sea."

Kate inched nearer to Anna in the doorway and took her hand and smiled as bravely as she could. Clarence went right on.

"We didn't have time…we didn't give a thought to grab our coats…so we got thoroughly wet and chilled when we finally did come back inside," he said. His eyes twinkled like an excited kid on Christmas morning. "The two of us…

we talked about it and decided that risking a cold was preferable to being killed inside of a falling house." They both laughed at this.

"Please. Please come inside and sit down," Anna finally said with a broad smile, motioning with her hand and tossing another loving look at her husband. "It's awfully cold out there my dear." She smiled as she shut the door behind her very young next door neighbor. Although Kate just wanted to make sure they were both OK she knew she needed to stay a while and chat, like good neighbors do. As Kate went into their living room she noticed that it was only slightly warmer than it was outside. She shouldn't have stood in the open door so long.

Once inside Clarence told Kate about the big Seattle quake of 1949. "I remember watching the plaster walls in my school crack open from floor to ceiling," he said. "The main crack went right down the wall behind a big picture of George Washington. You know, the one with the bottom corner still unpainted. He swung back and forth like a pendulum for a long time. I don't know why I've remembered that all these years."

Kate enjoyed listening to him because it took her mind off her own problems for the time being.

"Our teacher, Mrs. Thompson, I even remember her name…she herded us all down the stairs and outside like we were a bunch of sheep," he went on excitedly. "And when we all got outside we stood around on the lawn until someone rang the bell. I think she must have thought the whole school was going to fall down or something. I was real glad it was sunny that day…We've been sitting out there on our wet lawn waiting. Now I'm chilled to the very bone."

Kate just listened and nodded from time to time. It was clearly a vivid memory for Clarence, one that he had never forgotten—probably like this one that she would never forget. She noticed how ardent he got while talking about it. She reasoned quietly, "It really must have been an exciting time for him back then but then he was just a naïve student. That had been many many years ago. Life had changed for Clarence and his wife; old age does that."

Kate also learned that Clarence and Anna somehow had managed to pay their annual home insurance policy but they couldn't afford earthquake insurance! His son-in-law had told him that it probably wasn't worth the cost anyway since the Pacific Northwest has so few earthquakes. Unfortunately, he took his advice; fortunately, their home had survived relatively well, only one corner was raised up several inches above its foundation. Anyway, as long as there wasn't another earthquake, their house wouldn't fall down. It had faired far better than many others had.

Even as Clarence went on telling Kate about the money that they would need for repairs he had already decided in his mind not to spend any money at all. They were too old now and they would need the money for food and medicine. As Kate patiently stood listening her mind wandered. She tried to see herself in another fifty, no, thirty or forty years! How would she react if she had to live through another gigantic earthquake? How long would it take her to get over this one? Would she have a loving husband to stand beside her?

Anna said, "Now Clarence. You've done enough talking. I haven't even asked Kate if she would like a cup of tea…would you my dear?"

"Oh, no thanks…I've got to be getting back home. Maybe another time."

There hadn't been very much obvious damage to the elderly couple's house other than their foundation and several long diagonal cracks in their plaster walls, cracks that reminded her of photographs of lightning she had seen. She reasoned that the cracks would probably remind Clarence of his childhood earthquake when he thought about it. There were lots of little objects still spread across their carpet. Anna told Kate several times that she didn't want to pick anything up quite yet. It made perfect sense…if there were going to be more tremors, nevertheless, Kate couldn't help herself. Perhaps only as a symbolic gesture of friendship or perhaps a way of showing that she didn't think there were going to be any more earthquakes, she picked up some things and placed them on a nearby shelf. Kate didn't realize that the two old porcelain figurines she carefully put in place on a shelf weren't supposed to go where she put them. Anna just smiled warmly at her without saying anything.

Kate said, "I think the worst is over. We probably don't have to worry about any more big aftershocks." Of course she didn't really know if this was true but felt that it might give them a little reassurance. The risk was worth it. "Do you have enough food and water?" she asked after a pause.

Anna looked at her husband with a look of pride and joy and nodded. "Yes my dear. We've been setting aside some canned goods each week for years now and also a dozen frozen casseroles for this kind of event. Clarence has a lot of water bottles out in the breezeway too."

"Can I ask how long you think you can hold out then?" Kate asked.

"Well, we really don't eat very much these days…I think several weeks at least." Anna had never thought about losing her refrigeration or that even most canned goods have a finite shelf life. Anna asked, "And how did you fare, Dear? Is there anything that we can do to help you? You know we came over right after the earthquake but you weren't home." Ever since their first meeting Anna had loved Kate's laughing eyes. She reminded her of herself long ago.

This was when Kate told them her story. "I was on my way to work this morning, as usual. The earthquake struck when I was almost to the bridge, so I had to stop. Then some guy hit me from behind and now I've got to hassle with all that, too," she said. Then Kate said, "When I found out that the bridge had fallen down I just couldn't deal with it. I had to come back home."

The old couple both froze simultaneously in sudden disbelief. They hadn't yet heard about it. Clarence stammered, "You…you mean that the Deception Pass Bridge fell down?" Clarence slumped onto their sofa and closed his eyes.

Kate felt her throat tighten as she replied in a whisper, "Yes. It's completely gone. A lot of people went down with it they say, maybe my…". She stopped as her face suddenly clouded over; she burst into tears. Anna came over and sat beside Kate, wrapping her arm around Kate in a warm loving hug. Over the next several minutes Kate told them what she had heard and seen and also about her drive home. They listened in stunned silence. Still, the old couple didn't learn of her deepest fear.

As she left Anna said, "Could we have your cell phone number…in case we need to reach you?"

"I'm sorry but I don't have one yet," she answered, her face still showing genuine concern for them. "I guess it sounds pretty silly but I'm trying to get by without one if I can. You can dial 9-1-1 if you need to. I'll probably be home too for a while if you need me so just come on over. I don't know how to get to work anyway."

As Kate turned and was about to say good bye Anna asked, "Are the phones working?"

"Well mine is. Let's hope they continue to work; but don't worry. Things will be OK…I'll stop in again if that's alright." Then she left to check on the house on her other side.

As she walked across the wet grass (their front yards weren't separated by fences) she slowed down to listen to see if her phone was ringing. It wasn't. As she walked on she thought, "I'm so glad they're both OK."

She knocked and was surprised to find no one home. Their lights had been on and their car was still in the driveway when she left for work. Now the place was totally dark and quiet. It's renters or owners; she didn't know which, were a young couple with an infant. The husband had very short hair, almost shaved; she reasoned that he must be in the Navy. "Maybe they left today for a vacation," she thought. (Vacations in the winter were a euphemism for escaping from Washington's long cold gray wet weather). Kate didn't know until later that at that very moment they were driving south down the island hoping to catch the next ferry over to the mainland.

She had the presence of mind to go around to the side of their house where the natural gas line entered. Her house had a similar layout and that's where her gas line came in. She noticed that the pipe was bent into a weird vertical S shape and gave off a very faint hissing sound. The unmistakable scent of gas frightened her even more; she backed away trembling not knowing what to do. So she ran to a small pink house across the street and knocked hard on the front door. Its front yard boasted an old pickup truck that sat rusting away in the dirt driveway. She had seen it and the many apparently permanent piles of junk every day since she had moved in. Still, she felt relieved when an overweight, middle-aged man appeared at the door wearing a T-shirt and filthy jeans. The shirt said "Life SUCKS" in bold faded letters.

"What do *you* want?" he asked.

"I live across the street, over there," she turned and pointed. "My next door neighbors are gone but I think there's something wrong with their gas line. Would you come take a look?" She smiled at him, overlooking his unshaven face at least four days old, and terribly dirty fingernails.

Finally he gave a grunt and followed her, lagging several steps and observing her from behind more that anything else. After struggling with the main valve handle near the ground for less than a minute he was able to shut it off. He grunted something else under his breath as the hissing noise finally stopped. Neither of them could know that this hissing already had come to a complete and final stop over most of the city. Then Kate swallowed and said, "Could I ask one more favor? Please…maybe my own gas valve needs turning off. Would you take a look? I don't know about these things."

He grunted a third time under his breath, barely nodded, and stomped his way to the same side of her house. Kate began to wonder if he spoke English.

Miracle of miracles, her pipe wasn't bent, the valve worked, and she didn't hear any hissing sound before or after he turned it off.

"Thanks," she said.

Seconds later he grunted something a fourth and last time, stood up and shuffled back across the street. She didn't hear his front door slam and he didn't see Kate's broad gentle smile of relief as she went back inside her house. "The gas works...when I go and turn it back on again! At least I'll have heat tonight," she thought. As she closed her own front door she could hear several sirens off in the distance. She was glad that she didn't smell any smoke.

She'd done what she could for her immediate neighbors, for now at least.

All the rest of the day and evening she sat near her phone. She dialed Veronica's number a dozen times and got through some of the time, but no one ever answered. Her phone never rang either. "If only you would call. If only you would call," Kate whispered over and over. Kate didn't know it but she was beginning to face a grief-crisis because of what she didn't know more than what she did. Deep down inside herself she realized that she had to remain strong in spite of having no closure, no certainty about it. It was a very long day made longer by the even gray that was the sky.

Bill had slowly made his way back south to Oak Harbor in a flow of traffic that was frustratingly erratic. His truck was one in a long stream of vehicles brought to a complete halt many times along the way. Power poles were down; others were tilted steeply with their wires almost touching the ground. Tree branches weighed them down. He and the other drivers maneuvered out and around these obstacles where they could, there being very little oncoming traffic now. Most of the time he had to stop in a long unmoving line of traffic, hoping that someone would clear up the mess farther ahead.

Bill had plenty of time to worry about his family at home and to witness the extent of the damage all along the way. He dialed his regular phone number several times but heard only a busy signal. Could Nan be on the phone all that time? Each time that he tried her cell-phone number he heard a very loud, high frequency tone so that he had to hold the phone a foot away from his ear. Each time he punched its OFF button it only added to his anxiety about their safety. Bill focused all of his attention on his family's well being and on getting back to them.

He and Nan had been married while Bill was in the Navy and stationed at Naval Air Station Whidbey Island. Like many others their first two years together had been wonderful. They enjoyed outdoor sports, took in plays in Seattle, and toured the Pacific Northwest's assortment of Bed and Breakfasts as often as his work permitted. However, as Bill was away more and more on long overseas deployments, the cost of living shot up faster than their income, and a myriad of other inconspicuous circumstances occurred, (including the very conspicuous arrival of their first child), cracks began to appear in their marriage. Unfortunately, neither of them recognized these early danger signs for what they were.

It was during his tortuous drive home after the quake that he realized just how precious his family was to him. This thought came to him at the moment he realized he couldn't reach them on his cell phone! For the past four years or more he had been pretty self-absorbed. He really hadn't recognized their importance to him in many ways and he suddenly began to feel panic for their safety. It took the awful devastation of an earthquake to begin to shake some sense into him.

These thoughts kept his own terrifying memories at bay for a while; but his vivid images wouldn't stay submerged forever, as he was to find out in the weeks and months ahead.

For Bill expediency and getting home ruled the present. Some of the culverts running under the highway had collapsed but the drivers had simply driven over them or detoured around the troughs where possible. "I wish I had brought my four wheel drive today," he thought. As he reached the still flooded section of the highway east of the air base he watched the stream of cars ahead of him plow their way through over a foot of water that still covered the roadway. One of the cars unexpectedly came to a stop, its hot engine hissing in clouds of steam. The cars behind detoured around it without even slowing down, spraying it with water. No one stopped to help him. Bill didn't either!

Someone had set up a few 'road closed' signs along the way but there was neither enforcement nor explanation of why they were there. So upon reaching them some drivers simply got out, moved the signs out of the way, and drove on wherever they needed to go. Some drove directly over black, ominous looking electric power lines that crossed the road, power lines that might or might not still be carrying lethal electricity. Even a partly aware, objective observer would have recognized these small (almost inconspicuous) behaviors as the early signs of a breakdown in law and order.

He thought that things seemed to be improving a little between Nan and himself. He knew that he was supposed to spend more time with her but at the same time he reasoned that in order to make a better life for her and the kids, he needed to find a permanent, well-paying job. Doing that took time and focus; it took energy out of him as well, energy that he knew he should have been sharing with Nan and the kids.

After just over two hours of frustrating stop and start detours Bill finally arrived home. It was 9:45 when he finally drove up to his garage and stopped. He was angry because of all the idiotic behavior of all of the other frustrated and angry drivers who seemed to be everywhere on the roads.

Bill lived in a fairly new tract home southwest of town near a golf course, a home that was constructed to modern building earthquake codes He was relieved to find that almost everything looked normal on the outside, except for the porch roof that had fallen down against the front door and for several broken windows. Other than that it looked just as he had left it earlier that morning. For that he was thankful. Was his family OK? That was what really mattered. As he got out of his truck he could see and smell wisps of gray smoke in the air but he couldn't see anything burning or where it was coming from.

Bill stabbed his garage door opener attached to his sunshade but nothing happened. It didn't work for some reason. He jumped out of his cab and ran to the front door. After tearing away part of the roofing that blocked the front door he made his way inside. Bill found Nan and the kids huddled in the living room in the growing light of day, a day that now seemed somehow grayer and darker than usual without any electricity.

"Daddy, daddy," his kids yelled as they flew toward him in the hallway. The four of them clung together for a long time, sobbing and rocking, laughing and hugging each other more tightly than usual, yet no one cried. They were still a Navy family even though Bill had retired several years before!

As he looked around Bill noticed that almost everything seemed the same except for several wide cracks in the almost new plaster walls; he was puzzled to find that they were only in the east-west facing walls. Their new chandelier hung only by its safety wire and there was a light coat of plaster dust covering the dining table that the kids had quickly discovered and delighted in covering with finger doodles.

In the living room: Nan saw him looking at the light fixture and said in a sob. "It swung for a long time after the quake. It was terrible, Honey...the fires."

"What fires?" Bill broke in, again turning to look around the house as if he had missed something. His mind was still set on possible structural damage and other physical threats.

Both kids stood beside him wrapping their arms around his legs. Finally Timmy began pulling on his trouser pocket as if to say, "I want you to pick me up."

Nan said, "Two or three lots away from us, down the hill," turning to point out the kitchen window toward the southeast, "...that was one of them. You can still see some of the smoke. I thought the flames would come up this way. Nobody came to put it out! After a while I couldn't see their roof anymore." She began to cry again but more quietly. "And all those other ones too...".

"What other ones?" Timmy continued to yank on his trousers.

"Well there must be a lot of other fires because of all that black smoke over there." Nan pointed toward the northeast. "I think it's still there."

The kids were dragged a little as Bill edged closer to Nan and put his arm around her shoulder in an attempt to comfort her. Although his mind was still fixed on structural concerns he gave her his now familiar, light love taps. Thinking of the quake again he said, "Hon, it's all over, you don't have anything to worry about now. I'm home. We don't have to talk about it right away." Finally Bill reached down and picked Timmy up in his arms and said, "Let's all go sit down." He didn't think to go over to their picture window that faced the harbor toward the east to see if there was any other smoke in the sky.

The little family sat together on the couch with Patty on Bill's left knee and Timmy perched on his right, his strong arms around each one. He wished that he had a third arm for Nan but he didn't. She sat a foot away from him looking down at the carpet.

Although Nan was composed he could tell that she'd been crying hard. As long as he'd known her she had always been a fearful person although Bill had tried his best to help her regain the self-confidence that she needed to cope with life's challenges. He'd also discovered over the years that Nan usually took the negative point of view long before she saw the positive. He found this trait harder to live with.

She described the awful, low-pitched noise she had heard just before the house began to rock both times, "...it was the most frightening sound I've ever heard," she cried.

He moved nearer to her and let go of Patricia in order to wrap his arm around her. "I know. I heard it, too," he whispered. From his perspective they were all alive and well, he had somehow survived the falling bridge, and he knew that life would improve just as soon as his crossing was in place. But for now at least Nan and the kids were all he needed. Still, he couldn't bring himself to tell her about what he had just witnessed. He wouldn't do that to her. He would wait for a better time.

A few minutes later he said, "Hon, I think I'd better check out the rest of the house. OK?"

He could tell that she didn't want him to leave her but she answered, "OK, but come right back won't you?" The kids watched him go with looks of fright on their pure, clean, healthy faces.

"That's OK kids. Daddy will be right back," she said.

After looking around in the crawlspace with a flashlight Bill learned that their house had probably moved violently in different directions but still it hadn't come off its foundations. The whole thing must have moved together as a single unit. He'd noticed during his drive home that many of the older homes nearby had.

As he walked around the outside of his house Bill saw that two smaller kids' bedroom windows were broken. Strangely, one had only fractured its outer-most pane while the other had spread shards of glass across the lawn as if it had exploded. He would have to get it covered somehow before nighttime.

He came back inside through the side door to the garage. It was there that he heard the faint sound of dripping water in the ceiling overhead, just below the second story bathroom.

When Bill went upstairs and turned the faucet handle no water came out which was interesting because he could still hear that infernal dripping within the ceiling. So Bill went outside to the curb and turned off the main city water valve to the whole house. The dripping finally stopped after several more minutes. He added the dripping to his mental list of things to do later. As he passed through the garage again he looked with satisfaction at the row of five-gallon containers of drinking water he had stored several years before. He was relieved to see that they were still lying there on their sides unbroken. Bill had never found the time to renew the water…"they're probably pretty stale by now," he thought…"but they're still drinkable." He knew that each person needed at least one gallon per day just for drinking and more for washing and other needs. While he was glad that he had taken it seriously he wondered how long their water supply would really last. He carried one of them into the kitchen.

Back inside, the multiple temblors had knocked almost everything off their shelves; the floor was covered with broken dishes, cracked floor tiles, wall mirrors and framed pictures now fractured on their hardwood floor and others embedded deep into the carpet. His favorite old grandfather's clock that he had inherited from his Dad was lying face down in the entryway. He'd actually stepped over it when he came in but hadn't even consciously noticed it. That family treasure, now almost a real antique, seemed to symbolize a part of Bill's inner man, virtually dead or at least numb, face down, still and silent. He wondered if the clock would ever run again, if he could ever be the same.

After lunch he was able to get his motor generator working and fortunately, his house wiring was still intact. With half of his electrical circuits powered the family returned to some degree of normalcy. They had no natural gas pressure so their furnace didn't work, yet they had several electric radiator heaters that they moved from room to room as needed. All in all, physically speaking, Bill and his family had faired better than most on the north end of the island and elsewhere. However the emotional toll the earthquake had taken on both of them was enormous and long lasting.

Now that his family was reunited and unhurt things seemed a little better, yet Bill couldn't get those terrible images and sounds out of his mind: dozens of headlights and taillights that had suddenly dropped out of sight into the swirling water down below, huge rocks that had crushed people inside their cars, bridge beams that twisted apart like they were made of balsa wood, otherwise sane people panicking, and that awful noise coming from deep underground. These memories combined with surprising, irrational feelings of anger and frustration flashed into his mind at unexpected times. Bill didn't know why and he certainly didn't want to admit it but in some strange way these feelings were directed at Nan.

Each time he tried to figure out why he felt this way all he could come up with was her inability, no her unwillingness, to share with him whatever it was that she was afraid of. Nan seemed to be irritated all the time and pulling away from him more and more, but his need to deal with his own anxiety overpowered these thoughts. He knew the old adage that trauma either made you bitter or better, if it didn't kill you outright, but he wasn't sure which of the two applied to him; at least he wasn't dead, not yet.

Nan had studied child development in college and realized that both of her children were probably coping with their own fears that would call for her close attention in the weeks and months ahead. After finally getting the kids settled in their rooms with games that evening she and Bill went to the family room to talk.

"Bill, I...I don't know about the children."

"What do you mean?"

She wasn't as worried about Patricia their twelve year old as she was about Timothy. Pat was in the sixth grade already while Tim, precocious at four, was a preschooler, and full of life and energy. Nan explained, "Well, I think that Pat can process these events for what they really are but Timmy is probably going to feel helpless and unable to protect himself." She looked searchingly into his eyes, seeking some sign of understanding from him. She went on, "Bill, our Pat has the ability to understand about permanent loss, but when she hears about what has happened to her friends and their families she'll need careful watching. I'm going to need your help, Honey."

Now it was Bill who stared down at the carpet. He wasn't into psychology or emotions; he didn't know what to say or do so he just moved over closer to her and put his arm around her shoulder and hugged her again. He thought that would be enough.

After another long pause she went on, "I was so relieved when I saw the school bus finally pull up out front. When she didn't show up after the earthquake I was beside myself. Oh Bill, I was terrified when I thought about our little girl being there at school during the earthquake...she got home just before you did." Nan started to weep again but Bill recognized that now they were tears of relief. "When she came in she acted like nothing had even happened. You would have been so proud of her. I thought that she would have been in shock but she wasn't," she said. "Patty told me that her bus drove by many houses that were on fire but she didn't see any fire engines or police. She said that all the kids ran to one side of the bus and then the other as they past the burning houses. The bus driver yelled at them to sit down but they didn't. She said that she saw people standing out on their lawns just looking at the fires. She never cried. It was really strange the way she didn't show any emotion at all. Everything was just matter of fact." Nan paused again and as she did she snuggled more deeply into Bill's side. He said nothing. Finally she went on, "I think she was insulating herself from what she saw. She's a lot like me; she gets intensely preoccupied with details of all kinds. We're both going to have to help her through this."

As the weeks past Patricia didn't surprise them. She began to act out feelings of failure and anger at being helpless; she was afraid that another earthquake would come and maybe kill all of them this time. Nan was stretched to her limit to keep her family together emotionally; she wisely made sure that they had an unchanging daily schedule: meals, inside game time, naps, outside play, chores, and bedtime. She knew that her children picked up on both Bill's and her emotional reactions too. Actually she was proud of herself that she hadn't panicked more than she did during the earthquake. Nevertheless, both her children knew that the shaking and screaming, and the houses in the neighborhood that had caught fire, and all of the terrible smelling smoke wasn't part of a game. It was all for real. Nan needed Bill's strength now more than ever before, but he didn't have much to give her.

He didn't know much about providing her with the kind of emotional support (much less the other kinds of support) that she needed. Besides, he was fighting his own inner battles in the same way that most other men did, by suppressing his emotions and by shutting his mind off from those terrible images as best he could. He didn't want to go through it all again and again, he only wanted to forget it. Although Bill realized that in order to help Nan he would have to talk about everything and that would only bring his memories back up to the surface again; he just couldn't do it right now.

Meanwhile, Kate phoned her sister's number every hour but without success. Her heart sank lower each time she hung up.

Chapter 3
Day 2 Wednesday Afternoon

The Oak Harbor Police Chief, Fire Chief, and Island County's Sheriff met in the afternoon, the day after the disaster, to coordinate further details of their emergency response plan, a plan that had been developed years before but not needed until now. Each of them knew that they were far less prepared than they thought they were. It had taken the real thing to prove it.

They met in Oak Harbor's city council chambers. The building had been spared except for: ceiling tiles still hanging down from their T-bar support frames or littering the floor, several broken outside windows that had been hurriedly swept up, and cracked plaster walls, The gaping windows and lack of furnace heat forced everyone to wear their heavy winter coats. With emergency power generators supplying light and their sound off in the distance providing a constant low throbbing background for the discussions, the three leads and their lieutenants (twelve in all) began their meeting.

William Tate, the Mayor, had decided not to attend the meeting but had sent his new-hire instead, his Incident Commander. His Honor had hired Frank Metcalf, an outside man, for the position even though everyone had expected the Fire Chief to get the job. The chief wasn't at all happy about the appointment. Nevertheless, the chief knew that he was still in charge of the entire Department of Emergency Management, even though the boundary between his job and the IC's seemed pretty blurred in places. The earthquake had happened before they had time to iron out these incidentals.

Chief McGrath stood up and looked around the room at the others. The corners of his mouth turned up slightly into what those who knew him well recognized as the biggest smile he could manage; he shoved his hands deep into his coat pockets against the cold. He noticed that most of the others had done the same. Then he said, "Ladies and Gentlemen, I think it goes without saying that even though we've already established all of the basic procedures to respond to emergencies they really haven't been refined to any great extent beyond our All-hazards Comprehensive Emergency Management Plan." Everyone there (except Frank) also knew that Oak Harbor's participation in a regional emergency planning exercise some years before had gone very well but that it had also had the effect of lulling people into believing that they were fully prepared. This earthquake had quickly shown them that they weren't! While chains of command, top-level decision making authority, and voice communications had been carefully worked out back then few seriously considered the possibility that there could be such a large area disaster combined with the simultaneous loss of water, electricity and natural gas as well as a significant breakdown in telecommunications within the city.

The Chief picked up his own copy of the Emergency Management Plan and read from it, "It can also be assumed that a major, widespread catastrophe will most likely isolate our jurisdiction." He thought carefully for several moments before saying out loud. "As far as I'm concerned, *isolating our jurisdiction* is a just clever way of saying that the Deception Pass Bridge is no longer standing, although I'm sure there are other interpretations." No one said anything so he went on, "In the same paragraph of our plan it goes on to say that "…any significant assistance from nearby communities, counties, state or federal agencies would not occur for at least seventy-two hours or longer. The City of Oak Harbor will need to rely on available City resources and those of private organizations, businesses, and individuals within the City for the initial response to a disaster that is widespread in the region!" At this everyone nodded in agreement.

Chief McGrath went on, "It's already clear that loss of our water supply and poor communications between our assets are perhaps our weakest links so far…other than our limited manpower." He added, "This isn't the time to dissect our communications breakdowns. We've got to move forward quickly to maintain public safety and order," At this most of the men and women nodded in agreement; nodding particularly hard was the Sheriff and his deputies. He continued, "We've learned within the past several hours that there are only sporadic cell phone connections although we don't yet know why. Not all of the cell phone towers have their own power generators and those that do probably have enough fuel for only eighteen hours or less…and this assumes that the supplier's support staff will even show up at each of them to keep them running. I doubt that they will."

Just about then the sounds of fire sirens could be heard once again in the distance and the Chief suddenly stopped. He knew that he had to say something about the fires that were still breaking out or smoldering beneath gray ashes and blackened wood beams.

"Without going into a lot of detail I can tell you that we believe the major fires within city limits are all under control at this time." The Chief knew that this could change quickly; he needed to use all of the qualifications he could think of. "As you probably know, we've lost several blocks along Pioneer and a number of separated sections of apartments and single family dwellings between there and Whidbey Avenue to the north. We've recovered nineteen bodies there alone." He paused briefly when he noticed the shocked reaction to this announcement. Then he went on, "Water is our chief problem and we've had to draw it from the harbor and some wells in the county." He didn't mention the fact that during one of these recent *siphoning* activities (using gravity feed bladders) they had managed to collapse a water main that supplied over a hundred homes out in the county. Attorneys for both sides would have to work out the problems that were created later, after everything calmed down.

"For now, and with the possibility of more rain in the next day or so," he said, "I think it's safe to predict complete success over the fires. Having our natural gas supply turned off for us with the underwater pipe breakage has also made a positive difference as well. Oh, one more positive piece of news... during normal times we only get a little over half of our volunteers out in the county to respond to a call for one reason or another, yet over the past day or so since the earthquake we've had almost eighty percent show up! We owe a huge debt of gratitude to these men and women for their extraordinary service."

"Now let me address another problem that we're all going to face soon; fuel!" Again, almost everyone in the room nodded with understanding and tacit agreement even though they hadn't yet heard the bad news.

The Chief paused again to look around the group; his hands still pushed deep into the warm woolen pockets of his coat. He saw faces that already showed the strain of having worked through the night and the anticipation of facing many more. He saw men and women like himself who loved this community but who also knew they were extremely limited in what they could accomplish because of the widespread devastation that littered the landscape. Their frustration and fatigue were already beginning to show. He knew that he had the responsibility of bringing them hope in spite of the heavy odds against them. He had been receiving status reports from virtually all of the diverse elements of the emergency response organizations on the north half of the island and what he learned wasn't very positive. He had to find a way of balancing the truth with providing them hope. He would do his best.

"What about our fuel supplies?" he asked. "Island County's fuel farm in Coupeville is usually refilled about every three weeks or so. Even if it had been full when the earthquake hit we'll run out far too soon. Right now I can't say exactly when. As we all know, the ten-mile drive down there and back only uses part of it up without providing us here with any significant benefit. There's only about fourteen thousand gallons of unleaded gasoline and another twelve thousand of diesel fuel here in county shops right now. I'm relieved to say that we've got a 125-kilowatt generator there too. The marina has approximately another ten thousand gallons of each and the Oak Harbor school district's bus fleet supply might provide us more but we must first work out an agreement with them." He turned to a senior firefighter who was sitting in the back of the room, as far away from the windows and their cold breeze as he could get, a man who had been with the department for over twenty-five years, and said, "Chet, would you take charge of this right away?" The firefighter just nodded. The Chief knew that he had picked the right man for that job. He went right on, "There's also an unknown amount of gasoline in service station tanks here in the city; but, as you probably realize, none of these stations have generators to operate their pumps. Right now all of this gasoline is locked underground. We can do this; our generators can pump this gas…actually we may have to if the situation becomes worse…but to do so we'll need to bring in city lawyers to work up, let us say "voluntary donation" agreements or something like that, for each of the stations. This means identifying who makes such decisions for each station, contacting them, and getting them to sign this agreement as soon as possible." Then under his breath he muttered, "We should have done that years ago."

Chief McGrath looked around the room a second time, his eyes finally stopping on Jane, his executive assistant. "Dear Jane," he began, his eyes squinting a bit as they did whenever he wanted to ask someone for a favor, "would you please take charge of this?" She paused before answering. "Yes sir. You know I will." That was all she said; it was all that the Chief needed to hear. The Chief avoided looking at Frank and made no requests of any kind for his assistance. He was the Mayor's assistant not his!

After asking the others about their current fuel supply levels and needs and jotting them all down the Chief said, "I've made the following usage priorities for the remaining fuel that we have." He wanted to be absolutely clear about this with no chance of misunderstandings later so he wrote the figures out on the whiteboard, urging everyone to make a copy for themselves. "I'll document all of this later when things are more back to normal." Then he added, "We're gonna have to be flexible here I know…these are flexible priorities so contact me if you have a problem and…".

He was interrupted as the door flew open and a young Washington State Trooper entered. He was in uniform. The Chief smiled and nodded at him and then said, "Hello…Tom. It is Tom, isn't it?"

The young man smiled back and replied, "Yes sir, it is."

Realizing that he might have some new information to share and also to provide himself with an emotional break, the Chief said, "OK. Welcome Tom. You haven't missed very much and we all would like to get your perspective on the current status."

Without any hesitation at all the Trooper walked over beside the Chief and stood in a posture that fell somewhere between "attention" and "parade rest." He clearly commanded everyone's attention. "Well," he began, "the loss of the Deception Pass Bridge is already being felt in large and small ways from our point of view. I won't burden you with the small ways right now. You should be aware of the fact that the accident rate on both sides of the bridge has skyrocketed. The three of us can't handle all of them on this side. We really appreciate the close cooperation that we've already had with the Sheriff's office. Also, there doesn't appear to be any increase in what we would call highway crime, at least not yet."

Several deputies turned and shot knowing looks at one another.

Tom went on. "There's already a significant reduction of traffic passing through Oak Harbor from the north and only a small number of sightseers trying to get up to the bridge site. We don't have the manpower here on the island to do much about them. Our people are handling the north side pretty well. We've gotten in touch with patrol headquarters and they're sending additional personnel here in the near future; they couldn't say exactly how many or when they would get here. It's pretty bad on the mainland, too. That's about it, for now at least…Oh, yes," he said turning directly toward the Chief, "my Commander said to tell you that he'll try to contact you tonight sometime after ten o'clock. He's almost as busy right now as you all are." He said this with a broad grin that helped raised everyone's spirits. Then he sat down in the back of the room with others who shook his hand and thanked him for his service.

"Thanks very much, Tom," the Chief said. "Folks, there's no denying that we've got some tough times ahead. Remember the seventy-two hours that we're

supposed to have to wait before aid arrives?" he asked. "Well, I'll take long odds
that it's going to be far longer than that! I think we're on our own." With that
Chief McGrath turned toward Sheriff Williamson who was sitting in the back
row. It was a well-known trait of his…keeping his back to the wall.

McGrath went on, "The Sheriff will have his hands full in the county.
He's spread very thin as he's probably going to tell you in just a moment and
then Chief Townsend will conclude our meeting." With that the Fire Chief
smiled again and, as he moved to a nearby seat, nodded for the Sheriff to come
forward.

Sheriff Will Williamson was a large imposing figure in his emerald-green
uniform (he stood over six feet tall) and he spoke with a deep voice that reso-
nated with authority, authority wielded over many years. He had been a marine
sergeant in Vietnam long before being elected Island County Sheriff; that training and experience had served him well in his later civilian duties. He moved to
the podium far more quickly than most men his height and weight could have
and he didn't waste any time.

"Well guys…and gals…let me give you a quick rundown on what we've
been doing over the past twenty four hours. I've got twenty seven full time
deputies on duty right now and another twenty or so reserve officers, most of
whom have been able to show up for duty. About three-fifths of them are now
concentrated at the north end of the island. One fifth, or so, are down in the
Clinton area working the ferry landing and approaches. It's been pretty hairy
there and it looks like it's going to get worse before it gets better." At this the
state trooper nodded in agreement but didn't say anything. "The rest are spread
pretty thinly everywhere else. It looks like a lot of people are trying to get off
the island if they can. I've already suggested to all the Mayors down the island
that they should do whatever they can to facilitate this. It'll make our job a
whole lot easier." At that moment his cell phone rang. "Excuse me for a moment," he said and turned away from the group.

In a lowered voice, "Hello…yes, this is Williamson…Oh, hi Don. I
didn't recognize your voice right away…I understand…that's a lot worse than I
thought…alright, well *that's* good news at least…I'll check in with you as soon
as I can…goodbye…and thanks." Then he stabbed its off button and turned
back toward the group. It was clear to everyone that the phone call had put a
new frown on his face and that he wasn't going to tell them what the call was
about.

He went on, "Where was I? Oh yes, getting off the island. All the Mayors I talked to said that they would do what they could about encouraging people to leave Whidbey but they wanted it to be made clear that this was not an official evacuation order. We also talked about the importance of giving the people the bigger picture, about the overall scope of the destruction that is, so that they wouldn't just be escaping into a larger set of problems...this is just basic disaster education one-o-one isn't it?" he asked rhetorically. Then, with a quizzical look on his face he added, "I wasn't particularly surprised to find out that none of them were prepared. None of them had any kind of island evacuation information available." And then in almost an aside he added, "It was as if having such information ready wasn't even within their area of responsibility."

The sheriff studied the faces of the men and women in the room a second time and then said, "Well that's about it. From now on I'll be at the EOC, so if you need to contact me that's the place." With that he just stopped and began to return to his seat.

Chief McGrath cleared his throat and said, "I've got a question before you sit down if you don't mind, Will. I know it doesn't have anything to do with Oak Harbor specifically, but would you elaborate on what you see in the weeks ahead on crime here on the island?"

Williamson was ready for this question and replied, "Well Jim, as you know, we see all kinds of crime in the county, particularly the kinds linked to illegal drug usage." He meant "abuse" but knew he didn't need to correct the word with this crowd. "And, of course, if food runs out it could turn much worse very soon. As I see it, we've got to get food, water, and medicine over here just as quickly as possible. First priority! If that can be done the crime rate will probably stay relatively low." He stopped speaking a second time, looked at the Fire Chief for a sign that he had answered his question, and then went back to his seat.

Then it was Police Chief Rollie Townsend's turn. As he got up and came forward it was clear that he was very tired. He, too, was in uniform and he knew almost everyone in the room. That was one of the great benefits of serving in a small community like Oak Harbor. The level of familiarity and cooperation was high; both contributed to a more smoothly running operation. He reached inside his breast pocket and pulled out a sheaf of papers that he set on the podium. Although they contained a lot of numbers and emergency planning details he never looked at them. He didn't need to because most of them were indelibly embedded in his memory. He began, "Ladies and gentlemen. When I first came here to assume this job it was from southern California. Some of you probably didn't know that. Well, one of the reasons I accepted this offer was to get away from earthquakes!" Everyone in the room suddenly burst out in laughter. The laughter went on in waves that descended in volume and length like those that strike the beach from a passing ship. It had a wonderful cleansing effect. He finally broke in again just as the smiles were fading and silence returned.

"Yes, I can tell you that after living and working through some of the really big ones down there I vowed to retire to a calm and peaceful place like Whidbey Island." Several people chuckled. "God really has a sense of humor doesn't he? Actually, I think that dealing with the California quakes helped get me ready for this one. I only wish that the men and women of my department could have learned from them like I did. This situation has been pretty tough on them so far, but they've done a great job and I'm proud of them. That aside, I'd like to brief you on where we stand here in the city."

He glanced down briefly at the papers in front of him and then around the room. He could see the fatigue that was deeply etched on the faces of everyone present; to him they looked like he felt. Then he went on, "Today I want to cover seven points very briefly. I'm afraid that the first one is not good news. The Mayor has indicated that we're not likely to receive any major aid from the mainland at least for several weeks...or more. I know, I know, that's a lot longer than seventy-two hours! He's been in touch with FEMA officials as well as Olympia about this. We're on our own as Jim as already pointed out. No one knows what this really means yet but we're going to find out pretty soon."

"Secondly, I think that we're going to have to transition from dealing with trauma, physical injury, and property damage to law enforcement. This is probably going to happen fairly soon, too. As far as I can tell the populace just wasn't prepared and, like Sheriff Williamson said, we're going to be running out of food relatively soon. We should have worked much harder at..."

"I didn't say that we *were* running out of food, Rollie, I said *if* we run out of food," interjected Sheriff Williamson who was sitting ramrod straight in his chair. "We don't know what relief we're likely to get or when."

Chief Townsend nodded. "OK...I stand corrected. As I was going to say we all should have worked harder at helping the people get prepared and, as you all know, water is another matter. It's even more critical than food, but I'll leave that to others who know more about it than I do."

"My third point isn't good news either. We can't count on any major assistance from the Navy, at least not right away. It's clear that they have their hands full because of the tsunami. I spoke with the C.O. there several hours ago and he confirmed this. Their own water supply on base is intact, thank God, but under the present circumstances they aren't authorized to share any of it with us. Our preliminary request, or should I say Chief McGrath's request about this matter, is *in process* as they say, probably somewhere inside the Pentagon…as we speak. So it may still happen, but we can't count on it."

"Fourth, it's probably fair to say that the island's Public Health and Sanitation Department, Emergency Communication Systems, and Fire Departments are best prepared to carry out their missions for an extended period of time. What I mean is…on their own. They've been well planned and implemented, all things considered. Nevertheless, we all have to realize that they also depend on a sufficient supply of fuel, battery and generator power, and most importantly, staff. If we face an epidemic of some kind no one knows what could happen to their effectiveness."

"Fifth, I've recommended to the Mayor that he should issue an immediate order to the harbormaster to ration all gasoline and diesel fuel except for boats that are taking part in pre-authorized emergency runs to the mainland. There was some damage to the marina from the tidal waves. Some boats were capsized and mooring cables were torn loose along with some diesel fuel spillage when some pipes broke. Right now that's a detail; the HAZMAT people know about it on the mainland and said they'll be here as soon as they can get here."

So far Frank had been sitting in the back row silently taking all of this in. As the Police Chief went on with his briefing Frank thought about his own concerns. He had begun to wonder what his job really was supposed to involve. He had been led to believe that he would be coordinating most, if not all of these things. They were the kinds of things he knew he was really good at doing. Now even the Chief of Police was going straight to the Mayor! He began to feel anger rising up inside himself. He felt that his job hadn't been accurately described; the phrase "bait and switch" suddenly popped into his mind. Although his insides were churning he just sat looking down at the floor without saying a word.

"My sixth point is that while it's too early to go into details, I can say that the Mayor and I talked about requesting assistance from private boaters for such emergency transport services. Chief McGrath and I had agreed on this idea already," the Police Chief said. "If this happens we'll be contacting trucking firms, Island Transit, and smaller vans to transport the emergency supplies that are brought over by boat to several distribution centers that we're setting up. They could also take people who want to get off the island to the boats in the marina. It's a small step that's probably in the right direction but I doubt whether even this approach will be enough. What we really need is a bridge that can bring a continuous stream of supplies over to us and take a continuous stream of people off the island...oh yes, I just remembered, the Mayor mentioned some bridge project, I think there was an article about it in the newspaper several years ago. Do any of you know about it?"

A police sergeant replied, "Yes sir. I read about a feasibility study done back in 2001 by the highway department. They took a look at five possible bridge locations...but I don't think they found that any of them would work. As far as I know I don't think much has been done since then."

After a brief pause Sheriff Williamson responded. "Well, as far as I know Rollie, another group tried to go ahead with the idea...although they've really done a good job of staying out of sight. One of my deputies knows one of the organizers. I'll see what else I can find out and get back to you."

Chief Townsend hadn't gotten over four hours of sleep a night since the quake and the strain was obvious to everyone. He was due to retire officially in a little over a year but because his health had been deteriorating slowly for several years already he had considered *going out* early (he hadn't shared this with anyone except his wife and his doctor). His voice faltered briefly as he said, "Finally, I've been looking forward to making my seventh...and...last comment today. It's...it's that I'm awfully proud of each of you and your teams. I appreciate the courage and dedication that you've all shown in the past day or so to get the job done...I want to offer each of you the thanks of the Council members and the Mayor as well as the people of Oak Harbor. I also want to offer you my own support if needed, whenever needed, wherever needed." Having said this he sat down.

Chief McGrath rose slowly and returned to the podium. "I'm sorry, I must be tired. I forgot to mention something else. As far as I know the Mayor hasn't been able to reach the Governor yet. What that means is that without a formal Declaration of Emergency by him the Mayor doesn't have the authority to commandeer equipment or help from the citizens. Now, does anyone have any final questions or comments?"

One of the newest Sheriff's deputies raised his hand and turned toward Sheriff Williamson. He said, "Sir, I need some clarification about what to do if I have to use force to...".

He was cut off abruptly by the Sheriff who said, "Paul, let's discuss that offline, OK?" The young man nodded quickly and shut up.

"Are there any other questions?" There weren't so the meeting ended. Nevertheless, one question still lingered in a lot of minds. How many people on Whidbey would actually need assistance? No one really knew how many people were living on the island when the earthquake struck and how many might have been away someplace for the winter. Getting emergency information out to everyone was going to be of key importance in coping effectively in the days ahead, but that would be the easy part. Providing food and water supplies to everyone was going to be an even more demanding job. Knowing how many people were actually here would also impact both the number and location of the food distribution centers that would need to be set up. It was a critically important piece of information. Thankfully, the local chapter of the American Red Cross already had a good start on that task. In one way or another this information could also influence how well law and order could be maintained.

Sheriff Williamson and Chief McGrath were standing in the hallway after everyone except Frank had left the room. He'd stayed behind deliberately. As Frank approached the two men he overheard Williamson say, "If things go as I think they will, Jim, we'll need a lot more security to protect the food and water supplies than anyone can imagine. We're going to be stretched to the limit in the days ahead." Then the Sheriff turned and looked at Frank and said, "You were pretty quiet in there young man."

Frank was angry inside but he hoped that it didn't show. With a deliberately controlled voice he answered, "Yes, I guess I was. It seems like everyone else had things under control already...there really wasn't much for me to do." What he wanted to say was that he didn't feel he had the authority to do anything at all.

"Yeah, I know the feeling," the Sheriff replied, as if he had read Frank's thoughts. Then without pursuing the subject any further he said to both of them, "By the way, you know that phone call I got?"

McGrath said, "Yeah."

"It was from the Sheriff of Skagit County."

"Oh yeah? I know Don," McGrath replied.

"He told me that there's absolutely no traffic moving on I-5 and that he's heard nothing yet from any state officials about any relief coming. A big part of the problem is communication."

Chief McGrath nodded in understanding and pursed his lips. He didn't have to say anything. Frank also nodded but said, "I think I may be able to find out something more on that if you want me to...at least from the Seattle end."

The Sheriff said, "OK. That would be great Frank." Then he went on, "Thank God, Don also said that the death toll so far out in the county wasn't as bad as everyone had thought at first. It looks like we might have taken the brunt of it."

It was still too soon for the populace to feel the impact of gasoline and diesel shortages; for a while at least people were in shock and just wanted to stay home to recover, clean up the mess, and regain some sense of stability any way that they could. Some behavioral experts called it regrouping, others called it emotional consolidation. Whatever it was called it was a necessary step in people's return to normalcy.

Another impact of the quake had to do with local and regional businesses whose employees and management lived on opposite sides of the bridge. Now none of them had any way to get to or from work and, along with very unreliable phone service, most businesses and industries on Whidbey were soon to be crippled. The many fast food restaurants in town felt a slump in their business even sooner due to the naval base lock-down and the fact that fewer and fewer people were driving. The economic impact was going to be felt for years; many businesses would go bankrupt and close forever. Others wouldn't get back to normal, whatever normal was, for a very long time.

Similarly, some officers and enlisted personnel at Naval Air Station Whidbey Island who lived north of the bridge were not able to get to the base. Nevertheless, some of them still found creative ways to get to and from work. Several for instance, in typical Naval fashion, formed sea-going commute groups; they arranged for private cabin cruisers to bring them across the narrow water gap to a marina at Cornet Bay near the bridge; they took Navy vans to the base from there. Other personnel simply stayed home for days after the disaster. Eventually, however, the Navy was able to operate small personnel hovercraft between local marinas on Fidalgo Island and the western beach at the base each day. Local residents watched these daily amphibious commute activities with wonder. They seemed like wartime marine beach landings.

Although the North Whidbey Fire and Rescue teams were well organized before the disaster their eighty-five volunteer fire fighters weren't able to cope with all of the emergencies that kept arising afterward. For several days their High Angle Rescue team was kept extremely busy, as was their Water Rescue team. The bodies of several people were discovered trapped inside their capsized pleasure boats. The bodies of those deep underwater at the pass wouldn't be removed for several more weeks. Each of these highly trained groups did their best under taxing circumstances but the magnitude of this disaster was so much greater than anyone had planned for that they were doomed to only limited success. Rescue assets from other Puget Sound communities were called on for assistance but couldn't respond because they were needed closer to home. Whidbey was truly on its own as were virtually all of the San Juan Islands until some other way of transporting emergency goods and services from the mainland could be made available.

Yet another problem faced the county and city leaders; dealing with the dead. The temporary morgue that was set up in a small mortuary located near the center of town was soon filled with twenty-five bodies. A second and then a third morgue had to be established. Eventually the senior center (its roof had not collapsed) held forty-five bodies while a fraternal lodge farther north held thirty-six more and the number was still climbing. Most of the early fatalities were due to injuries from the collapse of buildings and fires but as the week progressed the cause of the deaths slowly changed. More and more people, particularly the elderly, died from dehydration, lack of special medicines, exposure to the incessant cold and damp, lack of food, contaminated water, and the stress linked with the trauma that they had experienced. It was agreed that temporary interment must be done as soon as possible to prevent the outbreak of disease; the Red Cross coordinated the details with the coroner and with as many surviving relatives as could be located. Family members would have to make final funeral arrangements later. Many bodies were cremated successfully until the fuel needed by the mortuary ran out. These events put a great strain on the local churches as well.

Many Christian churches did their best to continue holding weekly worship services soon after the earthquake but it became clear that many things were pressuring them to stop: gasoline shortages, unsafe buildings and leaking roofs, even their lack of electrical power, heat, and water. For the most part pastors still went to work each day to meet the needs of their congregations and minister as best they could; however, as time went by fewer and fewer people arrived for Sunday worship. Attendance at weekday events also dropped steadily. Over half of the churches finally announced that they were going to close until further notice. This meant that the other half had to cover for them as best they could by providing memorial services, stress counseling, giving out what emergency supplies they had, and otherwise demonstrating the love of God to and for the people. The disaster and its aftermath had brought many people's faith and belief in God into much sharper focus.

It's interesting to notice how, when life is going well, people can ignore matters of faith and religion. It's as if when man is happily ensconced on his earth he sees God happy in His Heaven. Nevertheless, anyone who knows anything about wartime conditions realizes that when death and destruction are near they bring man to his knees very quickly. Many people come to acknowledge the reality of their own inner spiritual being that, beforehand, they had either repressed or ignored altogether. Now this was happening on Whidbey Island and many other places in the northern Puget Sound region.

The disaster brought with it still other interesting developments. In addition to the two long runways at the naval base there were other shorter landing strips. The nearest one to Oak Harbor was a single narrow uncontrolled runway several miles south of the city. It was inspected late on the day of the earthquake and found to be unsafe for landings or takeoffs. Its surface had buckled in several spots; it needed emergency repairs. Thankfully, they were completed only three days later. Even so, only single engine and light twin engine airplanes could use the runway. This severely limited the amount of critical cargo that could be brought in. It was fortunate that city officials had carefully identified over a dozen suitable emergency helicopter landing sites several years before. A number of helicopters did arrive within the week (when the weather permitted) but most of them carried politicians who wanted to inspect the scope of the damage (only from the air) for an afternoon and the press who wanted aerial long shots of the devastation. None of them arrived with badly needed blood plasma, pharmaceutical or other medical supplies or food. The one helicopter that did land deposited a FEMA official from Seattle. He met with Mayor Tate for less than an hour in what was later termed a 'productive closed door' meeting.

Later the Mayor disclosed that the official told him that, because this had been much more than just a local disaster, FEMA couldn't be relied upon to deliver any supplies to them in the 'near term," as he had carefully phrased it. The Mayor was surprised to learn that the official felt the chief problem wasn't supply or demand as much as it was transportation. As the island was to learn time and time again, it was on its own for the foreseeable future. Even more significantly, the nature of the emergencies was beginning to change.

Whereas the collapse of buildings and fires had dominated the authorities' concerns for several days after the quake, now a silent and vaguely diffuse sense of panic was growing in the city as well as up and down the length of the island; it became evident in many little ways. It's earliest indication was the line of traffic that wended its way south toward the ferry landing at Clinton thirty miles south of Oak Harbor. Another stream of cars headed toward the island's second ferry landing at Keystone near Coupeville, much nearer and considered a safer bet by many. A lot of people just wanted to get off the island. When the 'refugees' at Keystone learned that the dock at Port Townsend had been seriously damaged by the tidal waves and closed they, too, headed south.

Someone long ago had planned for long ferry traffic backup by paving and marking almost two miles of the highway's shoulder. It extended from the ferry landing to the top of the long hill to the north; but no one had ever anticipated this much traffic. The line of cars was almost four miles long and still growing! The end of the line of vehicles was already at Maxwellton Road far beyond the official waiting area. People were expected to obey simple rules of driver etiquette like not sneaking their way into the waiting lane ahead of others; yet for some citizens at least the panic that was beginning to grip them swept away such etiquette.

Most of the 'refugees' waited patiently in the ferry lane queue for many many hours before they realized that the lane was hardly moving forward at all. Slowly but surely drivers began to run out of gasoline as they kept their engines running to keep warm or pull ahead as the cars ahead of them finally moved a few yards every twenty minutes or so. Few of them realized, however, that the line moved forward only because others ahead of them had pulled out of the line to try to find another route, to go back home, or to get across the water by walking onto the ferryboat...without their cars! In a growing number of instances the vehicles that ran out of gas were simply locked and abandoned in the waiting line causing still other problems. Some of their upset occupants tried to return home as best they could either on foot or by hitchhiking. Others carried whatever possessions they could and trudged down the long hill to the ferry terminal. As they neared the landing they didn't see any ferryboats running at all! Although it wasn't obvious many people were on the verge of pure panic; the cold air and gray overcast sky only deepened their sense of foreboding about the future.

Those who remained in the ferry's vehicle line and who were fortunate enough to be on the final long continuous downhill slope to the ferry terminal felt some hope of eventually reaching it with the help of gravity alone. Unfortunately, those who drove vehicles with power steering had to keep their engines running in order to steer and brake themselves; yet what no one in line knew was that all of the ferries had been stopped! Special inspections of their docking ramps and load and alignment checks (each required by law after every earthquake over 6.0 magnitude) were being carried out. During the state of confusion that followed this gigantic earthquake the DOT officials had failed to communicate this fact either on their website or over the radio. The ferry dock inspections were supposed to take up to a week to accomplish but had miraculously been expedited. Instead, it only took three days at Clinton and Mukilteo across the sound!

Ferry officials were greatly relieved to discover that by the time they had arrived around the southern end of the island the three major tsunami surges had decreased greatly in height and had done almost no damage to the piers on either side of the channel. These officials were equally relieved to learn that neither of the ferryboats had been docked when they struck.

The earthquake had also ruptured the main fuel line that stretched from the Naval seaplane base adjacent to Oak Harbor to the Naval Air Station several miles away. Luckily it hadn't caught fire. Without this fuel most flights would eventually come to a halt. The two 8,000 foot long runways could only be used for very carefully planned operations and these only after the runways had been repaired. Only helicopter and VSTOL flights could occur. For the time being all emergency flights would have to be refueled somewhere else.

Chapter 4
Day 3 Thursday Evening

By the evening of the third day the ferry traffic line-up at Clinton was over five miles long and still growing. Some people had been living in their cars for several days already hoping that they would get off the island before everyone else realized how serious the situation could become. Many of them lived with a deeply submerged fear that can grow out of control very quickly. While some of these modern-day immigrants had packed some food and water for their trip most of them hadn't. They hadn't imagined that they couldn't get off the island within half a day at the most. Things were getting serious as minor outbreaks of anger clashed with other displays of panic and fear both inside some vehicles and also between others. There were even some fights and occasional strong-arm robberies along the line of parked cars as people grew more and more desperate. Those who were timid simply kept their doors locked and, when the strain became too great for them, just pulled out of the line and drove back to the relative safety of their own homes. Because they left the waiting line the cars behind them moved forward hour by hour leading those who remained to think that everything was OK, that the ferries were running, that they would be OK. Yet another event was slowly but surely becoming apparent to those in the ferry line which made them lose hope.

Disaster relief authorities on the mainland started broadcasting news about the earthquake by radio. Many people listened to them on their car radios; nevertheless, very little was said about what the authorities were actually doing about it. General promises were made such as: "Food and medicines are on the way to the many communities in the northern Puget Sound region that have been devastated by the earthquake." However, the many thousands of people waiting patiently in their cars beside the highway never saw a single truck coming up the hill from the direction of the ferry landing.

Even though a Sheriff's patrol car came by every half-hour or so, it wasn't enough to enforce the 'no entering ferry holding lane' signs posted along the ferry traffic holding lane. Many people did it anyway. Other already tired and disgruntled drivers tried to keep these people from sneaking into the ferry lane

ahead of them; several accounts of gunshots and wounded people were reported. Yet these car-bound immigrants were no more or less fearful than anyone
else; they were just trying to get off the island, perhaps somehow they sensed
that even worse things might still happen.

A single white government pickup truck with the words *Incident Response
Team* stenciled precisely on the side on bold black letters passed the long line of
traffic several times in each direction but it never stopped.

The critical importance of the Deception Pass Bridge was becoming increasingly clear to everyone on Whidbey Island.

As occurs after all major disasters, people have to deal with the psychological trauma that lingers long after the physical trauma has healed. Even
though Kate was young and psychologically healthy her unconscious emerged
in dream-like memories each night. She didn't seem to be able to control that
particular part of herself; she began to sleep less and less soundly. Her sleep
loss brought with it other physical tolls that had to be paid. Kate's life began to
change in many little ways that she hardly noticed at first.

"I've got to sleep under extra blankets tonight," she thought. "It's terribly
cold inside." She hoped it wouldn't rain. She thought that her roof might leak.
With the power, water, and natural gas gone Kate was also beginning to worry
about the future. Her unconscious clung to her fears. When Kate finally did fall
asleep she dreamt about vague troubling events; they seemed much too huge
to overcome. Veronica or Jimmy or both usually appeared in her dreams. She
knew that she would survive but she also knew that it wouldn't be easy. Her
thigh was still painfully tender and she would have a scar there for some time,
but otherwise she was OK, physically that is.

Every hour of every day after the earthquake Kate tried to phone her
sister until her phone stopped working altogether on the third day. That only
contributed to her stress.

Perhaps Kate's most noticeable change was her overreaction to the noises
of trucks and cars that passed her house. Each time one passed she thought she
could feel the earth tremble; she would sit up straight, swing her head around
quickly to see if something was falling, and reach for something solid to hang
on to.

Again and again, her flashbacks forced her, against her will, back to that
terrible morning that she was trying to forget; but she couldn't forget it. Her

sister and her nephew...how close she herself had come to going down with the bridge...that rear-end collision! Some of her thoughts were becoming irrational; for instance, she vowed that she would never drive on that particular road ever again. This thought forced her to think about how she could get off the island from now on and also about her job. Would she have a job?

Her next door neighbors who had driven down to the ferry had come back disheartened and afraid the previous day; Kate realized that, for the time being at least, she and a lot of others were really stranded. Her nightmarish images only reinforced her troubled waking thoughts. One of her recurring dreams was that she was living on the mainland right next door to her job. Then a man in bib-coveralls walked up to the front door of the office and put up a sign on the door that said "closed." When she asked him why he was doing this he wouldn't answer her. Upon waking Kate realized that her dreams were little more than protective fabrications. She tried to find things to do at home to keep these conscious thoughts at bay.

There were no more local newspapers published for almost a month in spite of the brave promise the editor had made earlier. People had to get their news from battery-powered radios and local gossip. They learned about the devastation that had been experienced across a huge section of northwestern Washington but they weren't told about the increasing number of break-ins and even unheard-of daytime robberies in Oak Harbor and its suburbs, although not as many as law officials had thought might occur. People were afraid and fear led them to do bad things...and there was an ever-growing shortage of food and water. Small groups of hunters went out to shoot deer that lived in the island's forests. "Eating venison is a lot better than starving," they said.

Soon after the earthquake was over several amateur radio operators had been able to contact Olympia, Seattle, Everett, and Tacoma. They told the officials on the mainland that the situation seemed to have stabilized but that there were many deaths and injuries on Whidbey. Emergency supplies were needed immediately and that now they could only arrive by boat or by air because of the bridge. Several suitable landing sites for shallow draft boats were identified. Emergency planners on the mainland told them that if some way could be found to get emergency supplies across to Whidbey these supplies could be made available within two weeks or less. These amateur radio operators served as the first truly functional line of defenses the island had; they worked tirelessly around the clock for many days.

Yet try as it might the outside world just couldn't respond fast enough. The question that more and more people were asking was why hadn't someone planned ahead for such an eventuality? It seemed as if they had planned for the right kinds of disasters but had greatly underestimated the size.

Meanwhile most people stayed home huddled around fireplaces that filled the air with heavy palls of smoke. The wind didn't return for over a week. A few people ventured into town to gawk at the ruins along Pioneer Way; the police had put up "do not cross" barriers everywhere, but they only kept out the law abiding citizens.

After dark the sounds of breaking glass and running feet were heard with increasing frequency both down town and in the nearby neighborhoods.

Chapter 5
Day 4 Friday Morning

To someone watching from a distance, say hovering a half mile in the air, life almost seemed to go on as usual on the north half of Whidbey Island. Most of the debris had been shoved off the roadways and the cars and trucks that had run out of fuel or that had been in collisions were moved onto the shoulders as well so that emergency vehicles could get through. State Route 20 was open again even though there was almost no traffic on it anymore. County road crews had worked nearly fourteen-hour stretches every day since the quake and to top it all off, the sun finally broke through openings in the fleeting white clouds against a brilliant blue sky. The storm had finally and truly passed!

Everyone was elated when they heard that the Washington State Ferry System had decided to assign a third ferryboat across to Whidbey. It was the small boat that was taken off the Keystone to Port Townsend run and would transport people and cars down to Edmunds on the mainland many miles to the south. The other two would continue their normal runs between Mukilteo and Clinton, each making a crossing in about thirty minutes. The third boat went into service several days later; but because the captains were not used to the new procedures needed to keep the boats evenly spaced, a minor collision occurred that caused some damage to one of them. Still, things were starting to improve and the long line of cars was finally able to move forward in earnest down the long grade to the ferry landing.

Emergency officials were kept so busy with their many responsibilities that no one thought to ask the escaping island residents (as they boarded the ferryboats) where they were headed, under what conditions they would return or even when. Such information would have been of inestimable value to social planners on Whidbey.

Water was everyone's main concern. In Oak Harbor, the emergency wells were in full production but still, their water was being severely rationed. Public Works officials had discovered that only about sixty percent of all households were receiving water from the well systems' pumps. With the two above ground water tanks that had survived the quake running very low, everyone was asked to cut their usage back to only what was needed to prepare meals, for drinking, and only the most essential bathing and toilet needs. Officials had resorted to hurriedly printed emergency instruction leaflets that were delivered (at city government expense) to all local residents. Somehow the Post Office continued to function until its gasoline supplies ran out on the sixth day and when that happened it led to other serious consequences.

The aging population of Whidbey Island was a well-established fact. Retirees had continued to flock there over many decades because of its climate and its beautiful environment. Many of them depended on mail service for their prescription drugs, pension checks, and many other needed items, but now as an indirect result of the earthquake, they walked out to empty mailboxes, mailboxes that somehow seemed to symbolize their future. They felt a growing sense of insecurity in many different ways.

The elderly and those taking special medications were also among the first to feel another result of the earthquake. Even though three of the four drug stores in town had been put back into some semblance of service after the temblors it took a lot more tedious work for their pharmacies to become reasonably effective again. None of them had emergency electrical generators! The tremendous jolts had toppled their shelves and their staffs worked many extra hours to re-alphabetize and reconfirm by hand earlier orders of all outstanding prescriptions. Nevertheless, the pharmacies did an outstanding job under these difficult circumstances. The elderly gritted their teeth (or their dentures) as they had in earlier years, and held on. They had lived through times of war, economic depression, recessions and social upheavals before this and somehow they would weather this one as well.

Getting new medications from the mainland was also very uncertain. As the number of people who arrived at the temporary triage centers and hospital continued to climb new supplies of drugs were needed immediately. Poor communications with the outside world only made this situation more problematic. Several helicopter flights arrived with limited medicines at the Oak Harbor city park on the fourth day. Several others arrived near the hospital in Coupeville over the next several days. Nevertheless, they weren't enough and many people suffered greatly, particularly those with chronic health conditions.

Unfortunately, when Naval Air Station Whidbey Island had been locked down following the devastating tidal wave there was no access to its hospital facilities for civilians. Fortunately the building itself had survived much of the flood and earthquake damage but it overflowed with naval personnel who needed immediate care. The Commanding Officer contacted the Mayor with this discouraging news only hours after the tidal wave hit. Indeed, news of the lockdown came as a shock to many citizens who had assumed that the Navy would come to their aid in an emergency like this one. Now it was unable to do so. The Commanding Officer's first priority was to do whatever was needed to ensure mission readiness. Providing support services to civilians after the earthquake and tidal waves came second and this realization hit many civic leaders very hard. There just wasn't enough time right now to go through the long and tortuous chain of command in order to request such assistance, a chain that started with Oak Harbor's Mayor's office, the county's Department of Emergency Services, their counterpart at the state level, the Governor's Office, the Pentagon, and a lengthy assessment of damage that had to be done back at the Naval Air Station! Every chain is as strong as weakest link and there could be several in this very long and tenuous chain. There just wasn't enough time.

Another problem arose as a result of the earthquake. Because of the water shortage and fears of epidemic disease residents within the city were not supposed to use their toilets until further notice. Nevertheless, the city's water supply shrunk much faster than the planners had thought possible, more because of underground breaks in the pipes than actual water usage. Those who had gotten prepared ahead of time by buying camp toilets and by storing water fared much better than those who didn't; some shared some of their precious water with their neighbors.

Second in importance after water was the food supply. It was dwindling all over the island.

While city police and some Sheriff deputies tried to prevent them from doing so, people had raided the four major food stores in Oak Harbor as well as those in Freeland and Langley near the south end of the island. It was like an uncontrolled, shark-like, feeding frenzy and it was almost predictable. What wasn't predicted, however, was the strange yet welcome ring of overt community protectiveness that occurred in the many smaller rural grocery stores as well as in Coupeville. Not one of them was broken into because of the many citizens who patrolled the stores around the clock. Nevertheless, in the island's three largest towns the grocery shelves were almost empty within days after the quake although the Fire and Building departments had red-tagged all of them as being structurally unsafe. Nonetheless, people made their way inside climbing over crumbled walls and ranging like hungry animals amid heaps of food, some already beginning to spoil. The stench was already becoming unbearable. They took whatever they felt they needed; many of the things taken made no sense at all, contributing absolutely nothing to their physical survival. Witnesses saw individuals wearing bandanas across their faces like railroad bandits of the 1800s and dragging out burlap sacks bulging with boxes of cereal and canned goods, soap and sodas. Several groups snuck in after dark and stole many cases of wine and twelve-packs of beer. The fear and panic over what might lay ahead caused people to act irrationally. It was interesting how these thieves seemed to know just when the police would be somewhere else. None of them were ever caught!

Whidbey Island had been blessed for years with a well-planned free public transportation service. The Mayor's IC immediately commanded Island Transit, IT as it was commonly called, into emergency service. The fifty small vans and buses on Whidbey Island, almost all diesel powered, served as makeshift ambulances to shuttle the injured to the already overcrowded hospital in Coupeville or to temporary triage shelters that, because of insight and hard work, had already been identified by local American Red Cross officials. IT's diesel fuel supply lasted for almost five days before it finally ran out. Fortunately their radio communications system had survived the earthquake; the drivers of IT played a significant role in a great many recovery events, acting as many of the eyes and ears of the EMT responders.

As the days passed the number of motor vehicles on the roads continued to fall off. Fuel was running out which only contributed to the sense of general panic, isolation, and insecurity that people felt. They had never had to face this situation before. Even those who had planned ahead by storing extra gasoline, food and water at home began to worry. Would their supplies last until the island was finally supplied? Since nobody had told them when this might be it many imagined the worst. Only a handful of island residents had reason to believe that hope actually was on the way.

As any experienced emergency planner knows, physical injury and trauma are usually followed by longer-term problems such as diseases, infections and post traumatic stress. This was true as well following the Great Pacific Northwest Earthquake, as it was already being called. These symptoms were beginning to show up less than a week after the disaster. What the general public needed right away was hope, hope that they would receive the promised aid in time. However, both aid and hope would need to be massive in quantity and delivered very soon; with their only land link now gone people reasoned that almost everything would have to come over by boat.

Chapter 6
Days 5—7

Disasters can bring out the best in some people, at least sometimes. One such unplanned for event was the caravan of small trucks that arrived at a large parking lot on Midway Avenue a short mile north of town. Each driver brought containers of pure drinking water from their own wells in the outlying county areas. Their actions were totally unplanned; they were spontaneous acts of kindness and care for other human beings who were in need. In Coupeville large capacity rubber bladders were loaded onto pickup trucks, filled with potable water from well systems, and driven along several specified routes as well. Even while many citizens were still in shock others were doing what they could to help one another.

Previously, a number of Coupeville residents had taken three consecutive Saturday training classes in first aid, basic emergency repair, panic control, and related subjects led by a Community Emergency Response Team. It was part of a state run program; their actions contributed to saving several lives.

Washington State's Emergency Planning Department had announced that the island could expect some aid within three days of a disaster but as the days dragged on fewer and fewer people believed them.

Officials at Island County's chapter of the American Red Cross clearly recognized the impact that a major temblor would have on the state's response capabilities and had worked hard for years to try to educate the local citizens about the need for getting prepared. They discovered that this was a hard sell, however. It was easier for the people to deny that such an event would ever happen. Now it was too late to prepare! The first aid courses the Red Cross offered before the disaster had helped only several dozen citizens become better prepared. Still, several dozen is better than none!

The local Red Cross group, mostly volunteer citizens, had been meeting regularly for years to prepare for a disaster like this one and had already achieved several of their objectives: emergency shelter designations; defined Family Services, and a rudimentary voice communication system using several radio frequencies. Their operating manuals were also carefully planned. Nevertheless, words printed on paper don't always get translated into action.

Other Red Cross disaster services objectives for Oak Harbor had not been fully met when the big quake hit: stored cots and blankets; food and water; mass care facilities; and 100% effective communications all were below their planned levels. When electricity went out at their Oak Harbor headquarters their motor generator system had also malfunctioned for some unknown reason. It required more than a day to find out what was wrong and to locate a part for it. Fortunately the needed part was found in the school district's maintenance shop nearby. Red Cross staff often had to rely on sometimes tenuous voice links through the services of the Amateur Radio Emergency Services group, another virtually invisible yet essential group that worked tirelessly around the clock for the good of the whole island.

Outlying rural area citizens also played important roles in responding to the greatest natural disaster in northwest history. These county residents tended to be more self-sufficient and were therefore better prepared. Indeed, in general they had survived better than had their urban counterparts. This was due to several things: one was the greater separation between their houses that made it harder for fire to spread, another was the many wells that were in use; yet what contributed most to the high survivor rate of these citizens was their attitude about preparedness. Those who had lived on the island for several winters or more knew that their electrical power might go out at any time of day or night, windy or not, rainy or not. Because of this awareness a high percentage of people outside the city limits owned their own electrical generators; they also knew how to get them working. Many people also kept an extra supply of fuel at home. Nevertheless, their homes tended to be as old or older than those within the city limits were; a lot of structural damage also occurred in the county.

One particular problem did predominate in the county, however. Many county residents relied on propane to heat their homes, their tanks ranging up to five hundred gallons in capacity. These tanks often sat well away from the homes with a long connection pipe; the earthquake had broken many of these pipes causing the propane to be lost into the air leaving these homeowners without furnace heat or hot water. Fortunately, in some cases the homeowners had the forethought to shut the tank's main valve soon after the shaking had stopped.

Another surprising thing happened several days after the earthquake. Over thirty county residents who owned house trailers towed them into Oak Harbor to several large parking lots and made them available to the Red Cross for housing the homeless and the injured. No one ever found out whose idea this was or even who coordinated it. Each trailer served as a temporary motel of mercy; they quickly came to be called MOMs. It was yet another pure and simple, spontaneous outpouring of love and concern for others that had suffered and lost so much. Their owners didn't expect to be paid and they realized that when they were returned the trailers would probably be in worse shape than when they were first dropped off; surprisingly, most of them weren't!

The large parking lots where these house trailers were located began to take on the appearance of a small army camp. Someone had chalked off access roads, numbered lots, and other useful information. Trailers were aligned in a repeated series of chevron patterns to afford their occupants more visual privacy. Several people with a talent for organization assumed the leadership of these temporary little communities. Maybe this was just a natural result of having so many retired military people nearby.

The displaced families and individuals that moved into the MOMs were overcome by the outpouring of love and concern shown by others whom they had never met before. There were many small examples of genuine love shown by both the giver and the receiver, like a simple vase of flowers delivered to one trailer and several plastic garbage bags filled with clean blankets delivered to another. When a trailer owner arrived to check on how its occupants were doing they treated him to a folk singing festival; he was deeply touched. Yet another MOM owner dropped by one evening to make sure everything was OK and ended up sharing a special dinner the family had cooked for themselves.

Many of the churches on the north end of the island also played important roles after the earthquake. Their members not only prayed for those injured and the hard working emergency personnel who had struggled so hard already but they also began to mobilize what practical resources they had and to share them with others who were in need. It happened that many of the local churches reached out primarily to the neighborhoods near them because gasoline was in such short supply. Yet fewer and fewer parishioners showed up for Sunday church services as the weeks passed. Eventually, almost all mid-week meetings were cancelled. Nevertheless, pastors and priests, along with the elders and other senior members of the churches pitched in to set up special food and water supplies as well as stress counseling centers as best they could. Cots with donated blankets filled many of their undamaged rooms and were used by the homeless, homeless that still continued to grow in numbers. The churches' outreach helped many hundreds of people in tangible ways. The Golden Rule was clearly being demonstrated.

Then there were the resourceful and organized homeowner associations located at Strawberry Point, Sunrise Hills, Dugualla Bay Heights, and elsewhere who pulled together for the mutual benefit of their own neighborhoods. Several associations had already developed basic emergency preparedness plans, yet plans are one thing, actually acting on them is another. Some of the people in these neighborhoods, as elsewhere, weren't prepared for this disaster. However, some of their precious well water did reach the citizens in the city over the course of the next month.

Harder times were on the way and people finally began to realize it. Gasoline and propane supplies were starting to run out and the authorities weren't working fast enough to bring the heavy trucks across by ferryboat.

A law had been passed years before that all gasoline and propane trucks had to come to Whidbey Island over the Deception Pass Bridge. Ferryboats were not allowed to transport gasoline or propane because of fears largely related to fire and terrorism. Before the bridge went down about twenty large capacity propane transport trucks crossed the bridge every week, but no more! Special chartered water transport of propane had not been planned for and it would take several weeks or more to do so. Some people had already run out of gasoline and either stayed home or walked or biked into town when they had to go there. Others were running low on propane fuel as well.

As the days dragged by Kate felt that she needed to get out of the house. She couldn't wait by her phone forever. The sun was out so she decided to walk over to the nearest gas station quick stop. "It would only take ten minutes or so each way…and Veronica isn't likely to call right now anyway," she reasoned. Kate didn't realize it but this thought contradicted her subconscious belief that Veronica was dead. Again, a brief pall of dread swept over her.

When she was still several blocks away she noticed a long line of cars all aiming toward the gas station; they stretched almost out of sight up Cabot Drive and across SE 4th avenue. Kate headed for the quick stop to find out what was going on. As she entered the semi-dark store there were a dozen other people standing talking to one another in hushed tones. She made her way over to the counter.

"Excuse me," she said to the young tired looking clerk. "What's wrong? Why is there such a long line for gas?"

He shook his head back and forth slowly for the hundredth time and said, "I'm sorry miss we've got gas but we can't pump any. There's no electricity to run our pumps and we don't have a generator. Our cash registers don't work either. If you want something I can only take cash."

She said, "I don't want anything, thanks." She turned to leave when she overheard a man say, "Well that's not something that can't be solved. There are generators over at the home supply store, I saw them there just last week, a bunch of them."

His friend beside him replied, "I was there yesterday Hank and there weren't any left, I just tried to buy one!"

Indeed, none of the fourteen gas stations in Oak Harbor had emergency generators to operate their pumps! Of the twenty three gas stations on the entire island only four had backup power capability to pump gas on their own, and three of them were at the south end. Incidentally, the collapse of the bridge had suddenly stopped all refueling of these stations and unless some extraordinary measures were set up quickly the populace would be running short within another a week or so. Several stations at the south end of the island suddenly raised their prices by several dollars a gallon. Their customers paid it grimly rather than trying to find a better price. They really had no choice.

As Kate left the store she heard the young man call out to her, "Miss…I doubt if any of the other stations here are any better off. I heard that one in Freeland might have its own electricity but the lines there are probably pretty long by now." He didn't know that she hadn't even come in for gasoline.

As Kate started back toward home she had added yet another worry to her list; nevertheless, the sun was shining and the sky was pure blue, two reasons to be glad; no, there were three! There was no more smell of smoke in the air.

"I think I'll take another way home," she thought to herself and turned south down Southeast Ely Street. She loved the filtered patterns of sunlight on the sidewalk as she ambled along. She could just barely see her breath in the cold clear air. Tall trees lined the road and the shadows cast by their now bare limbs seemed to make the cool air even cooler. Rationally she knew that an earthquake couldn't change the chill of March "…still, who knows for sure?" she thought.

Kate loved to get out and walk whenever she could. It helped clear her mind. It was funny how, at least when she was outside like this, the vibrations she felt from passing vehicles didn't automatically make her think that another earthquake was happening; it always did inside her house. This was another reason Kate went for walks.

The small houses on each side of the street looked in fairly good shape as far as she could tell except for those that had caught fire, maybe every seventh or eighth one. It was strange how the fires had jumped over some houses and not others. She noticed that some of the trees that overhung the burnt-out homes were also scorched black. "They'll probably die pretty soon," she thought. She also noticed that many of the homeowners who had been burnt out had tried to save whatever they could. They piled their belongings on their front lawns; the whole neighborhood looked like one huge garage sale was going on. As Kate walked along she began to realize just how fortunate she had been through all of this. Her house hadn't caught fire. She didn't have to find another place to stay as so many others had and she was alive and well…except for her terrible uncertainty.

Kate turned the corner at SE 6th Avenue and headed east again where there were fewer trees but more litter covering peoples' lawns. Not all of it was earthquake-related debris. Kate continued left again onto SE Jerome Street and right onto SE 6th. As she was passing a small bright blue house she saw a young woman standing on her porch with two young children beside her. Kate smiled and said, "Hi."

The woman only scowled in return, grabbed her children's shoulders and herded them both back inside the open doorway without saying anything. Then she slammed the door shut. Kate was puzzled. "What was that about?" she pondered as she walked on. Kate couldn't know that the woman's husband had gone to work that terrible morning and hadn't come home.

With the wind beginning to pick up again it seemed to turn colder; she turned on SE 4th Avenue, the block where she lived. She wrapped her coat around her more tightly and pulled her neck down deeper into its warm neck folds. "The air is really cold," she thought. "I'm glad to get back home."

The ferryboats at Clinton had just been put back into service. Nevertheless, it would take many more days to get everyone who had been so patient in the waiting lane onto them. Fortunately there was another way to escape, by small boat. Small boats were one of the wonderfully distinctive features of the greater Puget Sound area; it seemed that almost everyone owned a boat of one kind or another. For several days after the earthquakes and tidal waves there was virtually no small boat traffic entering or leaving Oak Harbor or the small marina located just east of the bridge at Cornet Bay. Beginning on the third day, however, a growing stream of sailboats and powerboats left Whidbey in all directions until the island's marinas were nearly empty. The marinas' parking lots were now jammed with cars and trucks. Because there was virtually no security these vehicles were easy picking for thieves and vandals.

An "official" request to ration fuel that had been made by the Mayor to Oak Harbor's Harbormaster several days before had had almost no effect at all. People were scared and wouldn't follow procedures official or otherwise.

Some members of the Oak Harbor Yacht Club met and agreed to ferry people across to the mainland just north of Camano Island just for the price of the fuel. Club members had learned that a section of the concrete bridge linking Camano with the mainland had also collapsed and that the citizens there were almost as bad off as they were on Whidbey, yet Camano was separated from the mainland only by a stream a hundred feet or so across at the most. The same thing was true for Fidalgo Island to the north of Whidbey. Neither of them was nearly as isolated, as was Whidbey. Whidbey was truly an island; completely surrounded by seawater miles across in most places.

If only there had been another way to get supplies to Whidbey and people off of it. Many people realized that they really were isolated, almost completely trapped, and totally dependent upon themselves first and government authorities second for aid and assistance.

The U. S. Coast Guard played an important role for many days after the disaster. Not only did they rescue people who were stranded on several islands in the San Juan chain and from capsized boats but also they airlifted critical medicines to hospitals and temporary field hospitals. They also upheld their reputation as lifesavers by ferrying critical supplies from Everett to hastily established drop points on Whidbey, Camano, and Fidalgo island almost twenty four hours a day for several weeks. They had to temporarily overlook normal maintenance and repair schedules; several helicopters finally had to be taken out of service for this reason. As citizens tried to flee the island in their own severely overloaded boats the Coast Guard had to rescue some of them as well.

Just as things began to look better a new and even more serious problem arose. Garbage pick-ups began to occur less regularly and then stopped altogether in many places on Whidbey. The island had six landfill areas up until 1992 when they had been closed. After that about one hundred twenty tons of garbage were trucked off the island every day over the bridge. Now it couldn't be hauled away and was beginning to pile up!

The garbage-hauling firm faced two huge problems on the island, loss of the bridge and fuel. Island County's long-standing contract with a garbage-hauling firm specified that diesel fuel supplies would be the responsibility of the company and the county would simply reimburse these costs. But without a continuing supply of fuel their trucks began to run out on the fourth day. Even with careful replanning of their routes, loads, and pickup days some areas did not have any garbage service at all during the first week. By the third week Whidbey Island had no garbage pickup at all! Diesel fuel supplies had finally run out.

The few huge garbage trucks that were on the island when the bridge collapsed couldn't take their loads off of the island to the usual railroad car pickup site on the mainland. They had to be dumped someplace else. That place, by emergency edict of the County Commissioners, was a small but deep gravel pit north of Oak Harbor. While the decision to do this was made in haste both the hauling firm and neighbors living near the pit had time to repent in leisure. Their repentance largely took place in a number of law courts.

Eventually each homeowner had to deal with his own garbage situation as best he could; no one received any official guidance. Some simply piled their garbage up in nearby vacant lots or attempted to burn it somewhere. Fortunately, only a very few took their garbage out after dark to dump it beside the road. Some of the more organized homeowner associations quickly set up localized community garbage dumps where they used a backhoe to dig long, deep trenches and (wisely) to cover dirt back over the garbage. Most of the other areas began to accumulate garbage, insects, and rats, all precursors to disease. There were sewer-related problems as well.

Outside of the Oak Harbor city limits the residents relied on individual septic systems while inside the city limits a modern sewage system was in place well before the disaster struck. It was located downtown near the waterfront and city park. Unfortunately, the earthquake had severely damaged several main sewer trunk lines that fed into the plant; waste backed up quickly in spite of the fact that people were told to not use their toilets until further notice. It was clear that many people didn't obey the rules! Nevertheless, while it took several days to occur, many of the residents within the city eventually found their toilets clogged and unworkable. A few people who lived at lower elevations even had raw sewage overflowing back into their homes! Without having enough water the cleanup was very difficult and even more unpleasant. Many turned to using buckets or large pots as their forefathers had done long before them. Others did with their own waste what they did with their garbage, simply dumping it on top of their garbage! Health officials became very worried when they realized what was happening. The officials arranged for several public address systems to be set up on small trucks and driven through the city to tell people how to deal with human waste and garbage. They soon gave up doing this because of many difficulties.

County residents who had septic systems were a little better off because they weren't dependent on a centralized system and because a surprising number of these systems had survived the quake. It seemed to depend on whether the houses and their systems had been built on landfill or on solid ground. The pipes of many of those on fill literally shook themselves apart. Those fortunate people who had working toilets carried on life with only minimal inconvenience; particularly those who still had well water. The others soon discovered who their real neighbors were by their acts of *toilet* kindness. Nevertheless, the area was becoming noxious which only contributed to a growing sense of foreboding and fear.

Yet another unplanned-for event involved the sudden and unannounced closure of every bank! Private guards were quickly hired and stationed outside most of them on north Whidbey Island whether or not the buildings had been damaged. Two things had conspired to shut the banks: the Internet and electricity. Interestingly, the fiber-optic based Internet trunk that had been installed up and down the length of the island and used for electronic funds transfer (among many other things) worked sporadically for several days following the earthquake. Then it suddenly and mysteriously quit. Also, electricity was needed to run almost every piece of bank equipment. Although their power had been supplied by emergency generators for several days eventually their fuel ran out.

When people arrived at their banks and ATM machines to withdraw money to help them survive they went home without any. What they did take home was a growing sense of panic. How would they be able to get the food they needed and where would they get it even if they had the money? Water and food and, indirectly, money were now the main problems to be confronted. Heat, personal safety, and a good night's sleep had to come later.

Most of Kate's stress was caused by her worry about her sister and nephew. She hadn't been able to reach them at all and she took this as confirmation that they must be dead. Providentially, her positive, outgoing personality helped her counter her feelings of anxiety and fear just a little.

As the days dragged on Kate feared the nighttime the most because of her dreams or more accurately a repetitive dream that contained the same elements: she saw herself above the ground looking down. She saw small groups of people or animals running toward each other but never able to arrive for some reason. A beautiful doe was usually in one group and her young fawn in the other. Sometimes a wall of water or a high fence suddenly appeared between them. At other times there was a yawning crevasse that split the ground apart between the groups leaving them forever separated. It was like she was looking down, deep into the crevasse. In one of her dreams she could see all the way to the bottom. It contained a dull red-orange glow that gave off vaporous clouds, clouds that slowly rose up to where she was. As they choked her breathing she awakened trembling and afraid, wondering what her dream could mean.

Like many other people in the area Bill was also experiencing strange reactions that were totally new to him. They also happened mostly at night. Bill had prided himself on being self-reliant and goal oriented; his Navy career had gone smoothly. He joined the service several years after the Vietnam war had ended and had escaped the many hidden traumas of that debacle; however, his front row seat to this disaster had become his own Vietnam. Although he didn't recognize that it was happening he was slowly becoming a different person.

As the days passed Bill understood with his rational mind that he and his family would survive and yet he still felt an unexplainable sense of guilt. He turned many questions over and over in his mind: "Why didn't I go down, too? Why was I spared by only a matter of seconds? That guy...what happened to him? What was he doing there anyway? Maybe it was because of my participation with the planning group," he thought to himself. "Did God, if there really is one, spare me as some kind of thank you for my volunteer work over the past four years?"

Bill was feeling the kinds of emotions experienced by many others who have survived events that took the lives of people nearby them. He became more and more irritable with his wife and kids. In the darkest hours of the night he would wake suddenly from a dream, a dream that, like Kate's, never changed in its significant details. In it he was standing at the edge of a huge open field. Tall green grass swayed across the field in the invisible wind like slowly undulating ocean waves. Their rhythmic motion seemed to beckon him to walk out across the field; to walk on the water, so to speak. There ahead of him he saw two very large trees suddenly appear. Their huge trunks were only feet apart; their upper branches intertwined together as one solid living mass. As he crossed the field he knew that he had to walk between them, not around them…yet every time he got near them he became terribly afraid of something undefined and amorphous. He would awaken just before passing between their trunks, sweating and feeling relieved that it was only a dream. He pondered what it could mean, what little of it he could remember, but he never shared the dream with Nancy.

His unconscious mind seemed to be wrestling with the idea that one way or another, sooner or later; the earth would have its victory. It was like a game that his unconscious mind was playing against the conscious part of him. Deep down inside himself he realized that he was playing this totally against his will; he felt that sooner or later he would lose!

Another thought, fraught with other confused feelings, seemed to recur over and over, night after night…"I was so wrong about the rust and the vibration." This thought was followed almost immediately by another that somehow counteracted it…"Our project *is* going to make the difference." His thrashing and moaning scared Nan but she felt helpless to do anything to help him.

Each time this happened Bill couldn't get back to sleep; he lay in the darkness playing the series of events over and over again in his mind. Those awful disappearing taillights, those screams and the people buried alive under the hillside. How could the entire bridge be gone so quickly and completely? He couldn't find a way to turn the projector off.

As these nightly torments went on he also found himself thinking about the pretty young blond woman standing beside his truck that morning. He could see her face clearly, her blue eyes glistening with tears and then that brief look of puzzlement that turned to fear when he told her that the bridge had collapsed. Her pretty eyes reminded him of pools of deep, dark blue water with the dew of her tears hanging on delicate tendril leaves. Even now he could almost smell her scrubbed skin and another delightfully fragrant scent of some kind he couldn't define. He could almost feel the warmth of her delicate hand in his, a tender memory to a man who wasn't used to feeling very much tenderness.

The disaster had brought them together for only a few short minutes but as the days passed he found himself thinking about her more and more. He didn't understand why his unconscious kept bringing her back into his mind. He certainly hadn't consciously planned it this way. "Am I going through some kind of mid-life crisis?" he wondered. Bill quickly pushed this idea away. He didn't believe in mid-life crises and even if he did, they only happened to other guys. Yet like a single, brightly-colored yarn in an otherwise drab and rather plain carpet that was his life, Kate became more and more visible to him; she was interwoven into and through his thoughts, impossible to get rid of. "Maybe in some way she represents the pleasant, healthy side of my very unpleasant and unhealthy memory," he considered in an unusual flash of this kind of insight. "I'm not any sort of psychologist, but maybe she's balancing me out for the sake of my sanity, somewhere in my subconscious." He smiled to himself as he thought about how he was psyching himself out, something that engineers just don't do.

He didn't know her name nor she his. They were total strangers. As the days turned into weeks Bill knew that somehow, some way, he had to talk with the young woman again. He had to find out how she was and whether her family members had survived. He kicked himself for not asking her name back then.

As time passed he also felt the need to go back to that awful place where he had watched the bridge twist and writhe and fall out of sight. He made up his mind that he would go back soon.

One chill blustery morning Bill was sitting by himself in a small coffee shop, one of the few that had somehow managed to reopen. He had walked there from home beneath a low overcast of gray clouds. He wrapped both his hands around the steaming cup of coffee. There were two men sitting in a booth just out of sight around the corner from his; he could only hear their voices. He felt funny listening in on the conversation of others but their voices carried and there was nothing else he could do.

After several minutes he overheard one of them say, "Did you hear that there's going to be a memorial service next Saturday?"

Bill couldn't help wondering what they were talking about. He had heard that almost all of the local churches had been closed due to gasoline shortages or something.

"Do you know when and where it will be? Asked the second voice.

On a sudden impulse Bill got up and walked in their direction. This wasn't like him. He was usually pretty shy with strangers who probably wanted their privacy just as he would, but something inside him forced him to do it. He reached the corner and looked at each man; he had never seen either of them before. One of them wore jeans and a purple Huskies sweat shirt. He looked up at Bill in surprise while he answered his friend's question. "Yeah…I think it's planned for 6:00 o'clock next Saturday evening at the Bible church north of town, the one with the big white cross out on the front of their building."

Bill stood there just a moment glancing back and forth at each man and feeling stupid all of a sudden. Then he just nodded and grinned with a self-conscious look on his face and went back to his table around the corner without saying a word.

After a long pause he heard the second voice say, "Thanks, I know where that is."

Bill suddenly felt a tiny kernel of warmth ignite deep within him. He didn't really know why but he would be there.

Chapter 7

Saturday and the Meeting

As the days passed life on the island returned to a strange kind of normalcy. What seemed imminently important then now wasn't quite as urgent. People were learning how to cope with less, they were thankful to be alive, and they were wondering why they hadn't gotten better prepared for the disaster before it happened. The authorities were beginning to regain an obvious semblance of social control and even respect from most of the citizens who had watched their community break down for a while after the earth shook so terribly. Very small and insufficient trickles of emergency food supplies were finally arriving from the mainland, as was badly needed medicine. They came by pleasure craft and ferryboat. Yet, as Bill and a small handful of others knew, that would soon change. Local water supplies had been jury-rigged to work most of the time, at least until more permanent repairs could be made. Nevertheless, many many people still carried the invisible weight of their conscious and unconscious memories.

Bill and Kate finally met at church. It was during the special Saturday evening service held to remember both the living and the dead, a service that had only been advertised by word of mouth; it was more than sufficient. The relatively small church building northwest of town couldn't hold everyone who showed up. Fran, the Chief of Police, and the newspaper editor were there. Clarence and his wife were there. Several Sheriffs' deputies and firemen were there. People started arriving an hour before the starting time and, not surprisingly, its parking lot was soon jammed full. Although some families arrived by car or truck most of the others walked from their homes far away. Bill was there too but Nan didn't want to come. "I think that the service might frighten the children," she had said. She followed this with…"I don't want to have to get a babysitter either." Bill didn't agree with her and had left the house in a huff. He reasoned to himself that she didn't want to come only because of her own fears and was using the kids as an excuse. Yet he didn't recognize that he too was acting irrationally, pulled to the service by some invisible motivation that he didn't understand. He wasn't at all religious. He didn't even believe very deeply in God.

Bill was surprised when he realized that he had never even thought about God during the earthquake or for weeks afterward. To him the earth's movement and the resulting tidal waves were nothing supernatural, only the inevitable consequences of natural forces lying within the earth. His undergraduate engineering studies had taught him that! So why was he so drawn to this church service? The question puzzled him more than questions about the earthquake or his survival or God.

Bill was one of the last to get inside the sanctuary because of the huge and early turnout. The place was packed and already getting hot and muggy inside; he had to stand along one wall near the front. Many more people stood in the large lobby listening through the open double doors. The PA system was cranked up for their benefit. Even though it was dark and damp outside others stood at the side doors that were kept open for their benefit. The muffled sound of electrical generators could be heard outside. At least it wasn't raining.

"Hi," a middle aged man said. Bill turned to see if he was talking to him. He was. The man was also propped against the wall for lack of a chair.

Bill smiled weakly and replied, "Hi." That uncomfortable social silence well known to most men followed. Neither of them had much to say. It seemed clear, however, that both of them had experienced the earthquake's horrors. Finally Bill said, "my name's Bill, what's yours?" The other guy responded "Jeff… Jeff Daniels." They shook hands and smiled at one another but didn't say anything else.

Bill had never spent much time inside any church. To put it bluntly, he didn't have time for God or for religion. He was too busy living life. Although he didn't realize it at a conscious level his close escape from death was drawing him back toward deeper truths, a reality that he thought probably resided in places like this. At one level at least he understood why his wife wasn't where he was. She hadn't seen what he had. She'd survived within a relatively safe cocoon which is what home always should be, "but she could have tried harder to understand what I'm going through," he thought.

The leaders of the little Bible church knew that for some people the grieving process shouldn't be prolonged. Much like the posttraumatic stress of wartime, it was always best to give treatment sooner than later. On the other hand they also realized that grief lasts for different durations in different people and shouldn't be programmed or forced into submission. Either way holding this service was the right thing to do. Nevertheless, they had totally underestimated the response of the public and had only a vague idea of the deep spiritual needs that were carried into the room tonight. They realized that many people were still firmly chained to their personal losses while others were only curious about what Christianity and the Bible might have to say about this so-called "act of God." Others were present out of their reverence for and devotion to a Creator who had such great power at His control; but whatever their reasons for being there, each person was confronting the past in his or her own way.

As the service began Bill had a chance to look around the room. He saw somber faces, tear-stained faces filled with deep anguish and loss. He saw several rows filled by young men with closely cropped hair, obviously Navy, out of uniform. He identified with the unfamiliar, yet somehow familiar, faces of these total strangers. "Actually, I guess we're all related in one way or another," he reflected. Everyone had something in common tonight. Slowly, silently, secretly Bill began to cry.

His tears began when he heard an elderly man sitting near him begin to sob quietly. The old man's head was bent forward and moving back and forth slightly as if to say, "No. No, God. No. No." The old man had obviously lost someone dear to him and had started to cry just as the middle-aged pastor, wearing a light-blue shirt and dark slacks, offered a deeply moving opening prayer. The prayer reminded Bill of what a daddy would say to comfort a young child who had just lost a beloved pet.

"Oh blessed Lord God," he began, "We, your people, are in pain. We're here tonight to call out to You for Your mercy and peace, for Your protection and solace. We call on You to come and dwell among us tonight to bless our service of mourning and loss as we give over to You those who have died in this terrible disaster. We simply ask You to hear our prayers and confessions tonight, our heartfelt pleading for Your forgiveness for our hardness of heart."

At this a few people in the room were heard grumbling something under their breath. They didn't come to plead for any forgiveness. They had nothing to do with this "act of God." What did they have to be forgiven for? The pastor went on.

"Oh Lord, hear our cries tonight as we both remember our loved ones and also let them go. Help us to do both of these things in healthy ways and, Lord, as Your servant David wrote, 'For as the heavens are high above the earth, so great is your steadfast love toward those who fear you; as far as the east is from the west, so far do you remove our transgressions from us. As a father pities his children, so the Lord pities those who fear him.'

The pastor stopped briefly and looked around the room at the mostly still bowed heads. His eyes met the eyes of a half-dozen men and women who were looking at him. Some had tears in their eyes. He just smiled gently and nodded to them before going on. "Finally, Lord God, we're here to celebrate the lives of those who are now gone from us and to thank You for Your great goodness to accept everyone who trusts in you. Amen." An audible "amen" was heard from some in the room.

The pastor raised his head, cleared his throat, and smiled a bigger smile this time and said, "Dear friends, neighbors, and church family, we've all lived through an event that our children and grand children will be writing and talking about for decades to come. We survived but many others didn't."

"Beloved of God," the pastor went on, tenderly and almost quietly, "we're all here as one family tonight brought together by the same terrible events, events that shouldn't have happened…yet they did. Many of you have suffered great loss. We usually don't appreciate what we have until we have lost it, do we?" he asked. "And we can only thank God that it wasn't worse than it was. He does hold each of us in the palm of His hands and does care for us in ways we can't begin to fathom. Now we can begin to understand something of His very great power and His divine protection."

"As survivors each of us must now ask ourselves why God spared us; what are we to do in the days, weeks, and months ahead?" he asked.

Bill listened intently hoping to hear answers to those very questions, questions that he had formulated in a little different form from what the pastor had. He had heard the term *survivor guilt* somewhere but he had no idea what it meant. He felt confused, disoriented inside while on the outside he tried to present a façade of calm control; yet his tears betrayed him. "Why was I spared?" he asked silently. "I need to know the reason." As he processed these thoughts he heard the pastor's words continue.

"As I see it we have two basic choices. Either we can get angry at God and our fellow man, become really defensive or even offensive, take the law into our own hands, trust only in the power of force, and behave as senseless animals that are bent on survival or we can learn what lessons God has for us from these terrible events that we've just lived through. His is a totally different way. This is a choice that is up to each of us. It is a fundamental choice."

He paused to take a drink of water from a paper cup that he then carefully set down on a stool beside the lectern that also held his few notes. The pastor, a man in his early fifties, had led several congregations before coming to Whidbey and had experienced his share of disappointments over seeing how poorly men treat one another. He wondered to himself whether anything he would say tonight would make a difference to his listeners. He wanted to try to help the people act responsibly within the law; the law of love, that is.

Then he went on, "Of course, my friends, these are lessons that none of us would seek out voluntarily but which have been forced upon us. This evening I want to take a few minutes to share three lessons that my family and I have learned so far as we continue to cope with rebuilding our lives and our home. Hopefully they'll also be useful to you."

"My dear friends and neighbors, the first lesson I have learned is that this life really is perilous. I guess that sounds somewhat naïve and obvious to you. It's been a long time since my family and I have had to sacrifice very much and, I guess, we've taken a lot for granted; for instance a stable community, electricity, warmth, water to drink, food to eat, that sort of thing; but this disaster has made my family and me take a whole new look at just how fragile life is, how precious it is and at what really matters in our lives. I have found great peace in the words of Jesus who said, 'Come to Me, all you who labor and are heavy laden, and I will give you rest.' And many of us are heavy laden these days, aren't we? In the next verse in Matthew's Gospel the Lord said, "I am gentle and lowly in heart, and you will find rest for your souls." Now, my friends, isn't this what we all need right now, rest for our souls? You probably think that it's your body that's exhausted from all the stresses and strains of what you've been through, but it's actually your souls, that part of you that is a mixture of your uniquely created self and God's unique Spirit. It's your soul that needs renewal. He wants you to find rest for your soul here tonight, tomorrow, and for the rest of your life. It isn't hard to find this place of rest for your souls once you have come into a genuine, permanent relationship with Him. Having that daily peace is one important result of knowing Jesus Christ personally. A lesson that this disaster has impressed on me is that no matter how bad things may become I know that my personal relationship with God is intact, my soul is at rest."

Bill was surprised to find himself listening to the pastor's words while at the same time searching over the faces of the congregation before him. Gradually the pastor's words of comfort began to take root in his heart and his tears began to subside. He had never heard very much about what Jesus Himself had actually said, only how so many people had misused His name in angry oaths.

Now he was hearing the pastor describe the man Jesus in a way he hadn't ever known before. The ideas being shared were strangely new and fascinating to him. "Maybe he's right about my soul," he thought. "Maybe that's what my problem is; but I don't know how to find God. I don't know much of anything about the church."

As he was reflecting on these things he happened to look across the room almost opposite him, still through his blurred vision. It was then that he saw her. It was she! His heart jumped as he felt an odd feeling of relief flooding over him.

Kate hadn't moved at all but was looking intently at the pastor. She had a dark blue raincoat draped over her lap and wore a matching dark blue sweater that set off her short blond hair in striking contrast. Bill didn't remember that she looked so young. There was a boy on one side of her and a young woman on the other; she was partially blocked by Kate. In an instant he realized who they must be and he almost cried out loud with relief; all this time he had been grieving as much for Kate as for himself and his marriage; he must have somehow bonded with her that morning in the mist. Now he knew why he had had to find her.

Somehow during those few minutes when they had held hands, she had transferred some of her anguish and fear to him...and Bill had received it without knowing. As this understanding began to penetrate his mind he hoped that she hadn't recognized his anxiety back then.

"Friends," the pastor's voice found its way back into Bill's consciousness again," A second lesson I've learned from the earthquake and tidal waves is that we truly need one another. To me one of the things that makes America really great is how we help one another in times of need. Now I know that it's still too early to see much help for us coming from the outside world but it will come. This is one of the reasons we need one another right now, isn't it? What can you do to reach out to your neighbors? Can you share something with those who no longer have houses to live in? Will you do it? We're in this thing together and we can reach out in many practical ways to help others in need."

"Yes! That's the reason I've felt so deeply drawn into the design project," Bill thought to himself. "Even the pastor knows that we can't count on help from the mainland…but we can!" A broad smile filled his face while a feeling of warmth was filling his insides. His thoughts guided him back into the sermon once again.

"I'm sure you're all familiar with the story of the Good Samaritan in the Bible. That story tells of a guy who was mugged, robbed, stripped, and left for dead on the long dusty road going down to Jericho in Israel. Like some of us here tonight that guy lost everything. He even nearly lost his life. Now the writer, his name was Luke, tells us that several men came along soon afterward and just looked at the poor man lying there on the ground and walked on by. They had other things on their minds. They had their own important things to do that day and so they just left him. However, sometime later another man came along that road. He was a man who had compassion in his heart, a man whose conscience would not let him pass by. So he stopped, and as the text tells us, bound up the man's wounds, probably to stop the bleeding; took his own wine and olive oil that he was carrying on his journey and poured them on the man's skin wounds, probably as an antiseptic and to keep his skin from cracking and getting infected. Then this man from the region known as Samaria picked him up and placed him on his own four legged ambulance, actually a donkey, and took him to an inn and continued to take care of him there. He even paid the innkeeper for all expenses that would be involved." The pastor paused for another sip of water, a gesture as much to illustrate a point in the story as to sooth his throat. Then he went on.

"Now I won't tell you what happened because the story is probably familiar to most of you. This story came to mind as my family and I came out my front door during the first earthquake. As my house and houses all around me still swayed and bounced around, some of them actually came off their foundations and broke apart, an image suddenly came into my mind of this man lying on that hot, dusty road that went down to Jericho. I could see many people in Oak Harbor lying in the roadway, on sidewalks, inside their homes, and I had to ask myself which of the three men in this Bible story would I be?"

"It may sound a bit trite but I believe that every disaster brings with it opportunity for our growth and renewal, not only in the physical sense but also growth and renewal of our souls. They say that whatever doesn't kill us makes us stronger, but I'd like to make a slight change to this saying. Let me suggest that whatever doesn't kill us offers us new opportunities to help others who are under similar pressures. So what *did* I do? First I took care of my own family and then I checked how my neighbors were doing. I'm really glad I did because I found an elderly man, a widower, lying on his living room floor pinned under a bookcase that had fallen over on his legs. We got him to a local emergency center where he was splinted and treated for shock. Now I check in on him every day. We've become friends."

Bill had been looking over at Kate as the pastor was talking. He saw her nodding her head several times.

It was obvious to the pastor and the elders of the little church that not everyone had come to listen to a full-blown sermon. Some who were sitting near the back of the room were talking to one other in low voices, others had their chins on their chest, and eyes closed. They were apparently asleep. Perhaps they had only come for the coffee that was to be served after the service. Even when the pastor raised his voice they didn't stir. Nevertheless, most of the people listened intently just as Bill was doing.

During the pastor's second point Bill hadn't been able to take his eyes off Kate and her family beside her. He finally caught a brief glimpse of her sister when she leaned forward. He was surprised to discover that he recognized her! Nevertheless, she was out of context here and he struggled with her name then it hit him, it was Veronica!

The pastor went on, "My third and last point, err, or should I say lesson that I learned is that, just as we need one another at times like this, we also need the Lord Jesus in our lives. There really is no way that we can protect ourselves adequately from earthquakes, tidal waves, floods, famine, disease, sudden terrorist attacks, or other gigantically destructive events and yet, what if this earthquake was meant to be a wake up call for you and me? What if God is trying to get our attention and calling us to come back into his loving arms? And, God forbid, what if even worse times are coming? Please think about these questions my friends. God does wants to be real in your life."

The words 'sudden terrorist attacks' lodged in Bill's mind. They reverberated there, dragging him back to those agonizing few minutes when that young man had crossed the road out there in front of him…just before the bridge had dropped out of sight. "He very possibly came from underneath the bridge," Bill thought. "Could he have sabotaged the bridge? It's funny how I totally overlooked that until now. However, it was an earthquake not a bomb that did it! The whole idea of terrorism is stupid, isn't it?" he reflected. Bill wondered whether anyone else in the church had gone through the same thought process as he just had. As the pastor's words began to register themselves in his consciousness again, as absurd as it sounded, Bill wondered whether the divers who had examined the bridge wreckage found any evidence of explosives, whether they even looked for any. He knew, of course, that even if they had found any they wouldn't tell the public.

"I want to conclude my meditation by asking you to think about several important questions. First, what do you fear losing the most in life?" He paused to let the words penetrate. He noticed a group of guys sitting on the left side near the middle of the room nudge each other and lean forward a little. Then he said, "and the converse of this is what do you want to hold onto the most? Are things what you value most in life? Do you really believe that owning something can offer you real security? I've come to see in my own life that almost everything the world says has value actually loses value over time. Cars, televisions, appliances, furniture, boats and so on. As we all look at our city and the destruction that fills it right now we can see the truth of this, can't we? What do you fear losing the most in life? The earthquake has helped me to see that my family and friends mean far far more to me now than they did before it happened."

Once again his words seemed to take root in Bill's heart. They made sense. He knew that the pastor was right. He should have done more to help Nan with her problems and not focus so much on his own.

"My second question: What is it that you think will provide you the most personal protection in times of social upheaval? Think about this my friends. You may be surprised to discover that those things that the world says will protect you can actually end up doing just the opposite. Many of these things can turn on you and harm you, particularly if others in the society want them for themselves. We've already seen this happen right here in Oak Harbor, haven't we?"

At this point the pastor was prepared to quote from the letter of James in the New Testament that said, "Whoever wishes to be a friend of the world makes himself an enemy of God." He changed his mind at the last moment, however, and dropped it. "The context was wrong...and most of them probably wouldn't understand it anyway," he reasoned. So he just said, "My friends, I urge you to be careful to develop friendships with others that are based on loving and caring relationships not on gaining money or power or authority." The audience's reaction to this advice was mixed as far as he could tell but it didn't matter. He was delivering the truth not necessarily what they wanted to hear. He went on.

"Third, what is it that causes you to panic? Did you panic during the quake or when you saw that enormous wall of water sweeping in toward the island? Were you surprised to find out that you weren't the kind of person you thought you were? Panic quickly becomes an irrational, dangerous, and self-defeating thing, doesn't it? My friends, God's Word teaches us that perfect love will displace, actually do away with, our fear. So, as panic is a result of fear so love is the only sure antidote for it. Scripture also teaches us that God is the perfect embodiment of love, its very source. So there it is, the place to find peace and calm in the face of adversity is in God Himself…certainly not in things or your circumstances. How can you find this peace? It's really quite simple; I like to think about it in these four steps. First, you must admit that you have fallen short of God's plan for your life because of your sins. In other words you must admit that you are a sinner. Next you must ask God to forgive you these sins. Why would God forgive you if you didn't first believe that you really needed His forgiveness? My friends, He promises to forgive you, of that I am absolutely convinced. The third step is to confess out loud to someone else that you have asked Jesus Christ to come into your life as your Lord and your Savior. As many Christians sitting around you right now will tell you, your life will never be the same again after you do this. Your life will be a new and wonderful adventure; you'll no longer be walking by yourself you'll be walking with the Lord. The last step is that you go about the rest of your life believing that all of this has happened, that it's an accomplished fact. That's all there really is to it my friends. It has very little to do with religion or ritual. It comes down to personal surrender."

The pastor stopped for several moments to take another sip of water and to look around the sea of faces before him. A few in the room were shaking their heads in silent disapproval. They didn't want to hear the Gospel but many more did. Then his voice dropped to almost a whisper as he concluded his presentation.

"Most importantly, what is it that will cause you to doubt the faithfulness of God? If you trust only in money or possessions or power or social status to see you through this life I can tell you my friends that sooner or later you are sure to be disappointed, however, the Lord has promised to give you special strength in times of need such as this. He has suffered far greater pain than any of us have ever suffered…it was on the Cross. He died so that you and I might have life, genuine life. This is what Christians believe all around the world. It's what we put our faith in. This is our firm foundation even when the earth shakes and disintegrates beneath us. I pray that many of us in this room tonight have learned that God keeps His promise to remain faithful to us no matter what our circumstances may be, even when we stop being faithful to Him! That is simply His nature. I wanted to share these words of truth with you all tonight because all of us do need to hear them."

During points three and four Bill had been trying to get Kate's attention without looking really stupid. He didn't want to interrupt the pastor's speech. He wasn't a superstitious man at all, but he still tried to stare hard at the side of her head trying to get her to turn in his direction. "It doesn't work, I know, but there's nothing wrong in trying," he rationalized. Even after several minutes of prolonged and obtrusive staring he found that indeed, it didn't work! She never turned her head in any direction. Bill also considered coughing or sneezing or dropping something heavy however he quickly changed his mind. "Even if she does look at me she probably wouldn't remember me," he reasoned. He resigned himself to dividing his attention between Kate and the rest of the service.

It included a time of personal sharing about what had happened, a sort of secularized community catharsis. The pastor asked if people would like to stand and share memories about their loved ones. It was like a family memorial service except that the family had grown greatly in size and included mostly strangers. Scores of people stood up in front of total strangers and recounted who they had lost and how. It was terrible what most of them had lived through. The resiliency of the human spirit showed through along with accounts of bravery and selflessness. It definitely helped some of those present yet hurt others who weren't yet ready to cope with such traumatic memories.

As people shared their stories Bill's attention swung back again to Kate. It was clear that she was crying. He could see that from all the way across the large room; she was holding her sister's hand and the boy's. He felt a deep compassion for her; they had participated in a moment that few others had. He lost track of what was being shared from the crowd for a time as he began to think about what he would say to her. Would she remember him? Would she be afraid for some reason? It didn't matter. He had to find out.

When it was clear that no one else wanted to speak the pastor said, "We're just about to close our meeting, but we want to do one more thing tonight.

What I am going to suggest may seem uncomfortable to some of you but then again it may not. It may be reasonable and doable…we here at the church think it is," he said. "I'd just like to invite anyone here tonight who has a genuine need to raise your hand. After I acknowledge you I'd like you to stand up and just tell us what that need is. There may be someone else here tonight who can supply all or a part of your need. Now I'm *not* talking about a whole lot of money. I am talking about ten or twenty or maybe fifty bucks and I *am* talking about blankets and food, containers to hold water and even a place to stay for a while, those kinds of things."

He knew that both he and the church were taking a risk nevertheless it was the right thing to do.

A week before when the pastor was planning this sermon he had considered inviting those in the room who had specific needs to stay after the service and share them with the elders and him privately. He thought that some people might feel embarrassed about asking for help in public. He also felt that some of the things needed might already have been collected and sitting in the church's storage closets; but after carefully considering this approach, the elders had advised him against doing it this way. Instead, they thought that he should bring up the subject of immediate personal needs during the service; he should also ask if anyone present had what was needed. The idea could backfire but it did make sense. Indeed, it was the way the early church had operated and it was called "body life."

The pastor and the elders who were sitting amidst the crowd waited, holding their breath. This was asking a lot of churchgoers much less perfect strangers who may never have set foot inside a church before. Everyone just sat in total silence. The proverbial pin could have been heard dropping by everyone present. Some people began to feel uncomfortable and showed it. After a long period in which the pastor deliberately said nothing, but only looked around the sea of faces with a smile on his (actually only several minutes had passed) someone in the back of the room on the left-hand side slowly raised his hand. He was a very thin young man dressed in a bright red, plaid, long sleeve shirt. There was a lightweight, nylon windbreaker draped over the back of his chair. He almost pulled his arm back down again except for someone sitting beside him, a young woman with a baby in her arms. She looked over at him and nodded, smiling weakly. Hesitantly he raised his arm again.

"Yes. Thank you...and please stand up so that everyone can hear you better, and tell us your first name," the pastor said gently. He smiled warmly at the man who seemed to wobble on his feet a little.

"Will...er, William," he said quietly.

"Alright Will, I know that it takes courage to stand up like this but you don't need to feel afraid or embarrassed. We're all friends here. We're all in some kind of need aren't we?"

The young woman seated next to Will hugged her baby closer and rocked her a little. In a quiet whisper she said, "go on Will...please tell them."

"Well, you see," he stammered, "we lost our house last week, everything we had, which wasn't very much, my wife and daughter, we don't have any relatives anymore." He stopped again, looking down at his shoes. "We need somewhere...a place to stay for awhile," he said, his voice trembled and tears beginning to run down his cheeks. It was clear that he had been under a terrible strain and now, for the first time, he was letting it go. People nearby turned to look at him and his young wife and some of them began to cry. He went on, "We don't know what to do...". Then he just sank down onto his chair.

The pastor had thought that there might be requests like this one but he was totally caught off guard by his own emotional response. Here was real life, real pathos, and real need. His voice broke as he too began to cry. He just looked intently at the young couple for several more long moments before speaking.

"Will...is that your wife there with you, and your daughter?"

The young man replied, "Yes it is, sir."

"What are their names?"

"Angela, my wife, and Maryanne...she's eight months old."

The pastor smiled again and then walked around the lectern where he had been standing to the front of the raised stage, nearer the people. Then he addressed everyone present and said, "My friends. Will and Angela and Maryanne need a place to stay for a while. Can any of you help them?" That's all he said. It was all he needed to say.

What happened next surprised a great many of the unchurched who were there because at least a dozen hands shot up immediately all around the room. As the pastor looked at the owners of these hands he realized that most of them belonged to people he had never seen before. They didn't attend his church. He was a little concerned about what he had set in motion and sent up a brief prayer to God for protection. He and the elders had also prayed long and hard about holding this body life service and just leaving the results in God's hands. That is what he had just done.

When the service finally ended and an elder had given a closing prayer another forty minutes had passed. Yet these precious moments had seemed to streak by because of the depth of love that was shown by so many and by the genuineness each minute contained. A very long and emotion-laden list of real needs had been shared. Only three or four involved money and not much money at that. The people had been encouraged by Will's simple but heartfelt request and they, sometimes hesitantly, had raised their hands. The elders of the church developed a plan to bring giver together with those in need and helped to work out the details.

The people in the room were no longer a group of strangers. They were bonded together by their common pain, their shared testimonies, their losses and now through many examples of welcome, tangible assistance that had been offered. Even though most didn't realize it, they had moved a little nearer to God as well. They were seeing genuine Christianity in action.

As people started to leave Bill remained standing beside the wall, never taking his eyes off Kate, the boy, and her sister. As people finally moved out of the way he could see Kate's sister's face clearly now. It really was Veronica! He had worked with her years before on an important local project, a project that had suddenly now become even more important, but he had lost touch with her since then. "Could she really be Kate's sister? What a fantastic coincidence," he thought.

He didn't want them to disappear in the crowd. He watched for Kate's golden hair bobbing amid all the other heads that were migrating slowly toward the rear doors. Veronica was several inches shorter than her sister and her dark brown hair merged with many others around her. Still surrounded by many people in the aisle, Bill gradually made his way along the wall toward the same doors.

He was greeted with a smile and handshake from time to time. "We're really glad you're here," said a middle-aged man who was obviously a member of the church; he seemed to know many others who were there as well.

Bill just smiled and said, "Thanks." He hoped that his tears weren't visible.

Kate, her sister and nephew had just reached the double exit doors at the back when he caught up with her. He didn't know what to say at first but only stood beside her amidst the jostling throng. Finally, a few small steps further, she happened to turn and look at him. However, she didn't recognize him at first and only smiled. Then, without any forethought, Bill reached out and took her hand in both of his. He had to do it.

Suddenly she recognized him and burst out in a sobbing cry that startled people nearby them. She remembered that moment on the highway; she felt all of her earlier fear and anguish come flooding back in an instant: that poor man in the pickup truck! "Oh how shattered he had been," she recalled.

Bill wrapped his arms around her in a hug that lasted a long time and she accepted it, like a little girl who needed a big brother's comfort and protection. Veronica watched in surprise and drew back a little but she said nothing at first. She recognized Bill almost at once but didn't understand why he was hugging her sister.

When they finally pulled back from each other Kate looked up into Bill's face and sobbed, "Oh, I'd forgotten you. I've been so absorbed trying to get my own life back together...you were so kind to me then and...and you were broken and shaking...". She finally paused for a moment when she realized that she had been gushing. Then she said, "Oh, I'm sorry, my name is Katherine." Even though she was smiling tears slid down her cheeks once again. Bill's eyes also filled with tears but he wasn't at all embarrassed. They were oblivious of the crowd that continued to stream around them.

Bill had been so focused on her that he momentarily forgot her sister and nephew. Then suddenly with an embarrassed look he said, "This must be your sister, Veronica."

Kate looked at him with surprise. "How did you know her name?" she asked.

"Would you believe that we met years ago when we were working on a project together?" he replied.

Kate turned to Veronica and said, "Well, Vi, it's really a small world isn't it? Why don't you introduce Jimmy?"

Before she could do this Bill grinned and said, "Hi, Jimmy. Your mom told me all about you but you were younger then. I'm glad to meet you." He shook the boy's hand with a firm grip as the boy looked up into his face, a bit bewildered.

The boy just mumbled, "Hello." Again, Kate was surprised by it all.

Veronica smiled and blushed as Bill leaned forward and kissed her lightly on the cheek. He heard her say quietly, "I'm so glad that we finished that project, aren't you Bill?"

He didn't reply but only nodded.

Kate turned back to Bill and said, "Forgive me…this has been an emotional evening for me. I'm not all-together…I don't even know your name."

He smiled a little and said, "Well my parents used to call me William and that's on my driver's license but everyone else calls me Bill, Bill Arnold."

She smiled a really big smile at him in return, a smile that warmed his heart.

The four walked back outside to her car almost in total silence. Finally he said, "I've been wondering how you were and whether your sis…" he didn't finish his sentence. Now he didn't need to. Kate's face was barely visible in the darkness but Bill could tell that she was radiantly happy. He was glad for that; it made him happy too. Now he might be able to begin his own journey back. As Kate and the others climbed into her SUV and shut their doors Bill came over and stood beside her. She rolled her window down, reached out with both her hands, and took Bill's hand in hers. "Everything will be all right, Bill. You'll see," she said.

As Kate, her sister, and nephew drove away into the darkness he looked after her wondering if she was right. Could he get things back in order again? Could he find in his wife the comfort and support that he still needed? Yet the pastor had also made him think about his responsibility to Nan as much as to his own soul. "Maybe I've been pretty insensitive with her," he thought. He played with that thought and its ramifications all the way back home.

As Bill turned into his driveway another thought crept into his mind, "I should have gotten her last name and address. I'm so stupid!" It was the second time he thought this.

The special service had been good for Bill not only because of the words of truth and comfort that the pastor had shared or because of what had happened during the rest of the service, events that had opened his eyes to what true Christianity was about. It was also good for Bill because she had been there. Deep down inside he felt a bond with Kate. Was it the result of their simple physical contact that had lasted only moments? Maybe. Maybe somehow it symbolized the bridge itself. The sudden loss of the cold hard steel connection between Whidbey Island and Fidalgo Island when the bridge had collapsed had been replaced just as unexpectedly by two strangers who held each other's warm hands simply because of the trauma they had shared.

The day after the church service Bill realized that he had to tell Nan everything, everything that had happened to him at the bridge that morning. The time had finally come for the sake of their marriage and their family. It happened after breakfast; the kids were playing in their rooms. "Nan," he said, "last night the pastor shared some really important things with us all. I really wish you'd been there. He said that we all truly need one another, particularly in times like this. Nan, I've been keeping some things back from you ever since the earthquake but I can't keep them to myself any longer."

Nan's face blanched a little as she quickly turned to look away from him. She said nothing. She was expecting the worst.

"You need to know that as I was driving back from the bridge site that morning and couldn't reach you by phone I really panicked...I suddenly realized how much I love and need you and the kids. I couldn't wait to get home to make sure you were all OK. That pastor was right about a lot of things last night." Bill began. He motioned for her to come into the living room with him as he went on. "I've got to get some things off my chest. This has been weighing on me ever since then. Nan, my experiences were so terrible that...that I just couldn't tell you about them back then, but we've got to talk now. Come sit by me here on the sofa, will you?" he said patting the cushion beside him.

Nan smiled thinly and sat down near him without saying anything. She was trembling and her hands were tightly clenched; it was clear that she was afraid of what she might hear.

"You were going through your own thing that morning when I came home and I didn't think you could handle anything more so I just stuffed it all. I'm really sorry, Hon. I should have told you everything right then," Bill began. Over the next half-hour Bill shared all of the terrifying details about what happened to him at the bridge. He watched Nan's reactions carefully. She seemed calm and controlled but still didn't say a word. So he went on, "As I was driving back down the road from the bridge I saw this woman waving at me and flagging me down so I stopped. I thought that she needed help or something but she only wanted to find out what had happened. When I told her she told me that her sister and nephew had been ahead of her and might have gone down with the bridge. Then she started to cry."

At this Nan's face clouded as she looked down into her lap. She still didn't say anything.

"Well, I reached out my window and took her hand for a moment to comfort her and after that I just came home…but would you believe that she was at church last night sitting with her sister and nephew right beside her. Her sister turned out to be Veronica Tyler…you know, Veronica on the design team? I couldn't believe it, what a coincidence." When he had finally finished the account Bill felt exhausted but relieved. Finally she knew everything.

Nan sat perfectly still on the couch looking at him with a strange expression on her face that he'd never seen before. He thought that she was probably trying to process what he had just told her, maybe she was trying to see through her own eyes what he had seen at the bridge.

At length she finally said, "tell me again about Kate, Bill…I…thought there might be someone else."

Bill was literally floored by her statement, flabbergasted that she could have thought there was someone else in his life beside her. He didn't realize that Nan had resented Veronica and the other women on the design team that he spent so much time with over the past several years.

Finally in desperation he replied, "Nan, you've got to believe me on this. I met her right after the earthquake was over for only a couple of minutes. I never knew her name until last night and I certainly didn't expect to ever see her again. That's the truth. I still don't know her last name or anything else about her. You've got to believe me."

Nan looked directly into his eyes for a long time before responding. "OK. I can accept that…I do so want to believe you."

"You mean you don't?" Bill replied. "Tell me when I ever gave you any reason to distrust me? I've never been unfaithful to you. I love our kids. This whole disaster thing has made me crazy, I admit, but I think I'm getting over it…are you?" His voice was strained even though he tried to keep his frustration under control.

She answered, "I think so Bill. I hope so."

He went on, "You didn't answer me…when have I ever led you to believe there was someone else?"

"Ah…never, really," she said just as she broke down in a sob. "Oh Bill, I'm so sorry. I guess I'm just a jealous woman and I can't help it. You were gone so much that I resented it. The more you were gone the more I thought it was either because of me, that you didn't want to be around me anymore or there was somebody else." she sobbed.

Bill noticed that her hands were no longer clenched but relaxed.

They talked on well past noon about all kinds of things that they both had avoided for years. It was a time for total honesty and sharing of deep truths. The subject of Kate never came up again in their discussions nor of Veronica or any of the other women on the design team.

At length, Bill said, "Honey, you know, I'm still working through some stuff and it's going to take more time. I hope you'll work with me on it."

Nan looked up into his face and said, "You know I will…and I do trust you."

He sat there for several minutes in total silence, holding both her hands in his, before he said, "Nan, I've got to go back to the cliff up by the bridge. I don't fully understand why. I just have to. Maybe I'm looking for some kind of closure or something. I'd like you to come with me if you want to," he said in the gentlest voice he could muster.

Nan thought for a long while before she answered. "You know, Honey, that I'm really not a brave person. I've always been petrified of heights. That bridge frightened me every time I went across it. To be perfectly honest with you I'm glad it's gone. When I watched you get involved in your engineering studies and designing bridges of all things I guess I thought you didn't really care about my fear of heights. Maybe I translated that into believing you didn't care about me. I know that sounds absurd."

Bill just sat beside her listening but he didn't comprehend very much of what she was trying to tell him.

"Yes. I'll come with you but don't expect me to enjoy it…and I won't get anywhere near that cliff either!" she said with a little smile and a forced laugh.

Bill sat for several more moments thinking. Then he said quietly, "That's OK…I've changed my mind. It's something that I've really got to do by myself. I hope you understand?"

Nan sighed to herself with relief and only nodded.

Right after breakfast the next morning he grabbed a heavy coat and his old Navy cap, the one he had worn on-board ship, and jumped in his truck. Nan came to the door and waved goodbye. The road was slick with rain from the low gray clouds sweeping slowly overhead off the water. If it hadn't been for the later hour it could have been *that* day.

As he headed north out of town his mind wandered. Distractions often accompanied him in his truck. For some odd reason he wasn't worried about his job, work that he couldn't get to anyway. His boss had been more than understanding and had given Bill whatever leave he needed, of course without pay. Yet, no matter how his thoughts began sooner or later they converged on those same awful minutes. He'd replayed the scene over and over again as if by doing so they would be erased from his mind; but they still kept coming back. They were somehow drawn into his unconscious like the pull of two magnets; invisible, relentless, and powerful. The bridge site was his powerful magnet. It had pulled him here today as well.

Upon reaching the entrance to the Deception Pass State Park he saw that someone had put up barriers across the road blocking the rest of the way. "Apparently the authorities don't want curious onlookers driving up to the parking area at the bridge, although not much could be going on there now," he thought. Bill parked his pickup behind a deserted gas station, locked it, and hiked up to the bridge site through the cold drizzle; it felt even colder than it really was because of the wind that was coming off the water. His hands and face were already numb. The unmistakable fragrance of the evergreen trees that he loved was missing, but he could just detect the salty fragrance in the sea mist that drifted through the deep forest beside him. Bill passed a couple walking hand in hand, obviously returning from the spot; he didn't do anything more than nod his head at them as they passed in silence. They didn't notice him; their heads were bowed to the ground.

As Bill finally rounded the last bend and approached the parking lot and cliff-edge where so many people had perished he began to feel a totally new and strange feeling coming over him. It was as if the entire surface of his body was anesthetized. He had no feeling anywhere. He could move and see and hear, but he felt virtually nothing else. Even his thoughts seemed to be slowing down. "What's going on?" he thought. Bill knew that it wasn't simply his numbness from the cold that now buried its chill deep within him nor even the silence that ominously filled this place. Perhaps he had expected to hear that terrible, deep-throated growl come back from underground, a sound that he would always associate with this place. The feeling of numbness didn't alarm him, indeed, he was thankful for it because he thought that if those awful scenes did come back he would be more insulated, more protected from them.

He noticed that the cars and the truck had been dug out but their shells were all still there. Apparently earthmovers had been brought in soon after the earthquake to retrieve those who were trapped and alive and the bodies. Bill had heard that the Sheriff had supervised their removal and that they had been taken to a temporary morgue in Oak Harbor.

Door panels had been pried off. Their twisted metal bodies were dented and crushed by the huge granite boulders that had buried them, yet everything else was just the same as he had remembered it when he left that morning. "I guess there might be some kind of law suits and they don't want to disturb the evidence," he reasoned, "…but that doesn't make any sense. It was an act of God, at least the earthquake part of it. If there were going to be any legal suits they probably would be against the Department of Transportation or somebody else with deep pockets," he reflected.

The vehicles were empty now, filled only by a deathly silence. The wind that was usually audible in the firs overhead was also strangely quiet. Bill was glad that the moaning of the earth was gone. Even the pulsing rhythm he had first heard in his ears for several days after the earthquake, a repetitive whooshing sound that kept time with his heart beat, was finally gone. The sense of calm he was feeling was similar to those moments that he remembered from his Navy days during memorial services for the dead. In fact, this was a memorial site as sacred as any other on earth ever would be. It marked the spot where people had perished, against their will, against belief.

It was with slow hesitant steps that Bill was drawn over to the edge of the cliff where the bridge had once stood. They had put up concrete barriers there but he didn't really notice them. As he looked out over the water suddenly he saw the same terrifying images as before yet now they were a little dimmer, a little more blurred and faded. Bill felt some relief from this. "Maybe in time they'll go away," he thought. Yet, the longer that Bill stood there the more his feelings of raw fear continued to grow; he had absolutely no control over them. They overwhelmed him, forcing him to turn and run back from the edge. He knew that it was a fear of getting too close and going over himself, if the terrible shaking should suddenly started up again. He was experiencing the familiar post traumatic stress effects that are common in those who survive terrible disasters. "I'm so glad Nan didn't come," he thought to himself.

Then he noticed the small bronze plaque that was embedded in a slab of bridge concrete nearby. It proclaimed the bridge as a *National Historical Site*.

The anxiety and fear he felt inside distracted his mind from the now ambiguous and macabre new meaning of the words on the plaque. "All things of man must come to an end," he thought. "Even this bronze plate and its proud words—*National Historical Site*—would be gone someday, but for now these words had a new reference because the bridge was gone. Would they remove the plaque altogether? Would the words be changed? Would another plaque be inserted in place of this one to memorialize the passing of so many people?

When statistics of the disaster were finally published (for Whidbey Island alone), they showed: deaths due to injury or accident; two hundred thirty four, eighty-nine of which occurred at the Deception Pass Bridge. Deaths due directly or indirectly to disease and infection: sixty-eight. Deaths due to other causes: nineteen, for a total of three hundred twenty one. Reported injuries of all types: six hundred eighteen. Emotional and other Post Traumatic Stress: unknown but estimated to be in the thousands. Both Bill and Kate were two of its casualties.

Chapter 8
Geology 101
Far Beneath the Northern
Puget Lowland

The professor of earth sciences looked older than his sixty-four years. Although he was a short man in a nondescript rumpled gray tweed coat and equally unpressed trousers he still towered high in professional stature, indeed far above most of his fellow professors, and he knew it. He had taught at the university for almost twenty-one years after leaving civil service with the federal government at the National Weather Service's Research Center; he had spent another six years there. He had left because he hadn't been promoted into management as he had first hoped he would. His career, or more accurately the years that led up to its apparent failure, had helped age him prematurely, yet at the same time it had shown him where his real talents lay.

Professor Morrison had discovered that first and foremost he was a researcher. He loved all of its challenges, its call for creativity, and its continual novelty. Nevertheless, as soon as he had been hired by the university his teaching and counseling load quickly collided with his research interests. It became a game between him and the department. He usually won this game as he found various ways to carry out his own research while teaching as few classes as possible.

Other things also pointed toward the fact that all he really wanted to do was research: the emphasis he always put on research data in his lectures, his periodic absences from class when he went to scientific conferences, and his reliance on using the same set of lecture notes from year to year to year, a fact that had not gone unnoticed by the Chairman of his department. At the same time the Dean and the Chairman seemed to keep putting obstacles in his way of carrying out his research. The greatest of these was his annual teaching load.

Once again his Department Chairman had talked him into teaching another section of Geology 101 to a classroom full of youngsters most of whom had no interest at all in the subject. He had taught the same course at least one term a year for the past nineteen years! He knew every fact, every slide, and every data point by heart; he didn't have to prepare for it at all which pleased him immensely.

One of his primary tasks in teaching (as he had discovered over the years) was to try to identify the one or two truly gifted students each term who would go on to accomplish what he felt he had failed to accomplish, to go on to set new marks in scholastic achievement and make revolutionary break-throughs that would save lives. Professor Morrison looked through his thick glasses toward the current crop of young eager faces before him, wondering who the one or two might be. This afternoon's class dealt with the fundamentals of earthquakes.

"Class. I consider today's subject to be not only important in its own right as an academic subject with valuable interrelationships with many other disciplines, but now it's even more important, because of the huge earthquake we have just experienced in the northern Puget Sound region," he began.

Known to only a handful of people, Dr. Morrison had been waiting patiently for a massive slippage to occur someplace so that he could test out his elaborate theory of energy transfer within the earth's crust. Within an hour after the Great Disaster had happened he had begun collecting all of the seismic data that he could find not only for the entire region but also for the entire globe! He'd been keeping track of every aftershock and relating them to a vast array of other geophysical events: of course the position of the Moon, changes in air pressure and temperature, solar activity, stratospheric electron density flux, and scores of other variables. Each of them was fed into a computer program he had designed himself.

He went on, "Today we are going to consider the geology of earthquakes with special attention to the northern Puget Sound region where this one took place." Although his students didn't seem to show much interest in what he said he was feeling extraordinarily excited. "So let's begin at the largest scale to see what we can learn...considered at a global scale the earth's surface is made up of separate plates of more or less solid material as well as many smaller plates," he began. "Would someone over there by the light switch turn all of the lights off please," he said as he pointed across the lecture hall and then adjusted a well-worn but still colorful viewgraph transparency on the overhead projector. "Stresses build up when these plates collide or move over the top of one another. Much of the stress occurs at these interfaces right here." He moved his laser spot along two parallel lines on the screen. His very slight hand tremor was instantly amplified for everyone to see. He hated using these pointers. "One of these major plates, the Juan De Fuca plate…here, lies off the west coast of North America and British Columbia and, we think, is gradually sinking below the shallower North American Continental plate as the two slowly come together."

Professor Morrison glanced up briefly in the direction of his class (now hidden from sight by darkness) before going on with his lecture that was terribly familiar to him. "This area right along here," he said as he put the laser pointer back into his inside pocket and ran his forefinger along a dashed line directly on top of the transparency, "…is known as the Cascadia Subduction Zone. The process of one plate sliding beneath another is called subducting. Considered most simply, earthquakes are the result of the sudden sliding and breaking of rock within the crust of the earth." He delivered this last sentence with the force that comes from a long familiarity with the subject and an assurance that his words were completely accurate. Some of the other things he said were pure conjecture and he knew it.

"Geologists consider a deep earthquake to involve earth movements originating at thirty miles or more depth; they can last from fifteen to thirty seconds with magnitudes up to seven point five. That's using the energy magnitude scale developed by Dr. Richter," he interjected. "Usually, aftershocks aren't felt because of their great depth; the intervening earth muffles, one might say absorbs, the smaller energy vibrations." The professor paused again and peered out over the top of his glasses at his class who were sitting in semi-darkness. He wondered how many of his students would expect him to ask about these details on his mid-term exam scheduled in several weeks. He went on, "A shallow earthquake occurs in the earth's crust in the Continental plate at depths of about fifteen miles. They're usually under eight point zero in magnitude. A third and final type of quake is known as a subduction earthquake. Here in the Pacific Northwest they tend to occur about fifty miles offshore from the middle of Vancouver Island as far south as northern California and at great depth. I'm sure that many of you will feel some relief to learn that no earthquakes have occurred along this offshore Cascadia Subduction Zone since records were first kept in 1790."

The professor continued, "Nevertheless, as I was saying, these subduction events can produce magnitudes of eight and higher and last for sixty seconds or more. Damaging tsunamis can occur along with a great many large aftershocks just as this one did here in the Strait of Juan de Fuca." The professor knew that he was spouting a lot of facts, old facts, and that perhaps a few students in his class at least wanted something more. He wondered whether his insights about earthquake dynamics that he had developed over the years and which he usually presented in his upper class courses would be of interest or important to this class.

It was more than coincidental then that a young man sitting in the front row raised his hand. The professor stopped. "Yes, Mr., Mr. Jackson," he said with a noticeable pause as he tried to remember the young man's name. "Do you have a question or a comment?" The student answered, "I guess both."

"Alright, go on," Dr. Morrison said.

"Well sir, you're pretty much quoting these details from our textbook which we can read for ourselves. In fact I read all of them last night. Could you tell us about other facts that we might be tested on that are not in the text?" the student replied.

Professor Morrison wasn't particularly upset by this direct challenge to his style of teaching. He had met it before from a younger generation that seemed already, so in-charge, so impatient to get to the core of things. He only smiled and said, "Alright, Mr. Jackson. I'll be glad to do that for the remainder of today's lecture but only if the rest of the class agrees. Remember that the study of geology comprises many different things and one doesn't always know the best way of transmitting these things to students who come from so many different backgrounds." What he really meant to say was that he didn't know who in his class read the textbook at all and yet still expected to squeak through his tests merely on the basis of their general knowledge from having grown up in a fairly literate society. He turned to the class and said, "Well, class, what do you think? Would you like me to do as Mr. Jackson has suggested?" He thought he could see a reasonable number of students nodding assent in the darkened auditorium; he said to himself, "be it on your heads, people."

At this point another young man suddenly raised his hand but Professor Morrison didn't see him in the darkness. So the student said, "Sir, I have a question.

"Well...alright...who's speaking please?" Morrison asked.

"My name is Kenneth Martin," he answered.

Professor Morrison said, "Go ahead Mr. Martin," his voice was tinged with a little irritation.

"Professor. I've been on Whidbey Island several times and I remember that there are a lot of solid granite cliffs all around the bridge...I mean the bridge that used to be there. These cliffs looked pretty solid to me. When I saw on TV what the earthquake did I was really shocked. If the solid rock could move enough to fracture like that and bring the bridge down there must have been a huge amount of movement. As he paused Dr. Morrison began to wonder where this guy was going. He might carry the lecture off in some wild direction and waste time. Then the student continued," Well, I was wondering if you had done any research on faults in that area and what you might have found out? Did you think that there was going to be a really big one there?"

At this Dr. Morrison smiled again and sighed inwardly. "What a perfect segue into my advanced lecture. I only hope that this isn't too detailed for Geology 101. They're still going to be tested on it anyway," he thought.

He yanked the transparency off the light projector, suddenly filling the room with stark white light. He went over to his briefcase and reached inside for several other viewgraphs in a manila file folder labeled 'Whidbey Dynamics.' He selected one of them, placed it on the projector and stopped for a moment so that his class could study its many details. He hadn't planned to use it with this intro class but it seemed a little more appropriate now. Finally he went on. "Well, Mr. Martin, as a matter of fact I have studied that area. I've got to admit that I was totally caught off guard by this slippage as well as the significant venting from Mount Baker at least four days before it," he said, looking up and peering into the dimness to see the young man he was speaking to. "Now, my previous slide was taken from an orbital altitude. This one depicts a much lower altitude, a scale of twenty thousand to one".

"The deep almost vertical trough running nearly east to west, right here beneath Whidbey Island, isn't really very long as geological rifts go. We believe that it's a part of a larger system of faults that are related to the infamous Cascadia fault far out in the Pacific Ocean, a fault that parallels the continental coastline for over a thousand miles as my last slide just showed you. We also believe, from various ground, seabed, and orbital data, that these gigantic plates are in constant, but very slow movement. It's so slow that we just haven't had enough time to measure the deeper displacements. Some of our best sensors are only ten years old. There's so little precise information about the dynamics of these earth-crust processes that no one can predict what's really happening far underground, yet as we will see, fault lines can be and often are interconnected. Stresses can eventually reach their strain threshold and suddenly release the potential energy that's been accumulating in them for centuries or longer. I believe that this energy can be transmitted laterally along these interconnected faults." The professor glanced around the room briefly while at the same time running his finger along a series of thin, crossing lines. He noticed a young woman sitting in the front row who had her head in her hands. He couldn't see her face. He wondered what was wrong.

His last statement about interconnected faults triggered something in the second young man who had spoken up; he leaned forward studying the screen image intently, concentrating on the outline of the long, thin island in upper Puget Sound that he had visited. Without raising his hand to speak he said, "Man, there really are a lot of faults under that island aren't there? What if a slippage of one of them was transmitted to the others? It would be like a line of dominoes that all fall over in sequence wouldn't it?" he asked. The student had begun to understand what the professor was trying to explain.

Dr. Morrison's eyes brightened. He was pleased that he had been able to transmit an idea this clearly. Maybe he had just discovered who one of his special students, as he liked to call them, might be. He said, "Yes, Mr. Martin, it would if my hypothesis is correct…if fault lines are actually energy transmitters. However, there's a lot more work to be done to verify if this could be the case."

"There's another fault called Devil's Mountain…right here. It passes almost east and west beneath the entire northern end of Whidbey Island and it runs as far west as Vancouver Island. We refer to it as a left-laterial, oblique-slip, transpressional master fault!" Dr. Morrison forgot for a moment that this was only an intro class. He decided that he wouldn't require knowing this terminology on his mid-term.

He went on, "Even though it's not known for sure, perhaps this long fault was an extension of the Darrington Fault farther to the east." Using another transparency, Dr. Morrison pointed out that the Devil's Mountain fault was known to have a complex displacement history going back into the mid-Cretaceous era. At hearing this all of the students began taking notes furiously. They were sure it would show up on their mid-term. "Its main strand has many left-lateral strike-slip offsets and right-lateral faults. Tectonic maps showed as many as four sets of parallel faults running northwest to southeast beneath southern Whidbey Island and the greater Port Townsend peninsula," he continued, vaguely aware that his vocabulary had slid into *graduate speak*. Then he used a third slide to illustrate virtually the same region with different colored lines and legends.

Dr. Morrison pointed out that, "most of these faults are considered active; that is, each represents a potential source of an earthquake, but you also need to understand, class, that even though they're active faults little more than two point zero quakes have occurred along them rather regularly over many many years."

The class was almost over; nevertheless, Professor Morrison was getting more excited and it showed. He stabbed his finger at the transparency again and said, "Did you know that even now after the largest earthquake ever recorded in the Puget Sound region, the Devil's Mountain fault hasn't slipped as far as we know? Most of us thought it would, but it didn't! Nor have the newly discovered Strawberry Point and Utsalady Point faults to the east, over here! Our seismic data have already shown that it was another fault that slipped. It was much deeper and lying almost directly beneath the Deception Pass area and extending far to the west! The big one fooled us all."

These facts were largely lost on his class. Most of them glanced up at the slide and back down at the notes they were furiously taking. A few glanced at the wall clock. No one said anything.

He went on, "I suggest that whoever discovers the reason for this will be very close to winning a Nobel Prize."

The professor had fantasized about hearing his phone ring and being told that he was to receive this coveted prize. It was very nearly the equivalent of an Academy Award in science, but even better because of its monetary prize. With his adrenaline now pumping harder, he continued, "The energy dynamics are so complex that even powerful computers running algorithms containing hundreds of variables haven't been able to solve the equations so far, but we're *not* giving up."

"Now I suppose you're wondering why all of the many smaller magnitude quakes in the two point zero to four point five range that have been recorded in the Puget Sound region over the years haven't helped relieve this growing strain...didn't prevent this cataclysmic earthquake?" This was his standard classroom rhetorical question designed to get his students to think on their own. This time it didn't work. They all just sat looking at him or the slide. So Professor Morrison went on. "The National Geophysical Data Center's website posts actual seismograph records they have obtained at many sites down to about two point zero magnitude. These smaller ongoing tremors have led some geologists to think that the deeper zones of stress were being released with each new small earthquake; nevertheless, other equally eminent geologists have disagreed with this view for various reasons. I guess this is why the public feels justified in ignoring the whole subject." He gave a little laugh as if he had made a good joke; none of his students laughed or even smiled as far as he could tell.

"I believe from studying the seismic records of this recent event, that the first relatively small earthquake acted like a trigger that set off a much more powerful blast of geologic energy nearly sixty miles underground. As you all probably know, this happened about three minutes later. Here is what I believe happened. The massive plate beneath the ocean floor had been sliding sideways toward the east while the shallower Continental plate, many experts think, had been moving in nearly the opposite direction! It's a classic reverse fault; the first prying under and pressing upward beneath the second. It's my considered opinion, class, that if their two adjacent sloping faces had been smooth there would have been no great catastrophic consequences. I also believe that there probably was an interlocking, stair-step shape in each of their adjacent faces, probably created when each of them was formed; a vertical step in each one perhaps as much as a quarter mile deep or more. At first they were far apart. For aeons there was no problem." The old man stopped to look over his class again yet found little response other than in the two young men who had spoken up earlier. Each of them, at least, seemed interested in what he was saying.

Then he stepped to the side of the projector where its side-light illuminated his body in the lecture hall. He raised both his arms into a horizontal position in front of him and then slowly brought both of his palms together. Finally he bent his fingers and then slowly linked them together, his elbows still extended outward. Several students saw his motions as part of a modern-day handshake in slow motion. However to the professor it was a graphic demonstration of what he was trying to describe in words. Frustrated, he glanced up at the illuminated clock at the back of the classroom; there were only several more minutes to go; he knew he couldn't develop his hypothesis well enough in that time so he decided to go quickly to his conclusion. He went on.

"When the continuously sliding plates finally reached each other, each of my hands that is, these two stair steps met each other and slipped into place, they interlocked firmly together. I wouldn't begin to speculate on how long ago this happened. Nevertheless, some of us believe that the massive crustal rock behind them kept on pushing, building up the strain every hour, year after year, aeon upon aeon." He tried to illustrate this effect by forcing his hands together. He seemed to be straining his face and chin muscles at the same time, at least to those sitting in the nearer rows. "This is probably what created the conditions for the largest earth movement in the history of the Pacific Northwest." He delivered his assertion with a force that lent it far more credibility than it deserved. The students liked it and actually laughed and some applauded as the bell rang to release them to the real world.

Jackson, the first student who had raised his hand stayed after class and approaching the old man said, "Professor, I liked what you said just now. What you said made sense to me."

Dr. Morrison smiled and said, "Well, thank you. I wish that my colleagues were as open-minded as you appear to be; but to be honest, no one really understands these tectonic plates for sure. Nor do very many geologists or geophysicists believe that the crustal rock is so strong that the centuries-old build up of stress didn't actually fracture the rock prematurely creating many smaller earthquakes. Nevertheless, one thing is perfectly clear, as our two recent earthquakes have demonstrated; the two plates gave no prior warning whatsoever before they finally slipped out of place! I believe that they came unlocked because of a much lower downward pressure of the seawater added to an abnormally low atmospheric pressure, both of which had likely held them locked together for aeons…two events that had never occurred at the same time before at least since we began keeping records, I might add…. I was hoping to get to this conclusion in class before the bell rang. To me, it's the key that explains the whole terrible event."

The young student looked earnestly in the professor's eyes. He saw the fervor of youth still there, the excitement that discovery of a genuine breakthrough can bring to one at any age. He had a sudden glimpse of himself in thirty more years; at least if he could get good grades, graduate, find and keep a good job, and work hard.

Dr. Morrison looked at his young student and saw himself...himself as he still wanted to be: full of eager youth and energy, intellect and vitality. "Thank you sir, for your insightful comments," he said.

Chapter 9
Four Years Earlier
A Bridge from Nowhere

Four years before this story took place a small group of north Whidbey Island and Fidalgo Island citizens began meeting together. They all shared the same serious concern that one day Whidbey Island would need another bridge; even a temporary one would be acceptable, to bring needed emergency supplies across from the mainland. The initial group didn't agree on what might close the Deception Pass Bridge: old age and its inevitable companions of wear and tear and rust or perhaps terrorism, earthquake, or some other unforeseen cause. They knew in their hearts, however, that it would happen someday, probably sooner than later.

They all did agree, however, that the single event that would raise the need for another crossing to the mainland from Whidbey quickly into public consciousness would be a deliberate but poorly planned bridge closure or worse, a totally unexpected and immediate closure of the bridge for any number of possible reasons. The conundrum was that if this happened without proper planning it would be too late. If an emergency bridge was not already available by the time this happened the consequences would be gigantic (as this story has shown). They realized that an emergency bridge must be completed and ready to be put in place very soon after such an event happened. Their plan made sense. It really was the only sensible way. This is the story of how an emergency bridge was designed, built, put in place, and came to save many lives.

Dennis Hayden, 46, was an athletically built man and he obviously stayed in shape yet what wasn't apparent to those who didn't know him well was his health. It was borderline at best although he had tried to do things to mask his symptoms of excessive thirst and urination, weight loss in spite of eating a lot more than he should, and a frustrating lack of energy. A year before it had taken only one visit to his doctor and a simple blood test to verify the abrupt and totally unexpected onset of diabetes mellitus that he now faced. His pancreas had slowed its production of insulin for some unknown reason; now he had to inject himself with the drug several times a day and watch his diet carefully. It had taken several months for Denny's doctor to find just the right drug dosage and diet to bring about a "normal" carbohydrate metabolism for him. The whole thing was a bother but he could live with it. He had to!

He was the group's organizer even though the idea for a new water crossing had sprung into the minds of two others in the group almost at the same time. He was a complex man, a universal scientist who appreciated and accepted the physical and the spiritual realms at the same time, seeing the environment as a fascinating combination of creation and evolutionary development over aeons of time. Yet he didn't think in either-or terms; people liked him for that.

Dennis was also a deeply spiritual man yet he didn't force his beliefs on anyone else that didn't show an interest first. From time to time his quiet and respectful manner caused others to ask him why he seemed to be so at peace when many others seemed so angry and upset. Only then would he share the foundations of his soul: it was really simple in its singularity, its complexity; it was God and Dennis's past experiences with Him. These experiences had proven God to him over the years, shown him that He existed. In small and large ways He wanted to guide Dennis through the rest of his life if he would let Him. Dennis did let Him and it showed.

Dennis wasn't particularly eloquent or gifted in public speaking. At times he would stutter slightly as his mind raced forward to drag out a word or phrase that he needed for the moment. Nevertheless, it was his everyday, relaxed and friendly personality that made him liked by so many people.

He was a retired space program engineer newly arrived on Whidbey from California. His parents had lived on Whidbey for many years and he and his wife and kids had visited them practically every summer. He had fallen in love with the island during these visits. California had its beautiful parts yet northern Puget Sound was spectacular in every way. He had just known that he wanted to live there someday. Now he and his family were on the island…and he had occasion to drive across the beautiful Deception Pass Bridge spans several times a week.

Once he was living on the island he couldn't help but notice how important the Deception Pass Bridge was to the life of the island. He found himself becoming more and more focused on it; the bridge had become more than a fascination to him it had become a kind of obsession.

Dennis did a lot of homework at the beginning of the project. He realized that the life of the Deception Pass Bridge wasn't going to be as long as some said it would be. He had also studied how critical this vital lifeline was to Whidbey Island and, like a handful of other individuals, he had done some projections of what would happen if the bridge were closed for any reason. These projections really weren't very hard to do. In discussing the idea of an alternate, emergency bridge with several Washington State Department of Transportation officials, he had learned that they openly acknowledged that the existing bridge wouldn't last forever; nevertheless, they faced higher priority projects right now. Once again he noted, the present ruled the future.

They made it clear to Dennis that their budget was greatly over-strained. They told him that a study report had been published about the feasibility of five different crossing locations for a new bridge to Whidbey Island. It had been published in May of 2001 and announced that none of the five alternatives were acceptable for various reasons! Denny had already read it; he wasn't surprised to learn that virtually nothing had been done after that about a new bridge! Whidbey Island had merely been consigned to the consequences of its own actions, constrained by limited solutions (and budget) that were imposed upon it by others, mostly by outsiders who wouldn't have to share the terrible consequences when, not if, the old bridge no longer functioned as a bridge. Dennis also read about earthquakes that had taken place over the years, although he realized that it wouldn't necessarily be an earthquake that would cause the bridge to become impassable!

The first thing that Dennis and the fledgling group did was to agree on a general plan of action. "We've got to see how much local support there is for our plan," he said at their first informal meeting. "We have to talk to community leaders, elected officials, and key citizens."

Allen, a young newly graduated architect (later to become a member of the group's Site Selection Sub-committee), agreed. "Yeah, that's a good idea. I read some recent letters to the editor in two newspapers. One guy wrote that he was absolutely against any new bridge because it would change the complexion of the whole island." He went on, "The writer didn't say what he meant by "complexion" but he probably meant that traffic would increase, prices would go up, and lots of other things like that."

Another member chimed in, "Yeah, I think I read the same letters. What I remember was that this guy said the whole island would change…which is absurd. We're going to have to watch out for this kind of scare tactic. I doubt whether the whole island would be affected; but opponents may try to use this approach."

Dennis smiled at both young men before saying, "Yes, I noticed that too, but I think the writer raised an, an interesting point farther down in his, in his letter. Let me see." He opened a manila folder marked PRESS CLIPS and then said, "Here it is…. He wrote that he was certain that ta, ta, ta, taxes would have to go up to pay for a new bridge…hmm, I think he also said he was retired…yes here it is, retired! He said he wouldn't support anything at all that raised his ta, taxes. What do you…all think of that?"

Hank, one of the quieter members of the group replied, "Well Denny, I'm retired myself as you know, but I don't think that everyone would agree with him. I sure don't. We've got to support our schools, the senior center, our fire and police. That guy probably wrote to the editor because he's frustrated about his own finances or something."

"Maybe," replied Dennis, "but we need to do a lot more research to see if maybe he's right, about the ta…ta…taxes that is, before we jump to the conclusion that he came up with." Hank and Allen nodded and smiled.

Dennis read two more letters to the editor he took from his clippings that also contained negative comments about a new bridge. Then he shook his head and said, "For s, s, some strange reason it seems to be human nature for more people to speak out against something new than to speak out in favor of it. If we, if we…did everything on the basis of letters to the editor we'd end up with a, a pretty lopsided society wouldn't we? No one would start any new projects."

Allen spoke up again. "I remember an old saying my Dad taught me. Let me see if I can get it right. I think that it was that people see as much as they can bare to see." He paused only a moment before going on. "If I was living on a fixed income these days I'd have trouble voting to raise taxes too. The guy's got a point, but some things are more important than that. What would this guy say if the bridge went down?"

Over the next several months they talked with many individuals and groups and were surprised to find less opposition to their idea than they had expected. A public opinion poll done ten years earlier had showed less than majority support for a new bridge; nevertheless, that was a long time ago and opinions can and do change with the years, particularly after the 9/11 disaster. Dennis warned the group to be prepared to hear a wide range of opinions.

Several members of the team wanted to stay as informed as they could about disaster preparedness for the sake of their own families. They came to be known as the hunker down guys. They were called that in jest, of course, not because of what they believed but because the others didn't want to admit that they weren't prepared hardly at all. Everyone knew that most people, both on the island and off, were far less prepared for a major disaster than they thought they were. The team members were also smart enough to realize that scarcity for a few can become scarcity for all over time.

"I'm pretty typical, about being prepared that is," remarked one of the guys. "When I went through a Red Cross preparedness checklist last week I found out that I only had about a quarter of the things we would need if we had to survive without electricity and water even for the three days they said we should plan for...and I thought I was prepared!" When no one said anything he went on, "Yeah, I was supposed to have a first aid kit, an emergency plan on how we'd respond to various kinds of emergencies, and a lot of information. I only had a few gallons of drinking water stored out in my garage and, hey guys, it's been there so long that I'd hate to have to drink it now!"

The other committee members looked around the room and nodded again in tacit agreement. They knew that they were in the same situation, or worse, but didn't want to admit it.

Then another hunker-downer added, "I think that preparedness is some-thing like wanting to be wealthy, it's far more in our imagination than in reality. Actually, I think we should try to show how having a new bridge is a basic part of getting prepared." Everyone agreed but no one knew how to go about it.

Dennis had been listening to the discussion intently; he was listening for signs of leadership as well as common sense in the group. He found both. At length he said, "Well fellas, I've...I've got to agree with all of you. I'm probably n, n, not as prepared for a disaster as I should be myself, but that awareness is the first step in getting us prepared, isn't it?" Everyone nodded again but their smiles had been replaced with serious expressions. "So I'm going to ask Allen to, to...to get information from the local Red Cross office here in Oak Harbor for each of us by our next meeting. OK, Allen?"

"Yeah. I'll be glad to do that," he answered.

The hunker-down group seemed to realize sooner than the rest that their bridge project would have a deep and lasting impact not only on their own little world but on a much larger one as well. If they could pull it off it would set an example that others could follow when government wasn't able or willing to do the job. To them it was a demonstration of good old American individual initiative at its best. At the beginning at least, some others in the group admitted that they got involved just to leave their indelible mark (like their names) in future history books. However, as time went on they too came to realize the significance of what they had begun.

Another thing the hunker-down guys learned was that people were very creative in coming up with reasons for not getting prepared. As Hank pointed out several meetings later, "There are those who merely look into the past and say, 'well, it hasn't happened here in my lifetime so I don't think it ever will.' Others are willing to play the odds. You know what I mean. A few others will hide behind some physical disability claiming that it's not possible for me to get prepared so I just can't. Still others may claim that, because they're already giving care for someone else who isn't able to be evacuated, they won't be able to be evacuated either." Hank had saved what he thought was his most important thought for last when he said, "A few people even live in a state of psychological denial since they think that they're sufficiently prepared when they've done absolutely nothing at all to get ready!"

Wilson Talbot was also one of the hunker-downers. A man with a perpetual smile on his deeply weathered face, a face that, nevertheless, concealed his age. He could have been anywhere from thirty to sixty years old or more. Willy, had a disarming way of making people feel relaxed around him; he radiated a kind of joyful sense of power. Deep down he liked to be liked. He also read a lot but seldom let it show until now. Willy discovered some interesting facts from reading surveys about how prepared people were. One evening he decided to share them with the rest of the group; he was grinning from ear to ear which made the others listen even more carefully. They all thought that he was going to tell a good joke or something.

"I've been checking out what some national surveys say about preparedness. For example, I'll bet you all didn't know that if a person was employed full time he had the highest level of preparedness, according to this survey." Willy began, tapping on an article in his hand. Almost at the same time several others present cleared their throats and looked around the room as if to say Duuh!

"You mean that being employed full time is positively related to being well prepared!" one of them said with a faint smile lurking about his lips to help soften the clarification.

"Well, er, yes. That's what I meant to say." Willy always had a cheerful disposition that the group appreciated; he wasn't at all fazed and went right on. "Another thing they found was that people with school age children tended to be more prepared than others who don't have school age children. I wonder why that is?" he asked, barely out loud as he raised his eyebrows. No one said anything. They realized that Willy was serious.

It was at the following meeting that someone humorously announced that the bridge project group might better be staffed by lots of working family members who worked full time and had lots of children in school. The rest of the group chuckled as they glanced over at Willy who ignored the comment.

Tad, another group member who wasn't a hunker-downer, learned a little-known fact that he thought might be good for the others to know. He said, "Did you know that levels of preparedness vary greatly by region of the nation? Over three-quarters of the residents in Miami, for instance, said that they had a disaster supply kit while only 32 percent of Chicago residents did." He went on, "I think that Whidbey is probably in the Chicago column." The others nodded in agreement.

The second step forward that the committee took happened two months later. Even though the step didn't succeed it taught them all an important lesson.

Dennis contacted a number of university engineering departments in the greater Seattle area to find out whether any of them might help out in some way, perhaps by designing the planned emergency bridge; the group became discouraged when they couldn't find any local university engineering department willing to accept this challenge. It wasn't going to be their only discouragement.

The universities gave them many excuses. For one, the *plates* of several engineering departments were already too full to take on such an activity. Even when a member of the planning group tried to convince the officials that such a bridge could play a valuable role in many different Puget Sound locations it didn't seem to matter to the deans or to their faculty members.

Another reason given by one of the universities was that the only bridge designer on their faculty was away on sabbatical leave and probably wouldn't be interested anyway. In addition, such a project was far too big for any single undergraduate engineering student. Some other reasons given were that any new project had to be approved at least at the dean's level or higher and that a professionally licensed bridge engineering firm would have to co-sponsor the student project. With each new objection that was raised the small group grew more and more discouraged.

Yet another reason that a different university gave was that their undergraduate engineering students were already committed to participate in several annual engineering design competitions. One of the more popular of these was called the concrete canoe competition; its goal was to build a better concrete canoe!

Each year since 1987 students at many U. S. universities had competed against one another to design, build, and race twenty-foot long multi-manned canoes that they had made themselves, canoes made out of concrete! The competition was sponsored by the American Society of Civil Engineers. The Whidbey Island citizens' group only smiled and shook their heads at this seeming misdirection of valuable and needed technical talent. Following this annual tradition, however fun, exciting, and educationally fulfilling it might be, seemed to be more important to the students than contributing to solving an important and practical public need.

At the same time the group realized that if a university did take their bridge project on it would probably cause the college administration many difficulties. For instance, they might be opening themselves up to possible legal liabilities and their administrative staff workload would likely increase. Furthermore, the matter of who would raise the funds for the prizes would need to be identified. The main reason beneath all of these negative responses, however, turned out to be that the project was just too large and complex for even small groups of undergraduate engineering students working together to finish in a semester. Their end product would probably not meet enough of the design requirements for Whidbey to be worth the effort. The whole idea just didn't fit into their traditional ways of doing things.

More and more it seemed as if going to academia for help was the wrong approach. It seemed to several of the group members as if accomplishing such a bold and proactive plan simply wasn't possible unless the Department of Transportation carried it out from start to finish or perhaps the U. S. Army Corps of Engineers.

Over the course of the next year the bridge-planning group grew in size as it became much more attuned to the realities of accomplishing a project of this size and kind. The group held public meetings to gain support for their idea and to find out what kinds of objections there might be to it. They scheduled meeting rooms in the public library, senior center, and a public school over a three-month period. Attendance was not very large despite the outstanding advertising that was provided free of charge by the local newspaper and Chamber of Commerce. What they learned wasn't always what they wanted or even expected to hear.

Some citizens said that their island paradise would be ruined by all the outsiders flooding in over such a bridge, others argued that the Deception Pass Bridge had been responsible for a great deal of damage to *their* physical and social environment already! These folks couldn't seem to understand the difference between a temporary emergency bridge and a permanent one. Some even seemed to be opposed to both! The planning group listened patiently as still other people wanted the project stopped in favor of a water taxi system that would use high speed catamarans between the island and the mainland, an idea that had been tried in Gig Harbor across from Tacoma years before. Some citizens, using what they thought was faultless logic, were persuaded that such a bridge project could never be achieved because of all of the bureaucratic problems that had to be faced at the local, county, state, and even federal level. They argued that no citizen's initiative group could ever hope to overcome all of them.

All of the objections that were heard, however, seemed to boil down to these two: that the government would provide whatever emergency support might be needed after a disaster or that such an event would never happen in the first place. The group knew that failing to plan is planning to fail and the consequences of the Deception Pass Bridge becoming impassable were almost too terrible to think about.

Earlier research on computer-simulated earthquake effects along the greater Everett-Seattle-Tacoma interstate freeway had shown regional planners just how vulnerable this entire stretch of interstate highway was and how many overpasses and bridges would likely collapse or become impassable in quakes of various sizes and epicenter locations. It was during one of the team's early meetings that Dennis shared what he had learned from his study of population centers and the I-5 interstate highway on the mainland.

"I want to tell you what I've discovered about our situation here on Whidbey," he began. "I'm afraid that almost all of the major population centers north of Seattle that are located some distance away from the I-5 corridor probably will be overlooked by emergency responders for weeks or longer after a major disaster takes out even a few of its main overpasses and bridges." He noticed that several team members seemed surprised at his remark. He went on, "The I-5 corridor is seen…is seen as a major lifeline along which emergency services and supplies can be delivered. The security of the I-5 corridor is both important and also extremely tenuous. It is actually hung together by very thin threads indeed."

While he didn't say it out loud Dennis was thinking, "Actually, they should use Puget Sound itself as much as possible to transport their emergency supplies…by boat…to prearranged pick-up locations." Then he refocused again on the team sitting around him.

"The primary difference in transportation between communities on the mainland and Whidbey Island is simply this. Roads on the mainland are much more plentiful; many run parallel to one another as everyone knows. If one road is closed for some reason others still may be passable but on Whidbey Island, as we all realize, there's only one arterial and it's one l…lane wide in each direction down the entire length of the island! As you know, there are a few relatively short roads that run parallel with highway 20 but we…we…we have no other routes for end-to-end vehicle transportation. Whatever closes this arterial effectively stops much of our l…life support and commerce!" Dennis paused a second. He suddenly realized that he had been preaching to the choir so he concluded, "The Deception Pass Bridge is the beautiful, fragile jewel in thi… this crown or should I say the weak link in the chain!

During another meeting Janice, a relatively new member of the team, shared her view that the island was something like the human body. In a slightly trembling voice she announced "Well folks…I'm a little self-conscious. I hate public speaking, but you guys aren't the public anyway." With that she went on without any hesitation in a perfectly clear and controlled voice, "State Route Twenty in general and the Deception Pass Bridge in particular are much like the body's carotid artery…if you'll excuse my medical metaphor. If the blood is cut off there the body will soon become severely incapacitated and might even die without immediate first aid." Several of the others around the table glanced at each other to see whether or not they were taking her seriously. Everyone was. The young woman didn't need to expound very long to convince them of the aptness of her metaphor. "If the bridge isn't there we're going to need massive infusions by ferries or other kinds of water transport. Still, a bridge makes the most sense." Dennis beamed inside. These were his kind of words, his thoughts about the bridge, virtually his own vision for the project.

Veronica was another recent addition to the group. Janice who was a neighbor of hers in Anacortes had recruited her. Although Veronica was just a little over 30 years old (she looked ten years younger) she already held a Masters Degree in land-use planning. Dennis realized right away how valuable her talents would be to the group. She was very bright and had a pleasant personality and even more importantly, she was a team player. He discovered all of these things during his first meeting with her over coffee. He also found out that she had put her career on hold to have a family; she had a little boy at home and a husband whose work called him out of town for several days at a time.

During their meeting Veronica said, "I happened to pick up a small pamphlet. It was entitled "Preparing for Disaster" and was printed by the American Red Cross and the Federal Emergency Management Administration. It's very well done...and it really got me thinking...in fact, I've already started to stockpile food and water and other things myself."

"I think that our group would appreciate it if you'd give them a summary of it, that is if you want to," he said. "You could do it at our next meeting."

The following week Dennis introduced her to the group and summarized her background briefly. Then he just said, "Veronica, you've got ten minutes, OK?."

She smiled as she nodded and then began, "Dennis asked me to share some details from this little booklet from the Red Cross." She held it up so everyone could see its cover. Then she went on, "I found a couple of suggestions here that I hadn't thought of before...let's see, here's the first one. If our power goes out we're supposed to use up our perishable foods from our refrigerator and pantry first and only then from our freezer. Then we can eat our canned foods. They made a really good suggestion about taping a list of our freezer's contents on the outside so we'll know what's inside without having to open the door all the time. The food inside will keep days longer that way...Let me see... yes here it is, frozen foods are OK to eat as long as they still have ice crystals in their centers. They even gave out a list of emergency foods, for a family of four, for three days. I also thought it was interesting how they really emphasized the need for having lots of water as well as food, water isn't only needed for drinking. For instance, if we followed their three-day diet that included dry foods like cereal, soup mix, macaroni and cheese, dehydrated trail meals, instant coffee, tea and such we'd need about three and half gallons of water just to reconstitute and cook them. Of course we should save this water for the same use later." Veronica glanced up from her brochures for a moment before going on. "I picked up copies of these brochures for each of you...they're over there on the table. Oh, one last point that I found interesting, one of the handouts said that local officials and relief workers will be on the scene after a disaster, but they cannot reach everyone right away."

Dennis watched the group's reaction to her last statement. He noticed a lot of knowing looks, nods, and smiles passed back and forth across the conference table. Veronica ended by saying, "That final disclaimer was probably written by an attorney," and everyone laughed.

The team continued to grow in size slowly and mostly by word of mouth. If a member knew someone who might be interested and who had the right skills he or she was contacted. The group was only five months old when Bill Arnold first learned about the *bridge group* as it was unofficially called. Married for ten years, he had recently retired from the Navy as a Chief Petty Officer specializing in large diesel engine maintenance. He was now looking for a part time job to supplement their income. Secretly he hoped that someone in the group might know of something for him. This was why he had joined the group in the first place. Yet it wasn't very long before he began to realize how important this project was.

Bill had finally received his bachelor's degree in civil engineering with emphasis on bridge structure design. He had been able to finish it largely through a lot of hard work that involved extension courses and short, theme-project classes during the summer months. All during this time Nancy, his wife, felt increasingly isolated from him. He'd never found the time to explain to her how important his college degree really was to him or the impact it would have on his future earning potential. He saw it as his ticket to their future security. Deep inside himself Bill knew that he should have taken the time to tell her all this but for some reason he didn't. One result was a growing rift between them; at first she just resented his absence.

Nancy Arnold nee Phillips had been born and raised in North Carolina of a wealthy old aristocratic family whose origins stretched back many many generations. Her dad, Major Paul Gregory Phillips, with the Second Marine Logistics Group at Marine Corps Base Camp LeJeune, had taken to Bill right away even though he was in the Navy. The Phillips lived near Sneads Ferry in a posh gated community that boasted many waterfront homes. The Major had no difficulty buying one of the largest on Chadwick Shores Drive; it wasn't long before they joined the North Shore Country Club. He kept his small sailboat tied to the end of his private dock out front but never seemed to have enough time to take his family out sailing. As she grew up Nan had asked him many times to teach her how to sail but he'd only been able to cover little more than the basics. The Phillips didn't hurt for money at least.

Nancy's second story bedroom faced the ocean only a mile away. As she grew up she loved to open her window at night and, when the wind was just right, listen to the ocean surf and feel its cool salty breeze. The Phillips only child, Nancy got almost anything that she wanted, anything except boyfriends, cigarettes, alcohol, and dope. Her father took a dim view of them all, for his only daughter that is. He liked his liquor (when he was off duty) but he never smoked or tried any drugs. Nan's Mom arranged for her to take French lessons when she was starting junior high school, positively the worst time in life to do such a thing to an adolescent. She was the only girl her age taking them, but being a military brat had conferred a certain sense of stubborn independence on her that most of her girlfriends didn't have. Nevertheless, by nature Nan was more introverted, quiet, reserved, and sometimes touchy. Even though her Dad sometimes terrified both she and her Mom because of his temper she never responded back to him in anger. Her approach was simply to withdraw. It always seemed to be easier that way.

Nan was twenty-three and had just completed college when she met Bill. He had been temporarily assigned to an advanced mechanics school at Camp LeJeune, a very small component of the gigantic Marine amphibious training base, a base that covered one hundred fifty six thousand acres! Their meeting happened at a small quaint country market one Sunday afternoon where each had ordered the same exact espresso drink at the same moment from the same server. Both wanted a Grande-mocha-light-no froth-extra hot latte.

Nancy glanced over at the tall, rugged guy beside her at the counter. "Wow, that's a coincidence," she said with a deep and contagious smile on her pretty face.

"Yes it was. You go first." he replied with his own smile and a kind of gallant abbreviated arm-sweeping bow.

" Oh no. I beg you sir. You were here first." She replied with a wonderful lilting laugh. "Anyway, I'm in no hurry."

Bill laughed as he said, "I sure wish the guys on base were as courteous as you."

Nan paused as the girl behind the counter looked back and forth between them with a quizzical look on her face. Then Nan turned to her and said, "OK… did you get my order?"

The girl said, "It was a Grande-mocha-light-no froth-extra hot latte."

Nan nodded to her and turned back toward Bill. "I sure wish I had a memory like hers," she said.

Bill was basically shy but Nan wasn't. She invited him to join her at a small table beneath a colorful umbrella itself in the shade of a large leafy tree. He agreed.

As they sat down he held out his hand and said, "My name's Bill Arnold."

She took it in hers with a firm handshake that surprised him; she had learned it from her Dad. Then she said, "Mine's Nancy…Nancy Phillips."

It wasn't very long before they were meeting for coffee or just going for a walk, several times a week, whenever Bill's duty permitted it. He loved the way she took pleasure in the little things like the ever-changing view of the ocean and the way all the tiny birds darted around in the trees and especially the way she smiled at him. Bill also loved her pure joy of living. He couldn't find a better way of describing it.

When Bill found out that she had a sailboat he said, "Hey that's great. I love to sail…do you know how to sail?"

"Well, I guess a little, but Dad never has time to take me out with him anymore. Do you sail a lot?" she asked.

Bill grinned and decided to play a little joke on her. He answered, "Well I'm in the Navy aren't I? They give every man and woman sailing lessons so that if our ship sinks we can sail our lifeboats to land. It's really easy. I can…"

Before he could go on Nan interrupted him with a look on her face that was somewhere between seriousness and incredulity. "Whaat! You mean to tell me that all sailors are given sailing lessons? Somehow I don't believe it, and I bet you can't swim either."

"I can too," he replied, trying to change the subject before she caught him.

"Well then let's prove both of them at the same time," she said, "I'll see if Dad will let us use the sailboat and, if he will, I'll push you in the water." She broke out in a long, lilting laugh that lifted his heart.

Bill smiled back at her and said, "OK, how about next weekend?"

Next weekend found them both a hundred yards from the shore on her Dad's twenty two-foot long sloop in a mild breeze under an almost clear blue sky. Bill had hoisted both sails while Nan held the boat perfectly into the wind. As the sails suddenly filled and the boat heeled over and shot forward, Bill almost fell overboard. Nan laughed again as she watched him crawl on all fours back to the cockpit beside her. He looked just like a cross between of a long-armed chimpanzee and a drunken sailor.

"Well, Mr. Sailor, I though you said you knew all about sailboats," she taunted.

"I do. You can ask me anything," he replied, snuggling even closer to her side.

"OK. What's the difference between standing rigging and running rigging then?" she said with an equally taunting voice.

"Well, that depends," he said. "On a light cruiser the standing rigging is attached to the conning tower but on a battleship it's attached to the main mast." His eyes were twinkling; he knew that she could see right through him but when he went on about the running rigging being attached to the running board she gave him a quick kick with her foot and another laugh.

"I didn't say I could answer everything did I," he quipped. "But one thing I do know for sure, I love being out here with you. He'd noticed how Nan seemed to sparkle when they were together.

It was after they had returned to the dock and secured the sailboat that Bill said, "Nan, I think you have a pure joy for living."

Suddenly she stopped and faced him and said, "Joie de vivre…c'est mon expression favorite!" It was the first time she had spoken French to him.

He just looked at her in surprise; he didn't say anything. He'd hardly heard anyone speak French before. It sounded beautiful.

She laughed and said, "I thought I'd like to try it out on you. Do you know what it means?"

"Well, not exactly, but there's something in there about an *expression favorite*" he said, mimicking her accent as best he could. Then he laughed too and gently wrapped his arms around her as he kissed her for the very first time. He whispered, "You know, you're my *expression favorite*."

Nan melted into his arms. She knew that he was the right guy, the guy that she had waited for all these years. Nan kissed him back and held him even tighter than he had held her. She never did tell Bill what her special phrase meant, she didn't need to.

It had been a whirlwind courtship that lasted only four short months but it was sufficient, they were right for one another.

Even though Bill had graduated with honors he still didn't have a job. And although Nan seemed genuinely pleased to return to Whidbey Island and finally settle down; to get her home established once and for all, completing his final requirements for the degree had almost ruined their marriage. He had had to be in residence (live either on campus or near it) for his last two years so that he could attend classes full time. This had put Nan under even more strain as she moved their household down to Seattle, gave up all of her local girlfriends, learned where to shop in the university district, and dozens of other things that most husbands know nothing about. She was glad that Pat their daughter was only five so that at least she didn't need to look into schools right away. Although she was a Navy wife and accustomed to moving often, she had hoped that Bill's retirement would finally mean some family stability, like her Dad had provided her for those years she had lived at home.

One hectic week after having moved back to Oak Harbor again Nan was still unpacking all the boxes that were piled everywhere across their living room floor and hallway. She was at her wits end, barely coping with everything that had to be done. "Bill…Bill," she called. She thought he was out in the garage unpacking but when she didn't hear any reply she went to the front door, pushed it open, and saw him talking with a neighbor across the street. "Bill," she called again. He responded with a smile and a wave but didn't return right away. "That's just like him," she thought, "leaving me to do all the unpacking!" She reentered the house with her insides churning and other thoughts whirling through her head: "Why can't he ever help me? I know he can't help being friendly...but doesn't home ever come first? This is absolutely the last time I'll move, I swear it. He's got what *he* wanted...when is it my turn? I've got to control my temper."

Each night when darkness descended she also descended into her own dark pit, a pit lined with silent depressing feelings of dread and fear, yet there was no overt anger. Her pit was coated over with a thin veneer of self-control, very thin indeed.

She reflected, "Now that he's finally able to, he should want to stay home in the evenings. He should want to be with the kids and me. He's retired now... we've got a Navy pension...he's got his degree. Right now, at least, he's free from the routine of a job. So why does he seem to be drifting away from me?" These preoccupations insulated her from seeing herself as clearly as she might have from his perspective.

"I don't understand why he wants to get involved in this bridge project anyway...but it does seem awfully important to him. I know that he's got to live according to his own priorities," she reasoned to herself . However, to Nan it seemed like it was either the bridge or she.

As the weeks and months passed Nan became increasingly withdrawn while Bill immersed himself in "his project" as she called it. Like so many others on the island she liked things just the way they were. As far as she was concerned they didn't need any new bridge. To Bill, who had considered the many ramifications of living on an island with extremely tenuous connections to the outside world, the bridge project had taken on much greater significance. He convinced himself that it might possibly save hundreds if not thousands of lives someday.

Unfortunately, Bill never made the effort to talk about his feelings with Nan. As she increasingly retreated from him in little ways he felt less comfortable talking with her about anything, except their children. They both had changed. He didn't like her new personality. Now she was usually sour and quiet until sudden bursts of barely controlled emotion poured out of her, quickly enclosing them both within more sullen silence.

As Nan continued to withdraw from him, Bill began to wonder if his subconscious wasn't connecting his preoccupation with the bridge project with his marriage. "Am I running away?" "Do I need a new "bridge" of some kind? If I do, what kind?" he asked himself. Bill wasn't a particularly sensitive or philosophical type guy and he had trouble thinking about these possibilities. "Do I need some kind of new connection? He pondered the question many different ways but the answer always came back negative. I've got two kids, a wife, a home, a job of sorts, retirement income, and I'm healthy. What more could a guy ask for?" Yet even as he ran through this list of blessings over and over again he knew that something was missing. Then one day he knew what it was…it was leaving a legacy.

Up until now his life had been focused mostly on himself. Yet there was more to life than that. Bill began to understand that he should find ways to multiply himself not only through his children but also through other people. He knew that he couldn't do this through Nan. Increasingly, he realized that he must find ways to invest himself in the lives of others, share his own visions and creativity and encourage others to work hard and excel in their own lives. "Sure I can do this with the kids," he reasoned silently, "but they're not ready…it's too soon." Bill began to understand that he could do this through the bridge project. Yet once again, he hadn't thought about Nan's feelings at all nor had he shared his new insight about himself with her.

The small bridge group met weekly at first to plan different strategies to accomplish their project, if not to completion, at least to come up with semi-final construction plans. As the group met and began to touch the lives of many people it also grew in size. Bill discovered his ability to lead, a foundational part of his legacy.

Dennis, Bill, and the rest of the group (now numbering fifteen) agreed to form several semi-autonomous working committees. They settled on a Site Selection Sub-committee and a Political Action Sub-committee. A third group confronted the issue of funding while a fourth planned for their public relations. By mutual agreement, Dennis and Bill became co-directors of the entire project.

Each committee met by itself twice a month. It then came together as a single, united group monthly to review their progress. The high attendance at their meetings attested to everyone's genuine concern for their project. Each group had its work cut out for it as they soon discovered.

Bridge Location

For the Site Selection Sub-committee the location of a jumping off spot on north Whidbey Island and an adjoining spot on the mainland or Camano

Island to the east or Fidalgo Island to the north proved to be an extremely taxing and stressful job. Their first task was to study the pros and cons of various candidate bridge-landing locations. They did this quietly; taking weekend drives around the island with their cameras and notebooks. Although they tried to be as inconspicuous as possible, they were sometimes misidentified as realtors on the lookout for new property to buy or sell. They also made extensive use of a photomapping utility on the Internet that gave them high resolution color images of the virtual world. Whidbey Island was visible from far above in stunning detail. Because one of the committee members was a private pilot she took others up with her to survey and photograph the coastline from the air. Bill volunteered to be a part of this committee.

During their first several meetings no one was in charge and therefore, little was accomplished. Bill did share his fascination with the Deception Pass Bridge with them and how he had collected virtually every piece of information he could find on it. He told them that his files contained structural drawings, load calculations, old photographs, and other historical documentation. He couldn't explain why he was so fascinated by this beautiful structure. However, his fascination was clear to everyone else. They recognized what he didn't; namely, that he had fallen in love with the bridge, at least to the degree that a man can love an inanimate object. The rest of the committee agreed that Bill was "destined for the job of chairman," "perfectly cut out for it." When they put it to him he agreed without any hesitation.

Later that night at home:

"Nan, our meeting went really well tonight."

"Oh."

"Yeah, remember I told you we had broken up into four smaller groups, a couple of weeks ago."

"Yes Bill, I remember."

"We call one of them the Site Selection Sub-committee. We're trying to find the best place to connect the bridge at both ends, here on Whidbey and over on the mainland, the eastside." Bill turned to look into Nan's eyes as he said this. He saw no emotion at all, a total blank, neither concern nor interest. Still, he went on excitedly, hoping to see some sign of pleasure and acceptance from his words, "Well, would you believe that they chose me to be the chairman?" His words seemed to bounce off a deep void of silence that she had created around herself. It was a painfully deep void whose emotionless walls had grown out of her inner fears and resentment. He didn't realize that his neglect of her had helped build this void. He couldn't comprehend her total lack of response. In fact he wondered if he ever had understood her very well at all.

"Oh," she said.

"Yeah. It's really a great compliment.

"For whom?"

He only looked at her and shook his head several times before stalking out, slamming the garage door behind him.

Bill and his team had to confront a long list of public and private concerns. Some of them were realistic, others simply ludicrous. For one, Island County public officials hinted that they would not permit any private citizen's group to formulate any such grandiose plans without their approval or at least direct oversight; this edict seemed to make sense to the officials who firmly believed that they had absolute jurisdiction in such matters. At one point county officials quietly threatened a cease and desist law suit against the "little," "unofficial," "unauthorized," "citizen's" planning group but thought better of it as soon as the local newspaper got wind of it and threatened to publish a full report, a report that presented both sides of the matter. It was fortunate that the bridge group had several retired attorneys on board who knew their legal rights.

The unspoken underlying objection given by the county officials seemed to be that they knew more about doing such a job than the citizens who were proposing it, yet their objection was never stated quite this openly. Their position was shrouded in legalistic, bureaucratic jargon; nevertheless, what was plainly obvious to everyone was that, even if they had known how to do the job better, the public officials had never taken any concrete steps to accomplish it! It seemed to be yet another case of political reality; let the future deal with itself.

This realization had not been lost on Bill who found himself more and more captivated by the project. "If we don't do it, it looks like nobody else ever will," he thought to himself from time to time. He was convinced of its inherent value, its rightness. The group noticed that Bill had slowly but surely passed the point of being just a technically oriented member, possessing many useful skills, to a man with a mission in life and an ever-expanding social consciousness as well. He began to recognize this subtle change in himself. At the same time he was learning to not share any of his thoughts about the bridge project with Nan. It seemed to him that she neither understood nor agreed with them. He wasn't quite sure but he thought that, for some unknown reason, she might be becoming jealous of the bridge.

He poured himself completely into the bridge project, seeing it as a way to prove his own intellectual prowess and technical capabilities. "Maybe I'll even be able to land a good job because of it," he hoped. He also continued to find ways to help others on the team develop their own skills. His genuine encouragement of them helped mold the team into a far more cohesive group than it otherwise would have been.

There were also many concerns expressed privately against a bridge project and as team members heard about them they shared them. The concerns took various forms; the one that was heard most often was that no one wanted a bridge entrance or its access highway next to or even near their own property. Many of those surveyed informally said that if there had to be such an emergency bridge its access roadway would only be acceptable if it were at least a half a mile or more away from them. However, Dennis and Bill knew that wherever the bridge did end up intersecting the island there really wouldn't be very many folks affected and, in the end, all the rest really wouldn't care. An emergency bridge would be well worth the impact on a very few islanders.

Veronica helped the committee greatly with this issue because she was able to clearly explain the different kinds of zoning restrictions and legal rights the citizens had as well as give her perspective on the most probable points of view of government officials. Dennis and Bill saw in her a very competent woman who couldn't be pushed around. They respected her for this.

Others citizens argued (often feebly) that the heavy bridge traffic that was likely in both directions would scare off the wildlife living in the area and might also endanger school children going to and from school. Still others thought that *they* couldn't see how the community would benefit from having such a bridge and so, they reasoned a bridge simply wasn't needed. A few others thought that the authorities would, for sure, plan for gas, food, water, and electricity to be brought over to the island before anything was ever done to replace the Deception Pass Bridge! Other arguments trailed off in other vague directions: most of them meandered along a path that said people had lived on the island and survived its many storms and minor disasters so far and nothing could be so bad that they wouldn't be able to survive the loss of the Deception Pass Bridge as well. No amount of logical persuasion could get them to see how much they really depended on the thousands of tons of goods and support services that flowed across the bridge every day nor the fresh water supply to the city of Oak Harbor as well as the air base. It was perplexing to the site selection group that so many people could be so self-deluded, so self-centered, and so self-secure without having any really good reasons.

After receiving this rather negative public input the group agreed that, for the foreseeable future at least, their work should be kept as confidential as possible. This approach would also help control the panic and greed that sometimes accompanies real estate activities. The group realized that some people might want to greatly inflate the price of their land if it was critical to completing the bridge crossing. Indeed, the old adage was still true that says everyone listens to station W-I-I-F-M. That is, what's in it for me? Still other citizens said they dreaded the possibility that the state would simply take their land away from them through due process, for the public good (along with just compensation of course) which never seemed to them to be enough! They knew that the principle of eminent domain had been supported by the Fifth Amendment to the U. S. Constitution many many times before in the nation's history. The sub-committee debated the feasibility of other more open approaches but they always came back to secrecy, at least for the time being.

Site selection was a key issue in the project because it touched upon so many other different factors. Could existing traffic arterials be used or would new ones have to be built? If new ones were needed how would they connect with State Route 20 and the island's population centers? It was clear that they sorely needed a highway engineer, but they didn't have one. Even Veronica and Bill, working together with several others on their committee, could only rough out the most important of these issues.

It was at one of their sub-committee meetings that Veronica presented a number of the site selection factors. "For one thing," she said, "we've got to seriously consider if it would make more sense just to rebuild the original bridge where it is now? Still, all of the goods and services we need would have to be transported over to Whidbey during its reconstruction. Also…" She was cut off by Bill.

"But that's exactly what our bridge will do, isn't it?" he said. "Our emergency bridge can function as a construction back-up while the old bridge is being rebuilt, if that's what they decide to do."

She went on, "What specific environmental impacts would there be on endangered species on both sides of Saratoga Passage? I'm afraid that we're going to have to face up to this question sooner or later. I know that just preparing an environmental impact statement can cost hundreds of thousands of dollars these days…to protect a wide array of different creatures."

Her last comment pushed the hot button of one of the sub-committee members who was an avid environmentalist. He said, "Now, Veronica, you sound like you've got a pretty strong negative bias here, against environmentalism. You can't be sure what kind of species we're dealing with until the environmental impact study is finished. And another thing, there are a lot of people who think about our environment stewardship the way I do. They understand the fragile relationships between different species and man's dependence upon the entire chain. Let's not prejudge it, OK?"

She smiled faintly at the young man (newly graduated from Western Washington University and still reeking of academic fervor) as she continued. "We're also going to have to find out just how afraid of population growth the populace is and whether such fears make sense relative to an emergency bridge, *not* a permanent one?"

At this Bill jumped into the discussion. "You're right, Veronica! We've got to make it very clear to everyone that we're not building a permanent structure, only a temporary one! We've got to link this idea with that of survival. That's an important key to gaining public support."

Veronica smiled again, nodded in agreement, and went on. "Where are the private and publicly owned properties that would be used for the access roads? Will their owners sell them or even grant access rights?"

The best and final overall proposed Whidbey bridge site took these and many other factors into account as well; it took over a year to complete.

It was at one of the joint committee meetings when everyone was present that Dennis raised the question, "Hey, everyone, I've heard that one of the main arguments against any new bridge is that it would lead to a huge increase in population? How many of you think this would happen? Is it really is a valid argument?"

Tom, a newer member of the group who had moved to the island a couple of years before suddenly straightened up in his chair and said, "You know, I've heard the same thing from some of my neighbors down south of Coupeville but I think it's a red herring. We all know that the county's Growth Management Act mandates at least five-acre parcels. Now where I come from that's a lot of space. Five acres per family should pretty much control growth outside of the incorporated cities. At least it's a big step in the right direction." He looked around the room and grinned. When he saw several in the group nodding in agreement he felt good, energized, more assured and excited about contributing other thoughts as they came to him. Then he sat down and didn't say another word for the rest of the meeting.

"We've got to find out something else. We need some idea of how many residents don't live on Whidbey year-round." Dennis said. "It's a very different th...th...thing if the authorities have to cope with everyone or only half that number because the other half are away somewhere. We know that there are about sixty th...thousand people on the tax roles right now. Assuming that even one quarter of them happen to be...gone...when a disaster strikes," (he stressed the word disaster although he really didn't need to with this group and went right on) "...then the authorities will only have about forty-five thousand to c... c...c...cope with minus the seven thousand or so Naval personnel who, we may assume, will be taken care of by the Navy. This brings the total down to about thirty-eight thousand. Of course this is a best case estimate and it would very probably be a larger number than this." Dennis assigned this research job to one of the newer members of the group who only smiled weakly, gulped, and said he would do his best.

Over the months Dennis, Veronica and Bill continued their tag-team leadership. During a meeting late in the second year of their planning she said, "Proximity to the I-5 highway and to State Route 20 here on the island are very important considerations. Certainly, the shorter the connections the lower will be the land purchase and new road construction costs. We've got to factor that in as well." The others agreed with her without comment.

Avoidance of some already protected wetland areas was another consideration that proved to be an even harder nut to crack with so many environmentalists about. Several endangered species were known to be populating the proposed access sites in the earlier 2000 Department of Transportation sponsored bridge feasibility study. This government study made it appear that these non human species took precedence over clearly identified human needs, at least as far as a bridge was concerned. As Bill said during one of their meetings, "It's not clear to me whether very many environmentalists live on Whidbey Island. I think that they might change their rather idealistic, philosophical positions if they had to live through the consequences of a massive natural disaster like the one we're talking about." All but three of the committee agreed with him.

Once the bridge's east and west access sites had finally been determined the group agreed not to disclose them without the agreement of the whole team. It must be an all or none disclosure they reasoned. To announce these locations prematurely would set opposition forces in motion that might stop the entire project. After a good deal of prolonged and heated debate, the group agreed to keep it secret.

The entire bridge planning group concurred that it would make sense to hold several public lectures or debates on the need for a new emergency water crossing; but they also agreed that they wouldn't address the issue of where the bridge would be located. The first of these events turned out to be a flop because of poor planning, bad weather, and a breakdown in publicity, among other things. As Dennis pointed out, "A de, debate needs spokesmen who will speak on both sides of the, the…issue…spokesmen who are well prepared to present sound arguments and also counter arguments."

Unfortunately, the bridge group couldn't find anyone willing to debate them. Even a well-known national environmental protection organization declined to take part. So it turned out to be a poorly attended, one-sided lecture. Several committee members thought that this was probably a positive sign; that it showed the general public was in favor of their project. However, they were wrong. The actual reason was that few people like to speak publicly as it is and using a debate style intimidated them even more. The primary benefit gained from the first "debate-a la lecture" turned out to be that the team was better prepared than they otherwise would have been for the second one that took place a month later.

Dennis had finally succeeded in locating a quasi-official environmental organization that was willing to take part in their debate. Two twenty something, definitely college looking guys showed up at the lecture hall of the Oak Harbor main library on the appointed evening. Each carried a brief case and an armload of handouts. As the crowd filed in Bill introduced himself, "Hi. My name is Bill Arnold and this is Dennis Hayden. We're glad you could make it here tonight."

"Yeah, we are, too," said one of the two debaters after a long pause. He was very thin with long black hair tied in a ponytail and he stood well over six feet tall. He wore a dark blue sweatshirt and jeans. He went on, "I've never been on Whidbey before and it's really a job getting over here isn't it?" After another pause he said, "Oh, this is Anthony Place," looking at his friend, "…

and I'm Walter Tiffen…you can call me Walt. We're both members of *Sound Synthesis*, it's a student ecological organization at the U Dub…we're studying ecological synthesis…". He drew out the word ecological in a way that made it sound almost holy.

His colleague, Anthony Place, was five foot three inches tall with an almost perfectly round face and pale blue eyes. His crewcut made the top of his head seem even rounder than it actually was. He wore baggy tan corduroy trousers and a dirty cream-colored turtleneck sweater that was so tight the rolls of fat around his middle reminded folks of the Pillsbury doughboy. He looked virtually the same viewed from the front or the side. Nevertheless, Tony had a beautifully melodic speaking voice.

"We're going to be debating you guys," said Dennis. "Is this your first time?"

Tony Place answered, "Yeah, how about you guys?"

Bill grinned and said, "Don't worry, we've never debated before either." Bill looked at the two young men intently, wondering just how well prepared they were on ecological synthesis, whatever that was. He thought that he'd heard the term before but wasn't sure. They both looked so young. "Neither one of them could have had enough time to absorb very much information and besides, the field probably isn't that old in the first place," he thought. "Just what is ecological synthesis?" he asked out of curiosity.

Walt rose to the occasion; he was glad to meet a man his Dad's age who seemed interested. He replied with a grin, "Actually, it's a pretty old term, it's been around for at least twenty or thirty years. It refers to finding acceptable solutions to ecological problems, that's what the synthesis is about. You might think of it as attempting to increase the effectiveness of biodiversity conservation strategies."

Bill just smiled as he realized he'd not only never used these particular words before in his life but he'd never even heard them before! He studied Walt's face intently as he listened. He was surprised at the young man's fervor and his command of all this technical jargon. He saw a bright, enthusiastic, energetic young man with a passion, a bit like himself years ago. Bill hoped he still was like that.

Walt went on, "Tony and I are taking the same class and our professor thought it would be worth extra credit for us to come here and debate you. I'm sorry, did you say that you and…er, Dennis are the debaters?" he asked.

Bill only nodded and Walt continued, "We're studying the Puget Sound marine environment and the impact of man-made structures on it. Our joint project is related to best practice natural resource management."

At hearing this Bill realized that this could turn out to be an interesting evening if for no other reason that the other team seemed to be prepared with facts and not just opinions. He asked, "What do you call man-made structures?" Not waiting for a reply Bill went on, "do you mean undersea anchors or ferry terminals or barges or...what?" Just as Walt was about to answer him the meeting's organizer and judge announced it was time to begin. Bill would have to hear the answer to his question along with the other thirty-five people in the audience. Both Dennis and Bill were glad to see the editor of the newspaper in the room. They didn't recognize the Mayor who was sitting in the back row near the door.

"Ladies and gentlemen," began the judge, a retired high school English teacher and debate coach of many years. "My name is Wilson Jamies and I'm pleased to welcome you tonight to a debate on the question, "Should an emergency water crossing structure, a bridge, be built between Whidbey Island and the mainland? This is the question our four participants will be debating. We will follow the usual format used in international competitions. The first speaker will be selected by toss of a coin and he will decide whether to speak on the pro or the con side of the question. The second speaker from the other team will then have the same amount of time to give counter arguments to this question." He went on to explain how each team must also take the opposite side of the question and try to present persuasive arguments in its favor. The teacher had obviously done this many times before. He detailed what else would take place over the next hour or so. The audience seemed to settle down in their hard wooden chairs for a long and, they hoped, interesting evening.

Tony won the coin toss and chose to take the con side of the question; Neither Bill nor Dennis was surprised.

"Ladies and gentlemen. I am against constructing any kind of bridge across the beautiful waters surrounding this beautiful island and I am going to tell you why," began Tony in a voice that trembled from his inexperience in public speaking. Bill smiled a little as the young man went on, "However, before I do I want to tell you about what we call habitat selection. Basically, this refers to matching up the best naturally supportive environments with each species. It plays a profound role on such vital phenomena as species interactions, the gathering together of ecological communities, and even the origin and maintenance of biodiversity." He looked up from his notes at a sea of totally blank faces, faces that showed little comprehension at what he had just said and even less emotion. Unfazed, he went on, "Habitat fragmentation, modified landscapes, and most importantly, human incursion, have all contributed to disturbed special inter- actions and an actual disturbance in biodiversity. We've got to work toward sustainable models and practices."

Both Dennis and Bill began to relax a little.

"Now, with that as background let me get to my main point," Tony said. "Our...I mean my main objection has to do with the terrible damage that any bridge or any other manmade structure for that matter would do to the natural, the biological environment not only during its construction but also for a long time afterwards. Did you know that there are at least a half-dozen known spe- cies in the waters of northern Puget Sound that are presently on the national endangered species list? Did you realize that eelgrass habitats form a critical support for several priority fish species and other marine life, and that there is a lot of eelgrass around here? And I'll bet you didn't know that these eelgrass beds are thought to be irreplaceable once they're gone. We have a social mandate to protect them." He was becoming bolder in his presentation style, probably encouraged by his knowledge of these facts. Nevertheless, it was clear that so far at least, he had missed the key issue that concerned most of the audience and perhaps the judge as well, namely, their own well being; but Bill realized it and he knew what his main points of attack must be.

The student went on, "Did you know that just in the State of Washington there are almost twenty environmental organizations? I think the nearest to you is probably the Friends of the San Juans. All of them are focused on preserv- ing our natural environment. I'm sure that you will agree that you and I have a responsibility to protect all living things...because not all of them can protect themselves." He paused for several moments as if he was trying to figure out what he would say next. Then he went on, "Finally..." he said looking down at his notes, "OK...I'm sorry, I forgot to mention that the estuaries in Skagit Bay are considered as important wintering and staging habitats for many water- fowl and provide places for threatened Chinook salmon to spawn and rear their young, including herring, sand lance, and smelt."

Bill knew that many of his own generation held a somewhat different worldview than Tony and Walter's generation did and he wondered to himself about the young man's presupposition here. "Who said we must protect all living things?" he thought to himself. "That kind of position is being used by the present environmental movement all over the nation and it was threatening to undermine many vitally important social and even cultural human development projects across the state and the nation."

Tony continued on this same train of thought for several more minutes. Then it was clear that he had run out of things to say. He looked at his watch and returned to his seat without having given a concluding statement.

Bill and Dennis both noticed that Tony had mentioned the subject of a bridge only three times and had never linked its construction with pollution or any other kind of environmental damage in any concrete way.

"Thank you Mr. Place," said the judge, smiling." You do have another two minutes if you would like to use them."

Tony looked quickly over at his companion and then at the judge. Finally he shook his head and said, "No, that's about all I have to say."

The judge then turned to the second team to find out who would speak first. After he saw Bill nodding he said, "I will now call on the opposing team to argue in favor of this proposition. I believe Mr. Arnold is going to speak next."

Bill rose and walked over to the podium. "Yes, that's right sir. My name is Bill Arnold. My family and I have lived here in Oak Harbor for over nine years now. I retired from the Navy during that time." He paused briefly to adjust the three pages of notes he had in front of him, smiled broadly at the audience, as he thought to himself, "The average person listens for about twenty eight seconds before getting distracted. I've got to get their attention right away." So he said, "My friends, I am not going to debate the fine points that would, I'm quite sure, counter my colleague's statements just now because I want to spend our time on some far more important issues, issues that affect you and me here on Whidbey. To me these issues are very simple and they can be summarized in simple words: life, liberty, and the pursuit of happiness, to use an old and familiar phrase to us all. I'd like to consider each of these three words in order." He glanced around at the audience again to see if what he had said had had any sort of impact. Bill was relieved to see most of the crowd looking back at him intently, probably waiting to see if he was going to hit their own particular hot buttons or not. He had a pretty good idea that Tony hadn't. "My friends, a new bridge crossing is needed to save lives. This is my first point. Now this probably isn't very obvious to us all right now because we have the Deception Pass Bridge that makes it possible to bring a large percentage of our needed life support supplies over to us. However, that bridge is *not* young anymore and it has seen a huge increase in the number of vehicles that it carries, the loads it must carry, and the speed of the vehicles that speed across it every hour of the day."

He glanced down at his cryptic outlined notes before going on. "What would we all do if for some reason that bridge no longer functioned as a bridge, particularly if it happened suddenly?" Bill did not elaborate on why this might happen. He left that up to the audience to think about. He went on, "Many of us here tonight would suffer and others could even die. Yes, I said die...and you might ask how could this be? The answer is that our city's water supply comes across that bridge; and even if the natural gas supply continued, folks it crosses over to Whidbey through a six inch diameter high pressure main that runs under Saratoga Passage from Camano Island. Our furnaces and hot water still wouldn't work without electricity. Our faucets would probably only drip at the most; our elderly would probably be the first to feel the terrible effects of these losses. Unless our medicines could be transported by ferryboat and then trucked up from Clinton or Keystone or airlifted in many of us would be further endangered. We know that there aren't any significant emergency supplies over in Port Townsend. Today our pharmacies stock a relatively small supply of their drugs. Yes, my friends, if the Deception Pass Bridge was...", he was interrupted as someone's cell phone began to ring with an insistent and loud presentation of the William Tell overture. Bill just smiled to cover his feeling of annoyance and went on. "As I was saying folks, if the Deception Pass Bridge was closed for *any* reason, particularly over a short period of time that did not allow us to get prepared, we would all face great hardship and I'm sorry to say that these hardships would happen pretty fast. There is another thing that would happen. Our supply of gasoline, diesel fuel and propane would also stop!"

Bill knew he was on a roll now and he almost enjoyed the intense concentration he felt from the audience. "Can you imagine not being able to drive into Oak Harbor after your gasoline runs out? Where would you find food? I worry that many citizens would suffer from over exposure, catch colds or the flu, and become malnourished."

Bill stopped for a moment. He wanted his words to sink in; apparently they did as many in the audience had stricken looks on their faces. Some people turned to their neighbors and whispered. It was apparent that many of them had not thought about the essential role the bridge played in their daily lives.

Then he went on, "Let me return to the matter of food for a moment. Did you know that a survey was taken several years ago in the mid-west on the subject of emergency preparedness? It found that only about one-half of the respondents said they had sufficient food put away for several days. Only thirty six percent had water stored for this rather short duration. My friends, it's very likely that people in Oak Harbor have about that same level of preparedness. Here's why I say this. First is our reliance on what is called the "just-in-time" supply chain. This simply refers to our present capability to transport what is needed quickly and efficiently from central storehouses rather than stock-pile these things more locally. You may be surprised to learn that the J-I-T approach, that's what it's called these days, applies to almost everything imag-inable. Some of you may have noticed that even the pharmaceutical medicines you need are not kept in full stock at your local pharmacy. Of course under normal circumstances they can be ordered and delivered within a day or two at the most from somewhere else. Notice that I said, under normal circumstances. The fact that major grocery chains require almost constant truckloads of food to restock their shelves shows that they use the same J-I-T philosophy and also that we require a lot of food. We are all utterly dependent on the daily arrival of trucked goods. I have learned that each of the largest grocery stores on the island require about two very large tractor-trailer truck loads every day, seven days a week! Long gone are the days of local self-sufficiency my friends. So I just ask you to think about what would happen here if all these trucks couldn't get here anymore. I personally think it would be like suddenly going back in time to the 1920s and 30s, or worse."

Bill paused again. He hoped the audience (and of course the judge) would be impressed with his research as well as his presentation. He continued, "I said that there were two things that contributed to our lack of preparedness for a major disaster of some kind. The second thing is the Deception Pass Bridge itself…yes, I said the Deception Pass Bridge. It handles about sixty eight per-cent of all vehicles arriving on the island every year. This includes about three hundred and fifty heavy trucks and another 1,300 smaller trucks, busses, camp-ers, and recreational vehicles every single day on the average! Because there are some eight million vehicles that come to Whidbey every year, again on the average, this sixty eight percent amounts to about five million, four hundred and forty thousand vehicles every year. Bill was careful to emphasize these large numbers even though he felt that not many in his audience would comprehend them very well.

Bill went on, "So why would I say that the Deception Pass Bridge contributes to our lack of preparedness? It's simply because, discounting our two ferryboat connections and their relatively limited carrying capacity, Whidbey Island has no other means of delivering these hundreds of tons of needed supplies except for the bridge. My friends, we've become hugely dependent on its survival. I could share with you many other problems we would all face if the bridge were no longer there yet I won't. I'll leave that up to your imagination; but I do want to conclude my first point by saying that our very lives could be threatened without having another way to bring needed supplies across to us from the mainland. That is why we definitely need a new, heavy vehicle crossing of some kind between Whidbey and the mainland."

"As to my second point tonight I need to say that our personal mobility, an important aspect of our liberty as it were, to get off this island would be severely restricted." Bill was warming to his task. He no longer looked down at his notes or over at the two young students sitting across the room to see their responses. He was searching the faces of his audience. Those faces held the answer to the question of whether or not the general populace would support the bridge project. He went on, "Can you imagine a great many people all trying to escape from the island at the same time? And why would they want to escape you might ask? Would it be the food and water shortages, gasoline shortages, and home heating fuel shortages? We all take them for granted, don't we? Would they be trying to escape from increased crime in our neighborhoods when these supplies run out? I maintain that many thousands of people would try to take the ferryboats to get away, all at the same time. It would be something like the mass exoduses that happened during World War II across Europe and Asia." He noticed the serious looks growing on many faces and knew that he had already made his second point successfully.

He continued. "Now I've had to wait in some long lines for the Clinton ferry, particularly on the week ends. Perhaps some of you have too. Can you imagine the chaos and confusion if the bridge were gone? The two present ferries we have that run out of Keystone and Clinton can only transport about two million five hundred and sixty thousand vehicles a year. That works out to just over seven thousand one hundred a day. Even if the officials somehow made another ferry available all of us couldn't get away for a week or more and this assumes that all of the ferries will run continuously without the need for main-tenance downtime, that there are no accidents, and other considerations."

"I think my time is running out," he said. "But I've also got to mention what could happen to the Naval Air Station if the bridge failed. If those in Wash-ington, D.C. thought that this strategic facility was as vulnerable as it is in a situ-ation like this they might consider closing it a little more seriously! However, having another bridge could significantly reduce their concerns." He stopped to let his words penetrate. He cleared his throat and went on to his last point.

"And what about my final point, our pursuit of happiness? How would this be possible for a very long time after our lives were so disrupted?" he asked. "Now I know there are some of you who will scoff and say it couldn't be as bad as I've made it out to be. You may well be right. I hope to God you are, yet what if our beautiful Deception Pass Bridge did fail someday? Can you tell me that this will never happen? I doubt it. Even our Department of Transportation of-ficials who are responsible for checking the safety of all state bridges admit that the day will come when we will have to replace it. Of course they won't say when and they didn't say how either."

He knew that he couldn't stop now even though his time was almost up. He hadn't made a strong enough case for his third point. So he said, "My friends, my fellow neighbors, we take the pursuit of happiness as a fundamental Ameri-can right. As a resident or perhaps just a visitor to Whidbey Island you know how its beauty and tranquility brings happiness with it. I can tell you on the basis of a lot of careful research and thinking, we won't be a happy people if the bridge is closed and there isn't an alternative crossing to the mainland ready to go and...". The judge stood up and announced, "I'm sorry, Mr. Arnold, but your time is up."

Both Tony and Walt seemed to be squirming a little and starting to sweat. The room was getting close inside. Bill enjoyed the moment; he thought he had done a pretty good job for his first debate. The debate judge looked intently at Bill before announcing, "Ladies and Gentlemen. We will now take a ten minute break."

After the recess it was Dennis's turn to lead off and try to argue that Whidbey Island didn't need a new bridge crossing of some kind. This was the way debates were held and it was a new experience for him in two ways. For one thing he'd never debated before and didn't understand the format or the fine points that were used. For another thing he didn't support the debate position he had to take.

Dennis stood up and walked to the podium where he set out his notes. Then he began, "Well La...La...Ladies and Gentlemen, according to the rules of debate I'm supposed to try to convince you that we really, we really don't need a, a, a new bridge. I guess I could do that by leading you to believe our present bridge will outlive us all and our ch...children. Or, I might offer to you the thought that our governmental officials will take matters in hand and develop a, a new way of bringing food and fuel and medicines and everything else we need over to us when the bridge is no longer there to do so. I...I really don't think that I could convince very many of you of, of that." A few people in the audience snickered, a few others felt uncomfortable at the occasional stuttering that Dennis displayed. He went on, "Or, I might even lead you to believe th...th...that emergency agencies at the state and national levels would begin stockpiling all of the needed supplies right h...h...here on the island long before they were ever needed. Yet if I said that I'd have to find a way of asking you to forget what happened for weeks, no, for months after the Katrina Hurricane in Louisiana back in 2005. No, my friends...my debate task h...h...here tonight is almost impossible. My debating colleague and I agreed before we came that it would be better for us to lose this debate because I...I couldn't, in good conscience, follow the rules of debate than lead you all to think something that just isn't true." With that Dennis turned toward the judge with a faint smile and returned to his seat. The crowd sat very still.

The judge didn't know what to say for a moment; he only fidgeted a little and shuffled his feet. Finally he rose slowly from his chair and approached the podium and said, "Well, Ladies and Gentlemen, I must say that in all my years of coaching and judging debates and hearing all kinds of arguments for and against different subjects this is the first time a team has decided to lose voluntarily. I have no other choice but to award the team of Anthony Place and Walter Tiffen as the winners." The two young men beamed with pride. Walt, who hadn't even been allowed to speak at all, was heard muttering under his breath, "Well I'll be damned. What a relief. I was dreading having to debate the need for a bridge... now I don't have to."

The four men shook hands and smiled at one another as the audience started to leave. Two of the debaters smiled because they had won while the other two smiled because they also had won, in a different way.

As the students were getting ready to leave Bill remarked, "I bet that was the easiest extra credit you ever earned." They grinned, turned, and disappeared with the crowd. As Bill and Dennis left the library they agreed that the next time a debate was planned they would let others on the committee have the privilege.

Crossing the parking lot to their cars they heard their names called out. "Mr. Hayden, Mr. Arnold. Can you wait a minute?" It was the Mayor. "I'm William Tate," he said as he walked up to them at a brisk pace. Dennis said, "Oh, yes. You're the Mayor of Oak Harbor aren't you?" Tate smiled and answered, "Yes, and I'd like to chat with you sometime, about your bridge project." Dennis glanced at Bill whose expression didn't change at all and then said, "Well sir, we'd look forward to that." They worked out the details and left for home.

At the first planning group meeting after the debate one of the members asked Dennis how it went and he answered, "We lost the debate but I think we won it." The other man had a quizzical look on his face. Then Bill, who was standing nearby chimed in, "I agree." The two of them grinned at each other and sat down without saying anything else.

Do Politics Help or Hinder?

The first thing the Political Action Sub-committee did was to find out who in the Washington State government controlled bridges, highways, and its transportation infrastructure. They discovered a complex bureaucracy centered in Olympia, the state capitol, but also distributed around the state in separate district offices. It appeared that each district competed against the others for special project funding and political support; it went without saying that money was always tight. The group also discovered that Washington's gasoline tax was the third highest in the nation and was considered as the "linchpin of a sixteen year, $ 8.5 billion dollar transportation program" as a government website had pointed out. Back in 2005 the legislature had voted the gas tax in to fund more than two hundred seventy projects that were supposed to make roads and bridges safer and to ease choke points in "the system." However, nothing had been earmarked for a new bridge to Whidbey Island in what had come to be called the "2005 Transportation Partnership Funding Package"! The aging steel bridge span was inspected biannually and declared to be safe. That's all there was to it!

The group also came to realize that if this project could be accomplished it would bring Whidbey Island to the attention of national leaders. Everyone was aware of the fact that much of the nation's transportation infrastructure was in need of immediate repair and upgrading; many of its elements were literally crumbling for lack of money and foresight. If Whidbey could act to design and build a bridge *before* a disaster struck they would be showing others across the nation the immense value of being proactive. They also would be helping others to help themselves by setting an example of what citizens can accomplish using advanced project planning methods. There is a sense of pride of accomplishment in doing this; a not inconsequential benefit for everyone concerned.

Counterbalancing these positive facts were many political realities that surrounded their plan. They realized that many county commissioners and state legislators didn't want to upset their constituents, particularly their more powerful and influential ones who were outspoken against building a new bridge. It was partly because of these largely hidden yet effective *influences* that all positive action to carry out a project like this one could be, if not stopped altogether, at least delayed for a long time. The committee members knew that such delaying tactics had worked in the past yet they also knew that the clock was ticking. Time was running out for the life of the bridge. The Political Action Sub-committee had to find a way to circumvent this dangerous attitude within some of their government leaders.

Both the Site Section and Political Action Sub-Committees came to another important insight at virtually the same time, namely that the whole Puget Sound area is largely defined by water. They discovered that when highway overpasses fail over land the amount of cost and effort to replace them is enormous, yet when a bridge fails over water nothing beneath it needs to be replaced; water access to support the reconstruction is also far simpler and less expensive and the technology needed to make the necessary replacements already exists. They shared this insight with the Public Relations Sub-committee who used it effectively in their own campaign.

Another important (but little realized) fact finally came to the attention of the Political Action Sub-committee. It had to do with support for their project by Island County Supervisors. When Dennis and Bill met with several of them about the bridge project they sensed that some of them held natural, if somewhat veiled, allegiances to certain regions more than others. While they were expected to represent the needs of the entire county this didn't always happen as consistently as it should have. Because of this reality public promises didn't always find their way into their final votes. The sub-committee was becoming more and more astute in the bewildering ways of politics while at the same time, they were becoming more and more cynical.

How Much Money is Enough?

Six people served on the Funding Sub-committee. Saul Menquist was appointed to be the chairman because of his extensive background in financing and corporate governance. As a former chief financial officer of a successful Silicon Valley electronics firm he was very familiar with both the financing practices and budgetary processes that underlay large ventures. In addition, Saul knew a lot of important people up and down the West Coast. His second-in-command was Lindsey Horning who, with several master's degrees (one from Harvard School of Business and another from Stanford's Department of Ecology), still served on two large company boards. Several more talented people rounded out the committee. They had all volunteered; Dennis wisely asked each one to serve on the Funding Sub-committee because they understood a great deal about economics and raising funds. All of them realized that money serves not only as a store of wealth but also a means for leveraging all kinds of things one wants and needs. Buying and selling goods and services with money was only it's incidental function. They also realized that their main task of raising money to design and ultimately to get the bridge built was not going to be an easy one.

The Funding Sub-committee developed an ingenious multi-phased plan of action. They thought that if they could raise funds to complete the initial bridge design phase it might possibly shame the State Department of Transportation into taking the entire project over. Of course, it didn't turn out this way.

The first thing the group did was to file papers of incorporation with a parallel application for 501c-3 State and Federal non-profit status. They also took steps to be recognized as an official non-governmental organization. As Saul explained, "Having this NGO status would make it easier to obtain governmental funding and would also lend the project an air of greater legitimacy." While their formal applications exposed their ultimate purpose and methods to public scrutiny (because these details had to be made a matter of public record) the group felt that they still had to take this step fairly early in the project. They were glad that the group included several attorneys who were glad to work pro-bono; they finished the application forms for state and federal approval in four weeks time and received tentative approval from the Secretary of State of Washington soon thereafter. They knew that federal approval would take longer.

As Saul, Lindsey, and their committee members encountered one roadblock after another they were forced to take their plans to higher and higher levels of government, to government officials whose politics seemed to be dominated more by money than anything else. Saul was outspoken about his own view, namely that they should follow a bottoms-up approach to seek approval and active support for their project. He felt strongly that they should accept the procedures that have been set up by the local, regional, and state officials. Lindsey, on the other hand, who saw herself as more progressive thought they should go to the top at the very start (she never said who was at the *very top*, however). As she put it, "All we're going to do is waste our time going through all those intermediate levels. The end result will be just the same." Her frustration with Saul's approach came out from time to time and caused a lot of heated discussions. What neither of them noticed was that the project was gradually starting to be accepted by more and more citizens, both on the island and off. It seemed like a grassroots movement might possibly work particularly if supporters would contact their representatives. At the same time the project began receiving small and large donations largely on the basis of word of mouth support. In the first twelve months they had received over two hundred thousand dollars in their bank account. This necessitated hiring an accountant and part-time tax consultant. By the end of the second year their account had swelled to just under one-half million dollars. From a financial point of view at least things were looking up.

The next thing the Funding Sub-committee did was to write a detailed proposal to Mr. Alynn Paula, a northwest philanthropist who was keenly concerned with the environment and quality of life in the Pacific Northwest. They asked him for a matching grant of three hundred thousand dollars to complete the design phase and all preliminary activities related to it. The committee's attorneys cleverly and wisely included several performance-related back-out clauses in their proposal. For instance, if the Whidbey Island Bridge Project Group (WIBPG), as they now called themselves, failed to raise a certain defined level of financial and political support for the project within the first year, Mr. Paula could back out with ninety percent of his initial donation returned. Next, if the WIBPG couldn't locate a suitable professional firm to design the bridge within the second year then he could back out with seventy-five percent of his donation, and so on. The plan made sense to everyone including several elected state and county officials who now wanted to become key players on the team since it had begun to gain in popularity with the general public.

As the Funding Sub-committee began to address the vitally important subject of estimating the cost of the pre-construction phase in more detail their job got harder. None of the members knew how to determine the costs of this kind of large and complex project. Bill sat in on one of their meetings when this subject came up. He listened carefully for a while and then said, "I'm sure you all know much better than I that the profitability of a large construction project like ours rests primarily on how accurately the cost estimates are done. Bridge construction firms that have been around for years know the ropes. They've developed job estimation software that take virtually every rivet and bolt into account. They have to these days." The committee members nodded. Everyone knew this already.

Then Saul said, "What do you say we include initial construction cost estimates as a part of our call for bids…say plus or minus six or seven percent?" The committee all agreed after they had disputed several points.

It was during one of their round-robin discussions that Lindsey came up with an interesting idea. Dennis happened to be sitting in on their meeting. "You know. I've been thinking about bridges in general…about stepping way back from all of them," she began. "What do a lot of them have in common? Water underneath them!" She didn't notice any obvious reactions from the group so she went on. "Well Whidbey isn't the only island surrounded by water is it?" She gave a broad grin that was followed by a short, chuckle. "What if we do this project, at least the design part of it, on behalf of all of the inhabited islands in Puget Sound…even the whole country?" She added. "We're not the only place that might need an emergency bridge for some reason." As the others around the table caught on they said they thought this sounded reasonable.

They decided that by focusing in their public presentations not only on Whidbey Island's needs but also on other locations as well (all having certain basic characteristics in common) they might gain the support of a significantly larger populace, particularly those who lived around the shores of Puget Sound. Nevertheless, they quickly discovered that by using this approach to *sell* the project their work was easier in one respect but harder in others.

It was Dennis who shared this particular insight with them. "Lindsey, that's a good idea. We'll have to take a close look at it. I wouldn't be surprised if the Army Corps of Engineers didn't show some interest in what we come up with but we've got to face the fact that they have the mandate here not us. Also, it seems to m…m…me that they have to follow a top-down model. They have to wait for orders to come down to do a project and then they go and do it. It's probably about that simple. Nevertheless, as we all realize, if the Corps isn't ready with an emergency access bridge to Whidbey *very* soon after its needed it won't matter whether they have the mandate or not! Finally, we need to realize that no matter who does the job special permits have to be obtained to work over the water. We're going to have to deal with these kinds of hurdles when the time comes."

They reasoned that raising money to design and build a water-crossing bridge would be easier if the bridge was sufficiently generic in design and construction that it could serve the needs of virtually any island in Puget Sound (or elsewhere) that might need one someday.

This new, more generic, approach led to an interesting discussion between Dennis and Bill. They were drinking strong fragrant coffee together in downtown Oak Harbor one morning. The two of them had developed a close friendship over the months that was linked both by their shared interest in their project as well as their similar family backgrounds. Dennis was born and raised in the Puget Sound area just after the Second World War had ended. Bill was only fifteen years younger, a Navy transplant to Whidbey Island. Both loved Whidbey, both were married and both were college graduates.

"You know Denny, as we've been meeting together I've wondered why a water crossing to the mainland has to be a traditional bridge structure like the Deception Pass Bridge?" Bill began.

Dennis looked at him with a funny look and said, "What do you mean? As far as I'm concerned a new bridge doesn't have to be like the old one at all and it doesn't have to be at the northern tip of the island either. We already agreed on that a long time ago didn't we?"

Bill nodded and then continued, "Well, what I mean is that we've had pretty good experience with floating bridges haven't we? At least we've learned a lot from the mistakes we've made in the past. I know about the Hood Canal floating bridge fiasco and the section of the Lake Washington floating bridge that sunk, but that's not exactly what I mean. There's no reason why it wouldn't work again. Why couldn't we direct the contractor to work toward a much simpler floatation design using state of the art construction materials that are both lightweight and very strong?" Bill had read about Chinese emperors thousands of years before Christ who had followed the same general principle with great military success. "I think that's what we ought to be urging on our bridge contractors," he said again. "If our aerospace firms can design fantastically strong airplane wing spars out of composite material why can't we use the same basic approach?"

Dennis only nodded and smiled; he was growing to respect Bill more and more. At length Dennis said, "I think you've got something there. Why don't you bring it up at our next full group meeting?"

The basic plan that Bill shared was to construct many identical floating pontoon modules that could be stored near the shore at suitable spots yet quickly deployed soon after they were needed, "...and wherever they were needed," he added. Nevertheless, this change in approach would require a number of costly additions related to the specific location that each bridge would serve. Among other things, each bridge site would require its own environmental impact study, perhaps a different anchor design or tidal force stabilizing cables, of course different land-access plans and structures, and most importantly, different kinds and amounts of local and regional political support. Yet, as Bill put it, "Let's remember that we're responsible only for our own situation here on Whidbey, the other sites would have to do their own analyses."

It took several more long meetings at which Bill presented his basic idea so that everyone understood them. Finally they accepted the plan with the provision that they should stay open to other designs offered by the bridge firms themselves. Nevertheless, they would try to work toward a modular, generic bridge design plan.

Near the end of the second year of activity a half-dozen bridge construction firms had been identified and contacted with a Preliminary Request for Proposal, or PRFP, as it was called. A joint bidders' conference was also held six months later at which representatives of five of the interested firms attended. As Dennis had made clear to the committee, the objective of this initial conference was to make certain that all of the bridge firms received identical bid information and that they'd have all of their questions answered in the same way and in the presence of their competitors. No one could claim later that special information had been given to a particular firm.

It wasn't surprising that the contractors didn't contribute very much useful information with their competitors sitting across the table from them. Within several more months three companies had submitted preliminary bids for the job and were invited to make closed technical presentations of their approach and preliminary costs. They were also encouraged to share any advice they might want to give about any aspect of the project from A to Z. Because the committee's PRFP had specified that a modular, easily executable, relatively light-weight, highly buoyant structure were important design objectives all three firms had considered them. However, one firm in particular took them seriously and brought forward a truly elegant approach.

Working with Dennis, Bill, and Veronica, as well as several other members of the WIBPG, the Funding Sub-committee eventually reduced the contractor candidates down to two, one of which wasn't located in the State of Washington. After a careful comparison of their past projects and cost estimates, obtained during a pre-bid conference, the entire WIBPG met to select the overall best candidate. Saul chaired the meeting.

"Well my friends. That moment we've all been waiting for has arrived," he began. "We've just received what I consider to be the semi-final cost estimates from our two best and final bid contractors. My group has gone over all their figures carefully. It wasn't an easy job let me tell you. Both firms meet all of our basic requirements and their bottom-line estimates are remarkably close to each other. One of them ranged between eleven and fourteen million dollars depending on several contingency factors, factors that we pre-approved. The other firm's bid ranged between ten and thirteen million dollars. If we use average figures that works out to either one point eight million per mile or one point seven million per mile, not all that bad. Even if the life expectancy is only twenty five years that works out to only about a half million dollars a year even for the highest bid."

It was interesting to see how the WIBPG had changed during the final contractual meetings with the bridge firms. The entire team merged into a unified group of citizens, diverse in background and beliefs, yet sharing a strongly held belief that their project was for the good of the general public. It wasn't possible for them to know that in two years time their project would save the lives and reduce the suffering of a great many people.

The entire group seemed to become more energized and there was a growing sense of respect for one another as well as excitement that something truly important was being accomplished. They modified their own individual sub-group strategies much more willingly now; the Site Selection Sub-committee and Public Relations Sub-committee both decided to expand, taking on new members who understood regional issues. The Political Action Sub-committee also began to expand its attention more upon Olympia than Whidbey Island's county seat. Increasingly, the group realized that they were part of something truly important, truly historic.

What Should we Tell the Public and When?

The newly reconstituted Public Relations Sub-committee developed detailed plans about what to say in their press releases and when they should be released. It was fortunate that one of their members had been a professional journalist before retiring to Whidbey.

The person that Dennis finally selected to head up the sub-committee was Barbara Waller-Jones, recently arrived from the Chicago area with her husband. Their two children were still in college. Barb had headed a PR firm that specialized in large public projects. She brought with her many useful contacts and a lot of practical experience; however she had a well honed, if hidden, abrasive side as well.

Barbara was an only child and had been raised by foster parents after her parents were killed in a plane crash. She was in the seventh grade when it happened. Her stepfather turned out to be very old-school strict to the point of using physical abuse rather than correct discipline more and more often as she grew. Barbara became perpetually afraid of him. Even her step-mom, a thin, mousy little woman much younger than she looked, was also afraid of him. She never took Barb's side or protected her. For the five years that she lived with them Barb realized that they really didn't like her very much. Beneath their cheerful and friendly social veneer, both were harsh and demanding. They lived on the edge of poverty and needed the state's money that she brought in. It was that simple.

During high school she planned to run away several times however she never went through with it. These adolescent experiences left Barbara with a deeply critical and offensive edge that she tried to conceal but that would come out when she least expected it. She was critical of men in particular and often told them why.

Barbara was very bright; she had a way of catching on to the fundamental principles in her studies much faster than her classmates. She also had a memory for details. Both of these traits took her nearly to the top of her class in grades. But her personality took her nearer the bottom of her class in friendships and acceptance. As she was completing her Bachelor's Degree she was slowly and painfully learning that she was her own worst enemy and that she wouldn't succeed in any career until she could find a way to control her anger and its servant, her tongue. She did manage to keep the lid on throughout most of her professional career, a career that had started literally at the bottom of a mid-sized public relations firm. From there she had leapfrogged up the management ladder and into the vice president's office. Her leaps had taken over twenty years of her life and left a number of angry executives behind.

Well before Barbara had even been appointed to this lofty if controversial position within the bridge group everyone serving on the Public Relations Sub-committee realized the need for some degree of information control. They just couldn't agree on how much or what kind.

Arny, a member of the committee, was a retired publicist who had worked in several national level congressional campaigns. It was he who tried to clarify the matter during an early meeting. "I hope you all realize that every word we make public has to be carefully planned. In addition, I think that premature disclosure of what we're doing could derail the whole project. There are a lot of people out there who don't want a new bridge to the mainland. All I'm saying is that it's very important that we should all agree on a carefully written and timed release of information about the project."

His suggestion didn't sit particularly well with Barbara. She just didn't like this guy for some reason; but it became apparent to her later. She hadn't wanted him on her committee in the first place but Dennis had overruled her stating, "We've got to learn to work together don't we? We sure don't have that many volunteers."

"Like all publicists, Arny's too opinionated and sure of himself...too self-important. I guess I'll just have to put up with him," she muttered to herself. She recognized some aspects of his character that resembled both her father and her stepfather.

To some people in the WIBPG the Public Relations Sub-committee re-sembled a top-secret wartime intelligence operation. Even some of the sub-committee members themselves didn't like working in the *black* as some had called it. However, when Dennis, Bill, Veronica, and several others supported Arny's warning most of the others reconsidered. It quickly became clear that the Public Relations Sub-committee had its work cut out for itself both in deal-ing with the general public and in maintaining its own internal unity and focus. Because of the importance of the project and the exceptional devotion to their ultimate goal that was held by everyone their work went on basically unnoticed for several years. The press hadn't yet noticed their public filings for incorpora-tion.

At the next meeting after her appointment as chairwoman Barb said, "I've been thinking about this a lot and I believe it'll be essential for us to describe our project as being carried out for the safety and well being of the public, not for economic or political gain of any group or individual, particularly the W-I-B-P-G!" She spelled the letters out slowly. Then she went on, "We've got to do this carefully or it could back-fire."

Dennis looked up from his notebook and asked, "What do you mean?"

"Well, there are two aspects here. The first has to do with those folks who have argued in favor of a new bridge mainly because a new bridge could cut off nearly thirty miles of travel to work in each direction, assuming that their going to Everett or Seattle. This would save a lot of people a lot of gasoline and travel time. Some think that a new bridge located someplace near Oak Harbor could save at least fifteen thousand gallons of fuel a day by not having to drive using the original route." She paused only briefly before going on. "Of course we can support and use this same argument, but the second aspect is more problematic."

Bill was sitting next to her at the large conference table; he was doodling on a sketchpad as he listened. Barb looked down and noticed his doodling with growing impatience and anger. She looked back down at her notepad quickly before he noticed her glare. Her face flushed as she thought to herself, "Why aren't you listening? Aren't my comments important?" She went on, "By even raising this issue of economics we will be putting the idea of the possibility of our own financial or political gain into the minds of some people who wouldn't have thought of it otherwise. It's very possible that some people will prejudge our motives for working on this project. So I think it would be best to take the initiative and state up front very clearly that no one on the WIBPG is earning a penny from it, except our accountant and tax preparer...we're all volunteers."

The group realized that this might be a hard sell in the present climate of political cynicism but it was still true and truth, properly delivered, carried its own weight of authority.

"Next," she went on, "the public should be helped to understand that our bridge installation would be temporary, lasting perhaps up to five or so years until state officials can design and build a permanent replacement bridge to the island."

She hesitated and looked around the room to see if anyone had a question. Bill was still doodling and no one else said anything so she continued, "And finally, with regard to our project, the public should not be led to believe that there's any relationship between our pre-construction work and the Deception Pass Bridge that's still standing. We certainly don't want to start any rumors or be the cause of any panicking, if it's at all possible not to."

Arny raised his hand and said, "Well, that's all well and good Barbara but I believe some folks are going to think what they want to think regardless of what we tell them? I think it's also possible that some people will even believe that we'll do something to destroy the Deception Pass Bridge in order to justify our new bridge."

Barb studied the man's face intently before answering. She still didn't like him but was working hard to not let it show; she knew that she needed to cut through his implicit assumptions and return to her basic point. At length she replied, "I think, Arny, that you're first statement is right. People *will* think what they want to think in spite of any evidence to the contrary, yet we've got to trust in the common sense and intelligence of the majority. We'll always have these outliers among us, but I believe they represent a tiny fraction of the total." Still staring down at his tablet and doodling, Bill nodded in agreement. She went on, "But I don't agree with your second point, namely that some people will think that we would deliberately destroy the bridge to justify building ours. As I said a moment ago, perhaps you missed it...the public shouldn't be led to think that there's any kind of relationship between our pre-construction work on a new bridge, temporary or not, and the present Deception Pass Bridge. We certainly don't want anyone to panic...like we know something about the bridge that they don't. I didn't mean to imply that. Nor did I even hint that someone might think that we would sabotage the bridge for any reason at all. I simply meant that we must not in any way suggest that we're building a new bridge because the old bridge is ready to fall down at any moment." It was clear to everyone that Barb had thought this through very carefully; all but one member was genuinely thankful that she had joined the committee.

She went on, "We're going to have to approach this aspect very carefully." Somehow she seemed to swell a little in stature as she said this. Even though she wasn't wearing one of her many dark three-piece business suits (as she used to in her previous high-level corporate job) her words of wisdom commanded renewed respect. "I just want to urge each of us to be very careful to *not* connect what we're doing directly with the Deception Pass Bridge even if they try to force us to. Keep the two as far apart as you can, if you can," she warned. "I guess that's about all I want to say for now."

During the pause that followed Bill never took his eyes off his doodle pad but he began tapping the tip of his pen on the tabletop indicating to those who knew him that he was thinking. Everyone else around the table remained silent. At length he said, "Barb, you've done an excellent job here. I think that each of your recommendations is exactly on target…Denny, what do you think?"

Dennis also waited several moments before speaking. He hadn't expected to be put on the spot like this yet he didn't mind it. He said, "Well, I agree that we have to trust in the common sense of the people but Barb has really raised a more fundamental question…namely, whether or not the will of the people really matters anymore."

At this the body language of several people sitting at the table clearly said, "Oh no, here he goes again. We won't get out of here until midnight if we get started on that subject." But no one said anything until Barbara broke in again.

"Denny, we've talked about your views concerning our loss of individual rights and freedoms in America. And I can respect your views, only that wasn't what I was talking about at all and I don't think that now is the time to go over it again. My main point was only that we've got to be extremely careful to understand the implications of everything we say to the outside world *before* we say anything. If we don't it could be too late to retract them or even explain them properly. That's basically what I was trying to say."

For the rest of their meeting the committee members discussed the kinds of media that would be most effective in informing the public and convincing the media to support the project if they didn't already do so. Barb was to prove herself to be an invaluable resource person as well as a team player.

It was ironic that it was the Public Relations Sub-committee that recommended to the rest of the WIBPG that they should keep their work quiet for as long as they could, certainly at least during the initial design phase. It sounded like an oxymoron to say the least…that they should be well prepared with public relations information but that they shouldn't give any of it out! As soon as prefab construction actually began on the bridge, however, they knew that they would have to go public. Indeed, everyone realized that it's impossible to conceal any large civilian construction project like this for very long. Some reporter would find out and blow the whistle. And, as they delved farther into the details of planning the bridge with the other members of the committee they realized that their efforts could blow up into an even greater political nightmare; having to deal with bureaucracy at the federal level!

One of the planning topics they discussed early in the project was whether the emergency supplies needed on the island, if they were available from other locations in sufficient quantities, might be better transported by boat than across a bridge. If so, deep-water access to the island as well as a sufficient number of barges would be needed. There were several possible beach access locations for shallow draft barges at high tide, one of them was at the Naval seaplane base just east of the city and another within Oak Harbor itself. Yet there were many practical matters to be considered not least of which were tides and weather, available tugboats, and many safety and security issues not to mention getting permission from the Coast Guard in the first place. All of these factors would affect the safe and continuous transportation of these goods. The group agreed that barges wouldn't be the most efficient way to transport commuters, a ferryboat system would but the high cost of the new docks and landings, diesel fuel, maintenance, and other traffic-related requirements would probably cost more, over the long run, than the temporary emergency bridge they were planning not to mention all the other incredible legal and bureaucratic complications that such an approach would create.

A consideration that was discussed in depth was whether or not there were enough commuters living on and off Whidbey to justify a bridge in the first place or if the two existing ferrys might meet all of these transportation needs. The sub-committee collected extensive data on this important question. Taking the transportation load capacities of both ferry runs into account, where the commuters lived and needed to go, the amount of fuel that would be needed by mass public transit versus individual automobiles, the need for a second private vehicle (probably required on the mainland side if only ferryboat walk-ons were permitted), and other factors, they discovered that a bridge located somewhere within the northern quarter of the island would better serve all of these needs than would many small ferryboats, even if such ferries were available immediately after the Deception Pass Bridge was shut down. Of course no other small ferries were available in the first place. This study alone would have served well as a doctoral dissertation at any major university; it was completed in seven months time!

Another important detail had to be analyzed, that of long term waste management on the island. Would ferries or a bridge work better to transport the more than one hundred tons of garbage off Whidbey every day? This analysis had to consider trucking distances and routes and the availability of fuel, among other things. Once again, a bridge won out for many reasons.

It was during a general WIBPG meeting early in its third year of exis-tence that Bill raised the issue of bridge access. "I think we'd better take a closer look at road access to the bridge on both sides of the channel," he said. "We've been putting it off but I don't think we can wait any longer." The others agreed somewhat hesitantly, eventually coming to realize the kind of hornet's nest they would be poking.

Then Dennis chimed in, "I agree. I think we've been avoiding that subject because it's where th...th...the rubber m.. m.. meets the road, so to speak." Several in the room chuckled as he went on. "The issue of bridge access is pre-cisely where the landowners can stop us if they really want to. We can't just take their land like the government can. So we're gonna have to plan for it very carefully. It's gonna take all of our th...thinking caps together to come up with a workable approach." Veronica nodded with a serious look on her face; smiles slowly vanished from all around the table. Dennis went on, "I think it's time that we talk with the Mayor and the Commissioners about it."

"Well, Dennis...I can call you that can't I?' the Mayor asked.

Dennis replied, "yes, your Honor," showing a broad smile that helped thaw the slight chill of formality with which the meeting had started.

The Mayor went on, "Bill...please call me Bill...Before we begin I'd just like to say that your debate at the library was very persuasive. It's been so long ago you've probably forgotten about it...but I didn't. I was very impressed with your arguments and I've been looking forward to this meeting." Dennis and Bill glanced at each other and grinned as they remembered the whole affair long before.

His Honor went on with a faint smile forming on his lips, "It's the first time that I've seen a team win a debate by losing it, and on purpose at that!" It was clear to both men that the Mayor was sincere and that he respected their carefully planned presentation. "That was a stroke of genius. Whose idea was it?"

Dennis replied, "Well to tell you the truth, your Honor, it came from another member of our bridge committee. She thought it might work...and we think it did."

The Mayor sat back in his leather chair and smiled again. "I'd like to have these guys on my campaign committee," he thought, while out loud he said, "... gentlemen, we'd better get to the point, I'm sorry but I've got another meeting in about a half-hour." He leaned forward with his hands folded on an obviously new blotter and a penetrating look in his eyes. "Now, tell me what can I do for you?"

It was Bill who answered first, "Well sir, you probably know that our committee, we now call ourselves the W-I-B-P-G, that stands for the Whidbey Island Bridge Project Group, has begun to look into the matter of access roads that would connect with our, er...the bridge on both sides of the channel. We're making good progress on the structural aspects of the bridge itself. Remember that it is only an emergency bridge, *not* permanent." He paused briefly to clear his throat and then went on. "We've actually done a lot of research and we realize that nobody wants a major highway right next to their property no matter what the circumstances are. On the other hand, probably like you, we've studied what will happen to Oak Harbor and the rest of the island if the Deception Pass Bridge is closed for any prolonged length of time without very careful planning ahead of time. As we said during the debate we need a bridge that can carry heavy vehicles continuously. The situation here could become very serious as I'm sure your own er...investigations have convinced you."

At this the Mayor sat more upright and looked back and forth at the two men sitting in front of him. He was obviously trying to find just the right way to say what he wanted to say; he was adept at doing that. "I was impressed by your arguments during the debate, however I must say that I'm not as convinced as you both seem to be that the present bridge won't stand for many more years.

Washington State's Department of Transportation thinks so too and I've been led to believe that it's very possible for a replacement bridge to be built *well before* the present bridge is closed for whatever reason."

It was clear to both Bill and Dennis where the discussion was headed. The Mayor didn't support a new bridge, not right now at least...not during his administration. Dennis cut in, "But your Honor...Bill. We agree with everything that you've said ex...except for one thing. You're assuming, aren't you, that the present bri...bri...bridge won't fail unexpectedly for any reason. God forbid, what if terrorists should somehow bring it down? What if an earthquake should bring it down? If we don't have an emergency bridge ready to put into place very soon after this unthinkable event the consequences could be catastrophic. That's the only th...th...thing our group is working toward." He watched the Mayor's reaction as he spoke; he didn't like the look on the Mayor's face.

His Honor replied, "Gentlemen. We've got a pretty fair emergency management plan worked out along with specific procedures to implement it." What he didn't say was that this same plan clearly stated that it couldn't guarantee a perfect response to every kind of incident but only directed a reasonable effort to respond given many different factors. He continued, "You've got to realize that my job isn't to administer our transportation system or safeguard the Deception Pass Bridge. My job is to run the City of Oak Harbor. While I understand what you're trying to do and why I've got to be honest with you. You're wasting your time. We can count on our state officials to do their job. If the bridge should become unpassable for some reason they would find other ways to deliver the things we would need." The Mayor paused. It was clear that he was trying to decide whether or not to say something else. At length he said, "I've been led to believe that they would be able to detect its failure before it happened."

He stopped abruptly and looked at his watch. Then he said, "You did ask about access roads for your bridge...well maybe I can be of *some* help. You probably realize that there are many existing statutes and limitations on land use inside the city limits. Pretty much the same is true in the surrounding county. Before this discussion goes any further I need to bring in our city attorneys regarding the possibility of building a bridge at all."

The Mayor paused to see their reaction but found almost none. He had another slight frown lurking about his face. It was clear that he had slipped into semi-bureaucratic jargon, probably (both Dennis and Bill thought) to give him some wiggle room in the future. Finally, after a suitable pause, "Are you really talking about inside Oak Harbor city limits or out in the county? He asked them.

Dennis replied, "we've looked carefully at m…m…many possible locations and identified an access location on this side of the passage that is about… er, well let's just say for now its outside of city limits."

His Honor shot Dennis a brief veiled scowl for not answering the real question that he had wanted them to answer. Then the meeting ended abruptly as the Mayor's phone rang. He hung up and announced that he was being called away; he glanced at his watch again as he said, "I'm sorry but I do have to go. I'll have someone look into the matter and get back to you as soon as possible. Thanks for coming in gentlemen." They shook hands and left.

A week and a half after their meeting with the Mayor Dennis' phone range. "Hello," he said.

"Hello Mr. Hayden? This is Bill Tate. Our attorneys have reviewed various codes and statutes about roads. Could they meet with you sometime at your convenience?"

Bill and two other members of his Site Selection Sub-committee sat across the mahogany conference table from two city attorneys; both middle aged, both wearing impeccable and obviously new suits and virtually passionless expressions. One of the attorneys began, "Gentlemen. Thank you for coming in today. My name is Jeffrey Poulst and my colleague is Harry Hoffstra." He turned to smile weakly at his associate. Bill introduced his committee members and then Poulst continued.

"Before we begin we need to make sure that we understand exactly what your concerns are. Would you please state them again for us? And please let us know if anything we say doesn't seem to reflect your concerns."

The Site Selection Sub-committee had spent many hours going over their plans for today's meeting. They really wanted to know whether or not the city would try to block their efforts in some way, yet they didn't want to state it quite that bluntly. Bill nodded toward Charley Nelson sitting on his right who had been selected to lead the meeting. He was one of Bill's favorite proteges. He was slightly overweight, middle-aged, and wore glasses with black plastic rims, rims that seemed ideally suited to the 1970s. Charley had been a member of the committee almost from the beginning and understood the site selection issues very clearly. He cleared his throat several times before saying, "Well gentlemen, we're mainly interested in what Oak Harbor statutes have to say about transportation right of way, particularly at the city limits. More specifically, who has legal jurisdiction over highway design and maintenance rights at the boundary between the county and the city?

At this the first attorney shot his colleague a brief frown and said, "I. . . I'm not sure that's what the Mayor told us your concern was but I'll tell you as much I can without doing more research. Harry here can correct me if necessary. Because highways must be maintained by an entity that has taxing authority, to pay for the work and to maintain it you see, specific agreements, land surveys, and other legal matters must be completed well before any actual construction begins. In the case of that part of State Route Twenty that runs through the city, its boundaries are spelled out by legal description and filed both in Island County and, I believe, Olympia. I would think that the courts would adjudge State Route Twenty as having precedent over the city in the kind of matter you're bringing up...but the Mayor led us to believe that you were concerned with new roads not existing ones. Isn't that true?" he asked. Without waiting for a reply he said, "If you're contemplating a public access road inside the city limits then we'll have to go through well-established procedures. But if your access road is in the county then you'll have to begin with the county planning commission...which one is it?"

It was becoming obvious that the attorneys were probing, setting them up in order to find out where the bridge would strike Whidbey. "That's probably just what the Mayor asked them to do," Bill thought to himself. It was clear that the other two guys sitting beside him thought the same thing.

Bill had anticipated their question long before the meeting and had briefed both men on how to reply. Nevertheless, he felt that it was getting tricky and would be better if he took the lead. He turned to Charley and shook his head only slightly. At the same time he motioned to him by lowering his open hand slowly to the top of the table. Charley got the message. Bill bought time with a drink of water from the glass in front of him. Finally he turned toward Mr. Poulst and said, "Well, our main concern, as you probably know sir, is to design and build an emergency bridge between the mainland and Whidbey. In the process of doing this we've had to consider a lot of other things. Obviously, one of these things is the connecting roadway. That's the reason we asked the Mayor about it." As he said this he was thinking, "The attorneys were almost asking outright where the bridge would be located...certainly they have no legal authority to know the location particularly since it actually was going to be outside the city limits."

Bill and Veronica had spent long sessions together going over every possible detail of this identical question: where would the bridge connect on Whidbey and on the mainland? Although the two attorneys didn't know it, after several months the sub-committee had come up with the best location on each side of the channel, two locations that seemed like they would fulfill virtually all of the public's needs. When they had finally shared their decision with everyone in the WIBPG they all seemed pleased; and surprisingly, no one leaked the location, as easy as it might have been to do so.

"Gentlemen," Bill finally said, "I'm sure you can understand how critical this one fact is to the success of our project. We're trying to act responsibly so that speculators won't rush in to take advantage of this knowledge." He didn't point out the obverse of the same coin, that government officials would have more time to bring some kind of injunction against them if they wanted to (it was obvious to everyone in the room). "All that I can say for now is that the site is outside of city limits."

Jeffrey Poulst looked over at his colleague with a weak knowing smile, nodded, and pulled all of the papers he had spread out on the table back into one pile. He unconsciously ran his fingers up and down their opposite corners to form them into a perfectly even stack. It was clear that he considered the meeting virtually over. He was surprised when he heard his colleague say, "I've been thinking about your project a lot. In fact I've had the same kinds of concerns you have for many years," looking back and forth at the three men sitting across from him. "Clare and I have lived on Whidbey for almost nineteen years now. We came up from Arizona to raise our children here and I have to admit that I feel relieved every time I get across the Deception Pass Bridge."

Bill smiled at him, feeling a tiny glow of warmth building inside his gut. "This guy is on our side. I can tell it," he thought. Mr. Hoffstra went on.

"I probably shouldn't admit this but I do believe it's true.... we've got to do something about the bridge and sooner than later. I believe that your project has real merit and, if the Mayor approves, I want to help you out if I can."

None of the three visitors had given even a fleeting thought about the possibility that his statements might not be true, that he might only be offering his services to gain admittance to the committee and its many pieces of valuable information.

The second attorney went on, "I've got some spare hours during the week if you need them." At least he seemed genuine; however, the smile on his face faded quickly as he looked over at his colleague who was obviously not pleased with what had just happened; there is such a thing as allegiance, talking things over before going public, staying the course, the Mayor's course, of course.

Bill accepted Mr. Hoffstra's offer graciously with the words, "Well sir, That's very kind of you. We'll get back to you in the near future."

The meeting ended.

The three were slated to tell the entire committee at their next gathering what had happened during their meeting with the city officials. Nevertheless, Dennis phoned Bill the day before and asked, "Say Bill, would you give me a quick run-down on what happened over at city hall before you guys brief every-one else."

"Sure," he replied. "We think that all the Mayor really wants to know is where the bridge will be located on the Whidbey side...he never said a thing about the eastern side. That tells us something doesn't it? However, we didn't tell them. I think that riled one of the attorneys, Poulst; the other, his name is Hoffstra...he's offered to join us...if we need his services. Oh, another thing. They said that Olympia would have precedence over the City of Oak Harbor concerning jurisdictional matters of State Route Twenty right-of-way should it come to that."

There was a long pause before Dennis replied, "O.K. I think I understand what you're saying but let's talk some more later. By the way, you know that we already have two attorneys working with us right now. Do you think we need another at this point?"

"I don't know. Maybe, maybe not. That's not in my camp. Anyway, we're so close to being finished that perhaps we should say no," Bill answered. Then as an afterthought he added, "...and it's probably a good idea just from the security point of view."

During their committee briefing the following night Bill let the two other guys give it. It went well even though it was punctuated by the usual unre-lated questions and comments interjected by the sub-committee members. As their presentation went on Bill allowed his mind to wander outside of the meet-ing room and across the dark waters of Puget Sound. He saw the fabrication yard and its efficient assembly line operations where the bridge was now taking shape, section-by-section. "It's almost finished...it's beautiful...it's really going to turn heads." His thoughts began to tumble over themselves; "…she's sleek and strong. She'll be much stronger than the old one and she's only feet above the water. She'll do her job well…and we'll all be thankful for her when that time comes, if it ever comes!" Then suddenly without warning he understood why Nan was jealous of the bridge. She had good reason to be! In some strange and incomprehensible way he had fallen in love with her.

Chapter 10
A Strange Armada in the Distance

The earthquake and tsunami had struck only a little over a week before. The public officials in Oak Harbor, Coupeville, and the other municipalities on Whidbey Island were becoming increasingly alarmed at the progressive breakdown in law and order and the seeming inactivity of state and federal officials to do anything of real value. The city police were already stretched to their limit as were Sheriff Deputies, State Police, and Marshals in the rest of the county. Food supplies were dwindling rapidly and the meager supplies that were arriving almost every day by small boats from the mainland (weather permitting) simply couldn't meet the huge demand. The officials knew that something had to be done to give the people hope along with water, food, and medicines.

Day 9

That hope arrived unexpectedly just before noon on the ninth day after the Great Pacific Northwest Earthquake. Residents near Strawberry Point, four miles east of Oak Harbor, saw them coming first: two large, ocean-going tugboats accompanied by a number of smaller log-raft tugs, approaching from the south, from the direction of Everett. Each large tug pulled what looked like a snaking raft of long thin sleek objects, not at all cumbersome. Each object looked like a huge Indian canoe! Each of the two odd-looking rafts stretched back for over a quarter mile and yet cut smoothly, effortlessly through the water behind the powerful black and white tugboats. As they neared it became apparent that this strange armada was made up of a great many objects attached to one other. Each successive row was linked together, three across, like a trimaran, held together by rigid lateral struts.

Residents standing at the top of the high bluff had the best view. They got out their telescopes and binoculars and quickly discovered that the tan colored objects were actually concrete, canoe-shaped floats sitting low in the water. The bow and stern of each one looked identical; they were pointed with curved sides very much like that of an Indian canoe. Each had oddly shaped metal protrusions along the gunwales of their upper deck as well as at both ends. There were also large piles of what looked like steel cables atop each one that weighted them well down into the water. Canvas covered heaps of other equipment on their decks. Almost at the same time this was happening the residents began to hear the sounds of trucks, diesel tractors, and other heavy machinery approaching them from the west.

A dozen dump trucks arrived near the beach access road to the new bridge, each filled with gravel. Highway department road graders, ground compaction rollers, and other kinds of vehicles followed. It was something like an invasion by an army of workers; over fifty people went to work immediately. It was clear that everything had been carefully preplanned. They had to clear, grade, and pave a stretch of undeveloped beachfront land that extended only six hundred feet from the county road on Whidbey's side. Even though the bystanders couldn't see what was happening on the mainland side many miles away basically the same thing was taking place.

Because of the very shallow tidelands on the East Side of the passage almost seven-tenths of a mile of roadway originally had been designed to be built on piling. However, by using these standard, carefully designed, shallow draft concrete floats, the entire span could now sit on the mudflats at low tide. This approach saved a large amount of time, effort, and money and did virtually no damage to the tidelands. The concrete had been sprayed with a special, extremely tough, biologically inert coating.

The number of curious onlookers began to grow rapidly; a few of them got in the way of workers who were starting to bulldoze a right of way through a small stand of low trees down to the beach. Most of the citizens got out of the way without complaint. A few others raised weak objections about what was going on. Yet the residents had already lived through so much confusion and stress in the last nine days that they took it for granted that what was going on was an official relief effort of some kind. They were partly right. What they would learn later was that during the fourth year of the project the WIBPG had been able to work closely with county planners about this last and very important phase of their project. The County Commissioners had approved it as well, voting unanimously in favor once they had studied all of the plans, been briefed by geologists on the relatively high probability of there being a major earthquake in the area, and receiving a tentative go-ahead (with reservations) from their environmental impact consultants.

The WIBPG had also set up a sub-group to work with the State Patrol, Sheriff's office, and Oak Harbor City Police. Working together with the Island County's Public Words and Engineering Department and Skagit County's equivalent the members helped develop plans for the right of way, signage, and temporary traffic light installation.

On the first day of construction Bill had arrived to oversee the grading preparations. He had helped the small team of civil and structural engineers (who worked for the bridge firm) plan the details of where the land and the water met. He had devised a novel way for automatically adjusting the height of the roadway on the land to match the daily changes in tide height so that the access highway surface wouldn't require the drivers to slow down at all. Indeed, his engineering education paid off handsomely; he also was proud to see that the long hours that the whole bridge group had put in were finally coming to reality. He was also extremely pleased when the bridge company's president asked him to join the firm. That night when Bill told her this news Nan was overjoyed. She had resented his being gone so much of the time. She couldn't understand why his "retirement project," as she called it, had been so important to him. Now she was beginning to understand.

When they had reached a point several miles from shore one of the two huge tugboats and its raft veered west right toward the beach on the Whidbey side of the channel. The start of the bridge was to be several hundred yards east of the Naval Seaplane Base property. The second tugboat turned toward the east. The tide was within ninety minutes of cresting; their time of arrival had been carefully planned.

The huge tugboat was then disconnected from its entire raft of floats only a half-mile from shore. The onlookers saw that there was a barge connected directly behind the tug. The barge contained two huge reels of a continuous cable; each reel was almost four miles long! The entire raft of floats was temporarily anchored at each end. While several of the smaller tugs stabilized their charge of concrete canoes men on another small tugboat disconnected the nearest set of three canoes and began pushing them slowly straight toward the beach! Nine men were seen standing on their decks. Then, only five hundred feet away from the shoreline, the tug stopped as the workers quickly disconnected one of the three canoes from the other two. It was quickly sleued around sideways and then pushed by a second small tug until it ground to a stop only a hundred feet out from the beach. Its upper deck was almost level and stood fifteen feet above the water's surface. Then men leveled it by pumping seawater into separate compartments and watched as it settled a little deeper into the wet sand. The first of the bridge pontoons had been put in place (on each side of the channel) in less than an hour's time after the armada of boats and canoes had arrived!

The next step (that Bill also had designed) was securing the land-end of the two main connecting cables from the reels on the barge to special land anchors. Again, men on the tiny tugs play central roles here.

As the hours passed virtually the same process was repeated farther and farther out across the channel. More concrete canoe-shaped floats were being strung out toward the east, each connected to its neighbor by the two continuous cables, cables that wouldn't rust and that were stronger than steel! As the entire ever-growing string of pontoons was stretched apart and aligned in the right direction by the largest tug boat several smaller tug boat crews carried anchor cables out from the bow and stern of each one, dropping their anchors into the depths below in turn and then winching them back to the correct length that took the tides into account. The spectators would not learn for some time that extensive research and development had been done to design these special *PSAs* or Puget Sound Anchors, as they came to be called, anchors that were optimally suited to the fine silt bottom of the channel at this particular location in Saratoga Passage.

While all of this was going on, the same things were happening on the East Side of the passage, the other half of the bridge that was progressing toward Whidbey.

The tide was beginning to run out faster now and the entire raft of concrete floats sagged a little to the south, pulling the smaller tugboats off to one side. Nevertheless, the thin cross-section of the canoes reduced their total drag significantly making the whole structure both flexible and also suitably semi-rigid at the same time.

The eastern landfall for the emergency bridge was carefully selected to be about a mile north of Stanwood. It lined up with 300th NW a two-lane road that intersected I-5 farther to the east. Clearly, the floating bridge would bypass Camano Island. This decision had been made mainly because the existing roads connecting Camano Island with I-5 were already overloaded. They couldn't reasonably handle the Whidbey Island traffic as well.

These same construction events happened day after day. It was like a carefully choreographed mechanical dance in slow motion, a dance with deliberately (almost boringly) repeated steps. Obviously, powerful virtual reality 3-D simulations had been used to refine each of the steps. Two days later two more tugboats arrived pulling the last raft of concrete canoes that were systematically linked to the others already in place. The construction crews on each side of the passage competed with each other to see who could connect the most canoes in their nine-hour workday. They each averaged sixteen canoes a day even though it was still winter and daylight was much shorter. As darkness descended in the early afternoon giant floodlights were used to illuminate the bridge's construction.

The two huge tugboats kept a continuous strain on their thick space age composite connecting cables that were slowly spooling off their drums, cables that were now pulled almost taut and anchored securely at each land's end; the two long parallel cables lay in a specially designed cradle on top of each end of each concrete canoe.

At this particular location Saratoga Passage (that separates Whidbey Island from the mainland) was just less than seven miles across! When complete, there would be 162 individual canoes evenly spaced 225 feet apart! It was the beginning of a floating bridge and it represented real hope for the populace as well as being an engineering marvel.

During the second day of its assembly Bill brought Nan out with him to see what was happening. It surprised him that she had really wanted to come. They stood side by side in silence on the high bluff overlooking the intense activity that was spread out before them. After considering it all and with obvious surprise in her voice she finally said, "Oh my…Is *this* what you've been working on?"

He answered, "Yes, Honey, me and a whole lot of other people." He turned to face her and saw a tiny tear appear in the corner of one of her eyes.

"That's OK, Hon. I should have told you more about it as we went along but," he didn't finish his statement. He was surprised by what he heard himself say next; he hadn't planned to tell her. Bill very gently took both her hands in his and said in a low voice, "Nan, when…when the bridge went down…ah…I, I was right there…I watched it fall…with all those poor people on it." His voice broke as he began to lose control, "I just couldn't do anything to help them…I couldn't…and I couldn't tell you what I saw. I didn't want to burden you with it. You were going through your own problems," he whispered, now pulling her against his body. "…but it's all over now, Honey."

"I never realized," she said in a lowered voice. Nan looked up into his eyes and said tenderly, "Bill, why didn't you tell me this, Sweetheart? I didn't know…". Then she wrapped her arms around him. They stood together without saying a word for a very long time, oblivious of everything else.

Finally Bill said, "You're getting chilled, Hon, I think it's time to get you home."

"No wait," she said, "I want to look some more. I've got a lot of thinking to do." She didn't say anything for many minutes but only looked out over the water. She didn't want Bill to see the tears that were flowing down her cheeks. They were tears of shame and remorse.

Bill stood beside her also looking out over the water but not seeing anything through his own tears, tears of happiness.

While it was obvious that Nan had been awestruck by the whole scene stretched out in front of her she'd recognized something else as well. "And it's right down really near the water level isn't it? I love it!" she cried.

Early on the morning of the eleventh day after the earthquake bystanders saw two huge barges approaching with a tall crane balanced majestically atop each one. Stacked beside each crane (as well as on other barges nearby) were many pre-assembled sections of roadway. The onlookers wouldn't know until they read later in the newspaper that the prefab sections were made out of a special space-age composite (basically a carbon-graphite material) that would last a century even in the corrosive salt water of Puget Sound! U. S. aerospace technology had made this material possible.

Just as the first two tugboats had done days earlier, one of the barges headed east and the other west. The bridge span assembly teams went to work immediately, starting from each shore and working toward the center of the channel. Each roadway section was quickly aligned, dropped into place, and connected to the previous canoe. The process was as elegant as it was rapid. It was clear to everyone that these composite bridge span sections could be installed at least twice as fast as the floating canoes that were still being positioned out ahead of them.

The design had been planned so carefully and its pre-assembly so accurately carried out that a new span was dropped into place almost every forty minutes! The long reach of the cranes made it possible to drop three sections at a time onto their concrete canoes before the barges needed to be repositioned. It didn't take those on the land very long to calculate that all of the roadway sections could be in place in another two or three days! They could certainly wait that long; they wouldn't be stranded much longer. Even though it was considered to be an emergency bridge it was built to last longer than five years.

Bill enjoyed coming out to the bluff after dark to watch as the work progressed. As he stood there even he was surprised by the scope of the whole thing. He'd been so involved with the details for so long that he hadn't had time to think about the reality of its final assembly. It was something like his own Normandy invasion in miniature, complete with bright red laser beams extending out over the water that were used to align the bridge sections almost perfectly. He also brought Nan and the kids out several calm but cool evenings to watch. The kids were delighted to see all of the little boats performing their methodical dances in the searchlights that played back and forth over the dark water.

Tim was too young to know what was going on but Patty seemed to understand the importance of what was happening. She announced, "Mommy. Now we'll have more food and light again won't we?"

"Yes dear. Now we will."

Fourteen days after the earthquake the last canoe was finally and firmly anchored in the middle of the channel and soon thereafter the final road section was dropped into place! It fit to within three inches! The workers had labored twelve hours straight on the last day and it was a momentous occasion that they marked by tooting their whistles for long long minutes! Some island residents joined in with their car horns out of joy and a sense of increasing relief.

Meanwhile, the bridge's land-access crews on both sides of the passage had long since completed grading, packing, and paving the access roadway down to the bridge. It was obvious that it would be smooth, firm, and safe. It would handle heavy trucks and cars on its three lanes, two open lanes heading east in the morning hours and two going west in the afternoon. There was also a separate pedestrian-bicycle lane as well as specially designed conduits for two large water mains (they would not be completed for several more months so that water trucks had to bring drinking water across in the meantime). There also were electrical and natural gas conduits. Special care was taken to save all of the topsoil from the roadway area; it would be replaced later when the bridge structures were dismantled, washed, and stored for another use. The dirt was formed into sound barrier berms on each side of the new access road.

Many smooth-sided, canoe-shaped concrete floats, floats that hardly drifted at all in the strong currents, now linked the entire channel. The idea of enlarging the much smaller concrete canoes (constructed each year by undergraduate engineering students as part of a design competition) had come from a member of the team who was a brilliant architect and also well known for thinking outside of the box. Only this time he had proposed to the WIBPG and the bridge construction firm that they should stay inside the box, a concrete canoe-shaped box! Obviously, the bridge construction firm had liked the idea.

The Coast Guard provided the security needed to prevent the pleasure boats that were arriving from all over Puget Sound from getting in the way of the construction, particularly after dark and in spite of the warning lights that now spanned the entire channel. They also arranged for the inland waters navigation charts to be changed to show the presence of the new emergency crossing bridge.

Dennis had contacted emergency officials in Olympia several days after the earthquake to tell them that authorization had been given to begin assembly of the bridge and that they could plan on bringing emergency supplies across by truck in about two weeks time or less, at least if everything went as planned. He would give them the final go-ahead when that time came. He also contacted emergency services personnel in Oak Harbor and county officials in Coupeville about how the bridge was progressing; his concern was to provide them a way to get the supplies onto the island, the rest was up to them.

Word of the bridge's construction had spread like wildfire down the length of the island. People were overjoyed and actually celebrated in the streets. Now there would be food and water, electricity and gasoline, medicine and much easier escape, if anyone still wanted to! There also would be the possibility of commuting to work again in both directions; however, people weren't quite as sure about that yet. Nevertheless, the rapid and impressive construction of a floating bridge to the mainland had quickly turned the whole frightening situation around. Where there had been hopelessness now there was renewed hope.

Where there is hope there is more peace of mind, and where there is peace of mind there is social order.

Bill never saw Kate again. Several days after the bridge opened Veronica unexpectedly showed up at the bridge site when Bill was there. She told him that Kate had moved back home with their parents and that she was still trying to get rid of her memories of the whole thing, like so many other thousands of people.

He replied, "Yeah, I know. I'm still going through it too, but I think I'm making progress…it's gonna take a long time…but Nan's helping me now."

"I'm really glad to hear that," Veronica replied. "Bill, I've got to say that you and Denny and the others are heroes to me. Everyone on the island owes you a debt of gratitude for what you've done."

Bill just looked down at her and said, "thanks." Then he said, "Veronica. I've got to ask you a question…it's really been bothering me."

She looked at him with a slight smile, anticipating some weird question, the kind she'd gotten used to over the years that she'd known him.

"You don't have to tell me if you don't want to…but…what happened to you and Jimmy right after the earthquake? Why couldn't Kate contact you for so long?" he asked. He knew that his question might dredge up memories that she'd rather forget but still he had to ask.

Bill was a little surprised when she answered without any hesitation. "Well, obviously we *had* crossed over the bridge just a little while before it went down. Thankfully, we were mostly out of danger, but when all of the other things happened up in Anacortes and farther to the east I thought that I'd better get us as far away from it all as I could. My husband was gone on travel and we never set up any sort of emergency plan to meet somewhere other than our house, and we didn't agree on someone who lives out of the area that we both could contact either. I know, I know, we should have done this…but we didn't. And I don't have a cell phone either. Kate and I are sort of oddballs aren't we?" She stopped for a moment to see his reaction.

Bill was grinning but said nothing.

"So I never even drove home that day. You did know that we live in Anacortes didn't you? Bill the traffic was absolutely terrible. I guess I sort of panicked and didn't think about Kate trying to reach me. Well, I was able to get as far as Bellingham and found a motel…and they took my credit card!" she added.

"We were really glad to find a place to stay with so many other people streaming in over the next several days." Then she stopped again.

"But why didn't you try to call her?" he asked.

"I did! Many times, but my calls never went through, except for one. I heard her voice, but apparently she couldn't hear mine. At least I knew she was OK…that made me feel so relieved. I don't know if my phone at home worked or not."

Bill had worried over Kate's worry all this time but now he finally understood. He said, "Thanks Veronica. That makes everything a lot better. Oh… I've got just one more question. How did you get over to the island when we met at church? I thought you said you were up in Bellingham?"

Veronica smiled a much broader smile this time and said, "That's an easy one. After four days I heard on the radio that things had improved in Anacortes and I wanted to get Jimmy back home and clean up the damage. But as we got nearer and nearer I knew that Kate would be at her wits end so I changed my mind. Instead of heading north we headed for the beach in the Swinomish Reservation, you know, across from the northeast end of Whidbey. I parked my car and we hitched a ride with a guy who was taking some food across in his little boat. It only took us fifteen minutes or so. Then Jimmy and I hitch hiked into town, to Kate's. Bill, you should have seen her face when we walked in!"

Over the following months life on the island began to retrace its earlier familiar course and as it did Bill came to realize how much he loved Nan and that she really loved him too. Nothing could be more important than that. He also knew that it probably would be a long road back to the kind of relationship they had when they were first married, but they both wanted to work at it. He was willing to do whatever he had to do to repair their relationship and he wouldn't let his new job get in the way this time. Bill knew that he was ready to build a new bridge reaching over to his wife and he was willing to build it over half way.

Chapter 11
Local versus Regional Concerns

There were many different kinds of practical problems to cope with following these traumatic events. Most of them sprung from the fact that this disaster affected a huge region and not just a localized area. Indeed, what works well on paper for coping with a local disaster seldom works as neatly following a regional one, particularly of this magnitude. There were problems related to supply and demand, transportation and communication, political influence and decision making, individual and societal inertia, and simple human nature. Ultimately, they all boiled down to two things: insufficient planning and insufficient will. Each required a different kind of response.

Perhaps the greatest collection of problems had to do with the limited emergency resources that were immediately available for distribution! The Federal Emergency Management Administration had stockpiled many supplies in warehouses around Washington State over the years yet still, there were not nearly enough to meet all of the needs in the almost 20,000 square mile area affected by these massive quakes, tidal waves, and storm. No doubt armed with the best of intentions FEMA had underestimated the extent of the needs here just as they had done before the Katrina hurricane struck. Katrina left over eighteen hundred people dead and many thousands homeless; the nation had witnessed a mass migration on an historic scale.

Because this massive earthquake had affected such a large area transporting what supplies were available also became a major challenge. Because many communities on the mainland north of Seattle needed emergency assistance and the means of transportation were more available to them these communities were supplied earlier than were others farther away. It just seemed reasonable that these communities should receive the first tangible support.

Nevertheless, if the earthquake's effects had been confined only to the north end of Whidbey Island (causing the Deception Pass Bridge to collapse) then the needed emergency responses from the mainland would have been much faster and far more adequate. Receiving enough needed emergency goods in a timely manner basically came down to three fundamental factors, supply, demand, and the ability to transport the huge amounts of needed goods.

Because this wasn't just a local disaster but much larger each of the cities, towns, and villages on Whidbey Island were not the only places crying out for help. Competition for emergency aid between the almost one hundred separate large and small municipalities that were affected complicated the matter even further. Some cities had more political representation (otherwise known as political clout) than others did at the Capitol; it was suggested later that these areas were given higher priority when the emergency supplies were distributed; but this was only a veiled allegation at most with no firm evidence ever brought forward to prove it. In essence, Oak Harbor and the upper half of Whidbey Island along with Fidalgo Island and Camano Island were on their own for much longer than they had imagined.

One kind of problem that was related to the distribution of emergency supplies centered on the legal hoops that local officials had to cope with. Indeed, there was a long list of jurisdictional issues about what kinds of resources would be distributed and in what amounts to which areas. This disaster had proven that little effort had been made to plan for a truly regional disaster.

Many disasters that had taken place across America before the Great Pacific Northwest Earthquake may have sensitized people about the need to have emergency supplies and services already in place before they were needed, but Washington State seemed to be largely insulated from such realities. Human nature hadn't changed either. The power of apathy is very great indeed. It was clear that Whidbey Island's residents hadn't been very well prepared! The main reason for their unpreparedness was related to individual and social inertia.

Society has a way of constructing around itself many complex and largely invisible layers of perceived self-protection both before and after times of stress. One layer is built on a belief that it's always easier to wait and see what others will do to help *me* rather than to be proactive. Another layer asks, "Why should I risk acting now when I might end up doing the wrong thing or duplicating the efforts of others that are coming to my assistance?" Still another layer is more practical and is expressed in the words; "I don't have the money I need to get prepared even if I had wanted to." Yet all of them represent different kinds of inertia that prevent us from taking even minimal action to help our neighbors and ourselves. Unfortunately, simple human nature is simple and it's human. Taken together, these traits make for inherent weaknesses in coping in the most effective way with massive disasters.

One main reason why assistance didn't flow quickly or efficiently to everyone in need after the Great Pacific Northwest Earthquake was because of poor, insufficient, and even naive planning. In addition, State and Federal Government emergency planners, faced with their own budgetary and political problems, often found themselves hobbled because of a myriad of conflicting and outdated guidelines that had been put in place long before.

A second main reason why assistance didn't come as rapidly as it could have was insufficient will power. Once again, simple human nature is simple and it's human and herein lies the problem. Year after year there had never been sufficient willpower to tackle the matter of a new bridge to Whidbey Island. Such an idea had always seemed to be too huge, too costly, and too impossible. Simple human nature had led people to live in the false security of the past, a perpetual present that denied the possibility of any really large disaster.

If foresight is defined as the capacity to look ahead and plan for future eventualities then thank God there are people who actually have some. Yet it takes more than foresight to cope effectively with large natural disasters. It also takes perseverance and stubborn resolution to follow through on what needs to be done because there will be so many different roadblocks along the way. The greatest earthquake in Pacific Northwest history had shown this.

Epilog

Where Do We Go from Here?

This story was written for two reasons. The first one is far removed from pure entertainment. It is to help you to become more aware of what could happen after this kind of extreme natural disaster and, more importantly, to encourage you to take positive action now, before such a terrible event like this takes place.

So what can you do right now to start getting ready for that awful time, if it should happen, when no one can cross the Deception Pass Bridge again or when emergency personnel aren't able to reach you (wherever you happen to live) for any number of reasons? Several things are possible at the individual, family, and community level. Here are some useful suggestions provided by the American Red Cross, FEMA, and the Washington State Department of Health. A great deal of clearly written information is available without charge from your local city government offices as well as from the Internet. Here is some useful information concerning water, food, sanitation, and security.

In a brochure titled *"Treatment of Drinking Water for Emergency Use"* it says to boil water for at least three minutes or more to remove bacteria and parasites. Boiling will not remove toxic metals, chemicals or nitrates however, only distillation will. If one hasn't stored enough drinking water (at least one gallon per person per day for most needs and two quarts per day just for drinking) then potentially unsafe drinking water can be purified by adding liquid household chlorine bleach which usually is sold having a five to six percent concentration (check its label). Simply add three drops into each quart of clear water or five drops into each quart of cloudy or very cold water. Then mix thoroughly and let stand for thirty minutes or (preferably) longer. Serious problems of severe illness and even death associated with a parasite known as Cryptosporidium (Crypto), will *not* be avoided by using chlorine bleach, only by boiling the water. If one suspects that the water is unsafe because of oils, chemicals, sewage or poisonous substances do not even attempt to purify it or drink it even in very small quantities. Of course, the best solution is to plan ahead and have a large supply of drinking water already available kept in a cool dark place.

Having enough of the right kinds of food is the second subject of emergency preparedness; however, healthy people can go days without any food at all and without serious ill effects. A Red Cross/FEMA booklet titled "*Food and Water in an Emergency*" suggests that we should take our family's unique needs and tastes into consideration when stocking an emergency food pantry. Familiar foods lift morale and provide a sense of security in times of stress. Foods that don't require refrigeration, water, cooking or other special preparation are best. Here's what they said about storing foods: keep all food in a dry, cool, and dark place if possible; close all food boxes and bag containers tightly after each use; wrap perishable foods (e.g., crackers, cookies) in sealable plastic bags and place them in air-tight sealed containers; keep sugar, dried fruits and nuts, etc. in screw-top glass jars for protection against pests; throw out any canned goods that appear swollen, dented, or corroded; use foods (from your emergency pantry) before they go bad and replace them with fresh supplies; and inspect all foods for signs of spoilage before eating them.

The Red Cross suggests buying the following foodstuffs for an emergency food kit (list is not necessarily complete): instant cereal and coffee; granola bars; Top Ramen (dry soup mix); individual boxes of raisins; individual cans of fruit, beef stew, pork and beans, peaches, pears, fruit cocktail; dry cocoa; crackers; M&Ms and hard candy; and assorted small packets of salt, pepper, sugar, coffee creamer, ketchup, hot sauce, etc.

As far as cooking is concerned, canned foods can be eaten right out of the can; keep one or two manual can openers handy. A source of heat for cooking can come from a BBQ grill, fireplace, camp stove, etc. Eat at least one well-balanced meal every day if possible and take in enough calories to enable you to do any necessary work. Many emergency food menus call for 1,600 to 1,700 calories per adult per day. Finally, after eating make sure the leftovers and garbage of all kinds is securely wrapped and sealed in a plastic bag. Rodents are likely to get just as hungry as humans in a pre-famine situation.

Personal sanitation is also of key importance during a prolonged emergency. Effective solutions to personal body waste management are found in Boy Scout Manuals, camping books, and on the Internet. The details of digging and correctly using a pit latrine aren't discussed here except to say that it should be at least 200 feet from any water source or drainage, it should be wider than deep, and no disinfectants should be added that would kill the natural bacterial action (cover the waste with a layer of dirt). It's a good idea to buy several extra boxes of Handi-wipes, paper towels, and toilet paper as well as a roll of thick-wall plastic leaf bags with bag ties and smaller sandwich bags that can be zip-locked. They are invaluable.

Finally, a free publication titled "*Emergency Resource Guide,*" published jointly by the Emergency Management Division of the Washington Military Department and Department of Health (March 2008), contains a wealth of pragmatic information on personal and family security in many different kinds of emergencies including (but not limited to): Pandemic Flu, Terrorism, Radiation Exposure, Chemical Agents, Anthrax and Botulism, Power Outages, Household Fires, Tsunamis, and Earthquakes. It is available by contacting the Washington State Department of Health, P. O. Box 47890, Olympia, WA 98504-7890

I said earlier that there were two reasons for writing this story. The second one has to do with bringing hope to the hopeless. This fictional account brought hope to the populace of Whidbey Island in the form of an emergency bridge. While this bridge was actually built by a qualified bridge construction firm and finally involved County resources, it was first conceived and basically designed by concerned citizens. The story showed what American ingenuity and dedication might achieve. Of course it remains to be seen whether real life will deal differently than this with future disasters and whether government agencies will do whatever needs to be done before, during, or even after a disaster strikes. My own somewhat negative bias has probably shown through.

I left out (on purpose) most of the technical, engineering, and architectural details of building a bridge. They must be left to the professionals to add when the official history is written someday.

You may not know that the Deception Pass Bridge really *is* over seventy years old, it really does carry far more and far heavier vehicles than was specified in its original design, and that it does sit relatively near an earthquake fault line! Indeed, most of the facts presented in this story are accurate (as of the time of its writing). While crews from Washington State's Department of Transportation carry out periodic inspections of the Deception Pass Bridge and have found it safe, their technical assessment will very likely become immediately null and void when the earth moves excessively as it did in this story.

The beauty of Whidbey Island, its isolation and relative tranquility, and its modern goods and services have beckoned many thousands to move here, yet the beauty of nature and the tranquility of our life style will very quickly turn upon us all as false allurements if the worst should happen!

The choice of how we want this story to end is left up to you and me. Indeed, there's no clear cut ending to this story at this time. As is true for all large scale engineering projects, accomplishing the design, construction, and operation of an emergency bridge to Whidbey Island will call for dedicated perseverance by many creative people working together and it will call for a lot of hard work and cooperation.

Are you willing to do your part? If you are then offer your time and your talents. Become an organizing member of an actual Whidbey Island Bridge Project Group. Contribute money to help get this project started. Begin to gather the information that will be needed to pull it off. Buy a copy of this book for your friends. Thank you for reading my story.

About the Author

Richard F. Haines is a retired NASA senior research scientist who has worked on most of the nation's major space programs in California as well as managing several key aeronautical programs. He attended the University of Washington (1955- 57) in engineering before transferring to Pacific Lutheran College in Tacoma where he received the BA degree in 1960. He earned a MA degree in 1962 and a Ph.D. degree in 1964 from Michigan State University in the field of Experimental Psychology. He has authored many books and scientific journal articles in several different fields of science and aerospace technology and has been a member of numerous professional organizations before his retirement in 2001. His biography may be found in *Who's Who in America* and others.

Dick is married with two married daughters and three grandchildren. He lives with his wife Carol in the charming community of Dugualla Bay Heights north of Oak Harbor and almost in "eyeshot" of the wonderful old Deception Pass Bridge!

Made in the USA
Charleston, SC
19 January 2010